Anonymous

The Missing Link

Bible-women in the homes of the London poor

Anonymous

The Missing Link
Bible-women in the homes of the London poor

ISBN/EAN: 9783743355231

Manufactured in Europe, USA, Canada, Australia, Japa

Cover: Foto ©Andreas Hilbeck / pixelio.de

Manufactured and distributed by brebook publishing software (www.brebook.com)

Anonymous

The Missing Link

THE

MISSING LINK;

OR,

BIBLE-WOMEN IN THE HOMES

OF

THE LONDON POOR.

BY L. N. R.,

AUTHOR OF "THE BOOK AND ITS STORY."

" Lamps within the pitchers."—*Judges* vii, 16.
" The sword of the Lord and of Gideon."—*Judges* vii, 20.
" But we have this treasure in earthen vessels, that the excellency of the power
may be of God, and not of us."—2 *Cor.* iv, 7.

NEW YORK:

ROBERT CARTER & BROTHERS,

No. 530 BROADWAY.

1860.

PREFACE.

Tʜɪs little volume scarcely requires a preface. The greater part of it has already had many readers. Its publication in the present form has arisen out of the necessity of collecting together truthful details of acknowledged interest, which have been scattered through the pages of a cheap monthly periodical, called "Tʜᴇ Bᴏᴏᴋ ᴀɴᴅ ɪᴛs Mɪssɪᴏɴs." A summary of these is very frequently asked for, and they are here carefully re-arranged, in the hope that the blessing of God may follow them into a still wider circle, and use them for the further extension of the humble agency described.

Ever since the attention of the author was directed to a research into the "story" of the Book of books, an earnest desire has been felt that such story might be told in places like St. Giles's, and in a very unforeseen manner this desire is now being accomplished.

CONTENTS.

I.—THE LONDON HEATHEN AND THEIR MISSIONARIES...   7

II.—A MESSAGE, AND THE MESSENGER......................   18

III.—MARIAN'S TEA-PARTY IN ST. GILES'S....................   89

IV.—SKETCHES FROM LIFE IN THE SEVEN DIALS..........   48

V.—THE BIBLE-WOMAN AMONG THE DUST-HEAPS........   60

VI.—FRESH BEDS FOR THE LONDON POOR..................   74

VII.—A MIDSUMMER FETE IN ST. GILES'S....................   83

VIII.—CLERKENWELL AND THE BIBLE-WOMAN...............   91

IX.—BIBLE SELLING IN SPITALFIELDS   107

X.—THE WANT OF A BIBLE MISSION IN BETHNAL GREEN   125

XI.—THE WEAVERS AND THEIR FOREFATHERS.............   139

XII.—REBECCA IN SHOREDITCH   154

XIII.—SKETCHES IN LIMEHOUSE FIELDS, WHITE·CHAPEL
AND SHADWELL............   165

XIV.—THE BIBLE·WOMAN AT LONDON WALL.................   185

XV.—LEAVES FROM LIFE IN GRAY'S INN LANE.............   208

XVI.—ESTHER AND HARRIET; OR, TIMES PAST AND PRES-
ENT   224

XVII.—OUR MORAL WASTES AND THEIR MATRONS............   238

XVIII.—WESTMINSTER AND ITS BIBLE·WOMEN............ ...   255

XIX.—THE COTTAGE AMONG THE DUST HEAPS..............   261

XX.—A PAGE OF FIGUERS FOR BIBLE SOCIETY SUBSCRI-
BERS..   268

XXI.—OUR SUNKEN SIXTH....   279

XXII.—OUR AGENTS AND THEIR SUPPORT....... 288

　　　APPENDIX—

　　　　　LONDON FEMALE BIBLE AND DOMESTIC MISSIONS
　　　　　　—GENERAL RULES................................... 297

　　　　　INSTRUCTIONS TO THE BIBE-WOMAN.............. 297

　　　　　SUGGESTIONS TO PROPOSED SUPERINTENDENTS.. 299

　　　　　COOKERY FOR ST. GILES'S........................ 301

　　　　　CHEAP BEDS FOR THE POOR......................... 302

　　　　　NOTICE TO SUBSCRIBERS........................ 302

THE MISSING LINK.

CHAPTER I.

THE LONDON HEATHEN AND THEIR MISSIONARIES.

READER, are you disposed for a walk into one of the lowest parts of London—into a region which people of the better class seldom or never see, unless, indeed, business carries them through it as a thoroughfare? Let us explore it by daylight; and out of well-known Oxford street turn into Wardour street, the paradise of antiquarians.

We are not about to linger, and indulge our taste among quaint old carvings, candelabra, grotesque corbels, and antique church furniture; there are terrible scenes of squalor and misery to be found in some of the upper interiors of these Wardour street houses, which present us with such pictorial groupings below; but we are onward bound, to the left, into St. Giles's and the neighborhood of the Seven Dials, described in books as one of the "dens" and "rookeries" of London.   Novelists, and still more truly City Missionaries and Scripture Readers, have, perhaps, painted it in words to us before to-day ; but now we are going to see it for ourselves, as it existed in the month of June, 1857, for " seeing is believing."

We have threaded our way along one of the seven narrow streets to their centre.   A column formerly stood upon this open space : a column, surmounted with sundials, turning a face towards each street, and hence the place was named.   It was planned in the reign of Charles I, and was, for some time, a fashionable quarter.   The houses multiplied in the reign of Queen Anne, when Bloomsbury and Bedford squares were open heath, and when Great Russell street had gardens noted for their fragrance behind its noble mansions, and the prospect of pleasant fields in front, looking over to Hampstead and Highgate.

But as these gardens were built over, and the fine old dilapidated houses were let out in rooms to different families of low degree, about a century and a half ago, this neighborhood fell into ill odor ; the column was removed, and the Irish, who had first colonized in London in the reign of Queen Elizabeth, extended their settlements into the Seven Dials, since which the tenements have lapsed into the possession of those who had no objection to be their neighbors.

Could *we* endure to be their neighbors ?   An oppressive, fusty smell assails us as we pass along by the old-clothes shops ; we may scarcely stop to read the placards in their windows advertising for old lead and old iron, old glass and old bones. At the doors we encounter the cunning eye of the debased and de-graded son of Israel, looking out for customers. The dwellers in the cellars beneath the shops are come up this afternoon to breathe the air, the hot and fetid air. The "Seven Dials" seems to have its leisure hours ; so the streets are filled with loiterers and loungers. Lazy, dirty women are exhibiting to one another some article of shabby finery, newly revived, which they have just bought ; we search in vain among the lanky, sallow children for a bright face or a clean pinafore. There is not a true child-face among them all : noth-ing speaks of God or nature but one basket of flowers, with which a man happens to be turning the corner of the street.

Some of the dingy windows of those upper floors are open ; and oh, what dirty, haggard forms are peering out ! Many a pane is stuffed with rags, and all around bespeaks a want of light, and air, and water—God's free gifts to the country hovel, but not to the great city. We looked up the dark courts and alleys which had poured forth those squalid children, and which link the seven streets together, and would fain have entered them, but there was a something about them

1*

which seemed to say, "Seek no farther, or you may never return."

A group of undeniable London thieves were lingering round the gin-shop, that commonly answered to its fellow, at the entrance and the exit of such alleys. We glanced up one front staircase, and in at the open door of a room, where the dirt was thickly caked upon the floor, where a heap of rags in the corner was evidently all the bed, and where a few ashes in the grate spoke of what was said to be the case, " no work," and " no more fire !"

And this is day-time in the Seven Dials ; but " what of the night ?" If some who might be called industrious mechanics should be found here, even they—the parents, with, perhaps, six children—would be huddled into a single apartment, the sitting-room for all, and by night the sleeping-place for all together. But such would be a favored locality compared with the common lodging-rooms, where, in defiance of the law, each of the four corners is often occupied by a family ; and as many as sixteen persons,—men, women and children, some of them drunken and quarrelsome,— have been found crowded into one small dormitory. In places like these, the " new-born, the fever-stricken, the dying and the dead," as has been too truly told us, " are horribly intermingled." St. Giles's is tenanted by a most vagrant population. In six months of the year 1855, a City Missionary in Dudley street kept an account, which showed that during that period 536 families had left the district, and a similar number had entered it in their stead. This same missionary ascertained that two-thirds of the poverty, misery, crime and disease which came under his notice, were produced by the vice of intemperance. More than half the people were Irish, whose habits, prejudices and religion place great difficulties in the way of those who would reform them, and help them to help themselves. "They will be dirty, and nobody shall clean them ; they will huddle together, and nobody shall separate them." An Irishwoman, who was asked whether she did not feel comfortable when her old garments had been taken from her, and when, after full ablution, new ones had been supplied, answered, "Yes, thank yer honor ; I'm horrid clane !"

The occupations of the people in St. Giles's are very various. Besides the gin-palace keepers and old clothesmen, there are tailors, hatters, bird-stuffers, dogs'-meat men, crossing-sweepers, costermongers, street dealers in fruit and flowers ; also patterers, chanters, and song-sellers ; with sweeps, knife-grinders, and door-mat makers, to which may be added a thick sprinkling of professed thieves, and, indeed, of the vicious of both sexes.

"Many of them," says the *Times* of Thursday,

April 9th, 1857, in speaking of a similar district, "are the people who do the hard work of this metropolis; who rear its vast edifices, clean and pave its streets, construct and keep in order its innumerable ducts for water, gas, and refuse. They feed our hearths, and minister to our daily wants. They are not the beggars, but the porters, at our doors. To their dirt we owe our cleanliness; and they are the scapegoats of a thousand pollutions."

Their numbers are increased from various causes. A new street, with handsome shops and noble buildings, is desired for the extension of trade; as, for instance, New Oxford street: then Dyott street must disappear, that the neighborhood may be improved. It was a nest of vice and filth, that had strange old memories from the time of Queen Elizabeth, "when thick forests extended from the village of St. Giles's westward towards Tybourne." There was also the great black forest of Mary-la-bonne, into which the Queen used to send the Muscovite ambassador to hunt the wild boar.

Yes, Dyott street must disappear; but, as the stirring writer says again :—

"It is necessary first to get rid of some hundred, or even some thousand, people. So they are turned out, commonly by pick and crowbar, and no one asks where they go. No poet immortalizes the deserted alley and its touching traditions.   The rubbish wends its way, dead and alive.   Carts of refuse turn down one street, and dirty families another ; the one to some chasm where rubbish may be shot, the others to some courts or fallen streets, which are henceforth reported 'worse than they were before.' It is rather remarkable—and it is but common justice to state the fact—that the same state of things is found at this moment in all the other great cities of Europe.   Everywhere there has been a great congestion to the metropolis."

In the case of London especially, this congestion at heart would have been caused by the mere increase of her Irish poor population.   In 1851 the missionaries of the City Mission ascertained that about *one in every seven* of the families under their visitation was Irish and Roman Catholic ; this was after the famine of 1846–8 had driven them from their own shores. That same valuable City Mission, in 1857, reported the number of Irish families within their districts as 19,476, of which its agents had been able to visit more than 15,000, comprising 80,000 individuals.

But the funds of the City Mission are only sufficient to cover *half* the districts of the city with its most useful laborers, who for the last four-and-twenty years have gone, not " out into the highways and hedges," but up into the courts and the alleys, where few else had ventured to go, taking the Gospel to those who never come to hear it, and in every house, garret, and cellar, beseeching men to be reconciled to God. Their sphere is perpetually enlarging, for the population of London has increased by 60,000, even in the last twelve months. The mind groans under the added figures when all that they involve is realized. A witty speaker once said "that when things came to *millions* he could not understand them; the word tripped off the tongue, but he only felt that it meant *a great many*."

Reader, have you walked through St. Giles's? Do you live in London? Have you relations or friends that live there? and do you feel any interest in the "million-peopled city" for their sake? Know, then, that St. Giles's is nothing but the sample of a vast world unvisited, and supposed unvisitable, by the better classes, which lies behind the screen of their respectable dwellings. You breathe more freely as you escape into the neighborhood of the Museum; but henceforth, when you meet a living heap of rags and dirt which seems to have no business to cross your path along the open square, you may think whence such a being comes, and how it lives.

Into the physical and spiritual condition of such beings, it behoves all residents in London at least to inquire; for, again to quote the *Times:*

"When Lazarus has done his day's work, and betakes himself to his sty, he is a very unwholesome brute. Where he and his companions and his cubs feed and litter, the dirt ferments, and the very air is envenomed. Dr. Letheby, the medical officer of health, has analyzed it, and finds it charged with the vapors of death. Nature kindly dissipates it, and, raising the poison from the lair where it is generated, diffuses it to the dwellings around. Dives is, indeed, wise in his generation to fly o' nights from such a foul proximity."

But if such be the physical condition of hundreds of thousands, who rank below the decent classes in our great city, it is but typical of their moral and spiritual state ; and, indeed, the one reäcts upon the other. Such self-respect as they have left is shown in keeping themselves out of sight ; and they can only be reached by those who go forth diligently, after the example of their Master, " to seek and to save the lost."

The meetings of our great Voluntary Societies show that more and more is being done in this way by devoted clergymen and ministers, by Scripture read-ers, by district visitors, and by lay agency of a pastor-al aid character. Many churches and chapels main-tain also their own missionaries, and have their own home mission halls, in the midst of the courts and alleys around them.

A more recently established, and apparently a most

effective agency, is the now well-known Ragged School, which so truly begins at the beginning of the evil ; inviting the unwashed and uncombed young Arabs of the streets to " come ragged, come dirty, come just as they are," to be taught, first, the use of the basin and the comb, and the pleasure of wearing a clean garment ; and then to have poured into their young hearts those blessed Bible truths, all new and welcome to *them*, which *must* raise them into a grade of society above their parents, and will, by possibility, raise their parents along with them.

Still it must have struck many an earnest heart, in the above-mentioned class of workers, that there were depths to which their efforts never penetrated ; rooms to which they were always denied admittance ; moreover, that there existed home influences which perpetually defeated all theirs. "Much was doing for the children, certainly ; but oh ! that in past time as much had been done for the MOTHERS !"

CHAPTER II.

A MESSAGE, AND THE MESSENGER.

A LADY, who had long been engaged in promoting the circulation of the Word of God in country districts, walked, one midsummer afternoon, about two years since, with a friend through the streets of St. Giles's. The friend was a retired physician, who had known the secrets of the Seven Dials in the days of his early practice. The lady had recently become a resident in London, and the two having been village neighbors, this was a kind of exploratory walk to observe the condition of the London poor. Meantime, the question arose, how far these people, in their countless courts and alleys, would be found to be supplied with the Bible.

This inquiry grew into a determination to ascertain that they were so supplied, and led to a reference to one of the active missionaries of the district. He was asked if he knew of a poor, good woman, who would venture with a bag of Bibles into every room, as a paid agent for the Bible Society, and give a faithful account of her trust.

In reply, he said he thought he happened to have a letter in his pocket from a woman who might be trained to this employment—a good, grave person, of middle age, and whom he had known for some years. She was a resident in St. Giles's, and her letter to him, which was a remarkable one, expressed the desire, quite spontaneously, to devote three hours a day to the visitation of those sorrowful children of sin whom none else would go near. Of "that which she had," the treasure of time, though she depended on it for her daily bread, she was willing to offer a portion to the Lord, without money and without price.

The letter was as follows :

"SIR,—Aware that frequent opportunities occur for verbal communication, you will, doubtless, be surprised at my addressing this to you ; but, fearful of trespassing on your time on such occasions, I have preferred the present mode. It is unnecessary to relate the circumstances by which I first became acquainted with your efforts to make known the Gospel of Christ ; but you may remember the request I made the first time I ever addressed you. I asked you to lend me a Bible—you knew not my name or residence ; yet, with cheerful kindness, you complied with that request ; and, for the first time in my life, I brought a Bible into my home. It was on the 11th of February, 1853. That Bible I still retain : of its influence over me none but its Great Author can be aware; nor of the slow but certain means by which its precious truths have been revealed to my hitherto benighted soul.

"With my bodily sufferings during that period you are, to a great extent, acquainted. Twice compelled to seek surgical aid in a hospital—to all appearances I was sinking to my grave; but my God looked mercifully on me, and bade me live.

"You know, however, nothing of the wounds that defied the surgeon's skill—wounds that divine grace inflicted, and which divine mercy could alone have healed. That I have been the recipient of such mercy I humbly dare to hope; and, God helping me, I have devoted every moment of my life to prove my gratitude. I feel that, to testify my thanks for the precious pardon of an offended God, there are other ways than words; and I have thought over many plans, all of which I have dismissed but one, which is for me perfectly practicable; and it is to ask your coöperation in it that I presume to address you.

"During the time I was in the hospital I had frequent opportunities of witnessing the utterly friendless condition of many poor outcasts, who sought admission to its charity, the filthy plight of their persons and clothing proving their need of a female hand to rectify disorder.

"I have not to learn, sir, that in your missionary

visits to the abodes of vice, you meet with many such who have none to help them. Now, I would wish to dedicate the time I have to spare (it might be two or three hours a day), not so much to the decent poor, who have a claim on the sympathy of their neighbors, but to the lost and degraded of my own sex, whom, from their vicious lives, no tenderly reared female would be likely to approach; but to me, who, by God's mercy, was preserved in my youth from a like fate, such scenes will have no terror: and I shall esteem it another benefit received from you if you will at any time let me know where such a sufferer lives. No matter how degraded she may be. It will be enough for her to require my aid—such as cleansing and washing her, and repairing her garments. If she can, by your means, obtain admission to a hospital, I will, by frequent visits, take care that she has a change of linen, and in all ways endeavor to win such erring sister back to virtue and to peace.

"But while especially devoting my services to those who have none to help them, I shall ever consider it as much my duty to render aid to any desolate sick, who may at any time come under your notice.

"Accept, sir, my grateful recollections of your sympathy, to which I am so largely indebted for my restored health, and allow me to subscribe myself your obedient, humble servant,　　　　MARIAN B."

The Missionary felt no doubt that this letter was genuine. He said " it was like the writer when you knew her ;" and, after an introduction had taken place, the lady formed the same opinion. She felt convinced that this was the kind of person she sought, and that, in carrying THE MESSAGE FROM GOD to every door, various opportunities of usefulness would arise, and probably some of the very kind to which Christian readiness of devotion had been spontaneously expressed.

The history of Marian B. was a singular one. She earned a scanty livelihood in cutting fire-papers, or moulding wax flowers, or making bags for silver-smiths in London ; and her lot had been cast, for three-and-thirty years, in some one or other of the purlieus of the Seven Dials. A drunken father, who broke her mother's heart, had brought her, as a young girl of fifteen, gradually down, down from the privileges of a respectable birth, to dwell in a low lodging-house of St. Giles's. He died shortly afterwards, and left her and a sister, of five years of age, orphans, in the midst of pollution, which they, as by miracle, escaped, often sitting on the stairs or door-step all night to avoid what was to be seen within. An old man, who was her fellow lodger, kind hearted, though an Atheist, had taught her to write a little, and he bade her never read the Bible —" it was full of lies ; she had only to look round her in St. Giles's, and she might see that there was no God !"

She had picked up reading and knitting from gazing in continually at the shop windows. She married at eighteen years of age. Her husband proved sober and steady, but he was as poor as herself. When she went to church, she was without shoes and stockings, and he had no coat. Still, from that time she knew the meaning of that blessed word—" a home," though such home was but a room, changed from time to time in the same neighborhood.

Five years before the time at which the lady met with her, she was passing through the streets one rainy night, when she took shelter in an alley that led up to a little Mission-hall in Dudley street, and hearing a voice, went in to listen. It was almost the close of the address ; but some verses quoted from the eleventh chapter of Hebrews struck on her ear and touched her heart. She knew that the book always used in such places must be a Bible ; but her attention was further arrested by an announcement that books would be lent on the next evening from that place from a newly-formed library for the poor. Going early at the appointed time, she was the first claimant of the promise. She had intended to borrow " Uncle Tom's Cabin," but a strong impulse came over her which she could not resist ; it was as if she had heard it whispered to her, "Do not borrow Uncle Tom—borrow a Bible." So she asked for a Bible.

"A Bible, my good woman?" was the missionary's reply. "We did not mean to lend Bibles from this library ; but wait, I will fetch you one. It is a token for good that the Book of God, the best of books, should be the first one asked for, and lent from this place." He brought her the Bible, and asked if he should call and read a chapter with her. She said respectfully, "No, sir, thank you ; we are very quiet folk, my husband might not like it ; I will take the book and read it for myself."

The Lord's time was come. His MESSAGE then first entered her house, and went straight to her heart. The Divine Spirit applied the word with power, and the arrow of conviction was ere long driven home by suffering and affliction.

A twelvemonth after she had received the Bible, she was obliged to send to the missionary who had lent it to her, to request a ticket for the hospital. Then he visited her, and found how God had worked with her by His own word, and had thereby *alone* brought her to Himself.

Two years of much suffering followed, and during this period her husband had also been ill ; so that gradually, one by one, the comforts they had gathered round them by a frugal life vanished away under the gripe of want. They were *just able to live*, and from time to time received casual and temporary help. The missionary's visits were always warmly welcomed, not for what he brought, but for what he taught. Sickness and poverty are hard teachers ; but the discipline was all necessary to a naturally proud heart.

One evening, in the winter of 1856–7, "Marian" remembers sitting and thinking that "come what might, she would no more, to relieve present necessity, pawn her goods," as was the habit of her neighbors. "She saw the evil of it," and saw it so strongly that she "felt she would want food, and fire too," before she would break her resolution, made in the strength of God.

She received the offer of employment in selling Bibles, feeling that it was the work which, of all others, she should delight to undertake. Another letter to the missionary who had recommended her evinced the spirit in which she would commence her new duties, and it also develops her idea of what would come out of them.

"Sir,—After anxious and prayerful consideration of the path pointed out, I feel that I shall have much need of strength to overcome the obstacles that will meet me on every side ; but I believe with humble confidence that the grace which was able to subdue my own heart will never leave me in my effort to pour into the hearts of others that blessed message. I am myself too strong a proof of the power of Almighty God to dare to doubt in any case the mercy which broke down the strongholds of sin in me.

"And if I foresee trials in that path, what sources of joy and comfort do I not foresee likewise! An opening is made to me, which I never even dared to hope for, and I may be sent as the glad messenger of light to some poor sufferers who are anxiously wishing for a knowledge of the blessed Book, and, being unable to read it, have none to read it to them.

"What a sweet employ it will be for me in the evening, after having faithfully devoted the time required by the Bible Society for the sale of the books committed to me, if I can return to any poor home where I have seen the aid of a friendly hand to be needed. The performance of some kind office may be the means of my obtaining permission to read, and, as well as I can, explain the glorious truths of the Book, for which in the morning, perhaps, I had vainly endeavored to obtain an entrance.

"Indeed, sir, I feel I cannot write what I foresee, or tell you how my heart warms as I write it. It appears that God is graciously marking out a path for me in which alone I am fit to labor. I know nothing of the customs and manners of the rich; I could not undertake the most menial service in a gentleman's house; but I can talk to the poor outcasts among whom I dwell; my deepest sympathy is secured to them by the sad history of my own early days. I may help the poor untended wife and mother. I may send young children to school. I may have a word in season for the drunken and even the infidel husband. It will be a privilege for me to obtain admission to those miserable homes, and on what an errand!—with the Word of God! To its Author I look to direct me to turn all my opportunities to His glory! I cast myself upon His almighty power to aid me, and I will fear no evil. Accept my thanks for this fresh proof of your kindness, and I beg to be remembered in your prayers.

"Your deeply obliged servant,

"MARIAN."

We should certainly not give publicity to these letters had the usefulness they foretell been a mere dream of possibilities; but the history of the next year proved that God had prepared this woman for this purpose, and also to become an ensample to many others who have risen up to be missionaries to the "poor outcasts among whom they dwell;" and having provided the *executive*, or native agency for the work, He also elicited the *directive*, and suffered it to lack no means necessary to the development of His own design.

"The Lord shall rebuild Jerusalem ; He gathereth together the outcasts of Israel."

With desires expressed as above, and in a better strength than her own, this good, grave, middle-aged woman entered upon a district comprising places unimaginable except to those who have visited them. She was allowed her own choice of streets, and began her work in Soho, closely bordering on St. Giles's. In this district you may enter long passages, and perceive numbers of rooms on either side, then at the end ascend a flight of stairs into another long passage, with rooms on either side—"a forest of rooms"—then cross a kind of bridge over a small yard, and find, still further on, more galleries and passages, as if there had been once a garden to the first house, and these had been built out into it. So little light and air can penetrate into these rookeries, that the people may well prefer sitting out on the curb-stone, with their feet in the gutter.

The tenants were mostly Irish—they were civil to Marian, even when made aware of her errand as the "Bible-woman." Many were tailors hard at work, and answered that, when they wanted the Bible, the priest would get it for them. Great numbers of women in such localities were said to be "out," employed in making pickles by Crosse and Blackwell.

Some of her earliest visits were paid to courts in

which no one professes to get an honest maintenance, and where the children of Irish parents, who were frequently unmarried, have grown up, half naked and buried in dirt, having no knowledge of, or desire for, a better existence. By " tossing," by thieving, by passing bad money (for in Whitechapel they can get a shilling, that few can tell to be false coinage, for $2\frac{1}{2}$d.), by every species of vice, they live, sometimes in starving indigence, sometimes in reckless abundance : occasionally beefsteaks and potatoes will be tumbled on to a table, with no accompaniment of plate or fork. Their dwellings are like cow-houses—save that cow-houses are sweet in comparison—lighted by but one pane of glass, if that be not broken and stuffed with rags, and a heap of shavings or filthy straw for a bed ; some of them buy hare and rabbit skins, and, hoarding them till they have enough to sell, creates a stench which breeds fever ; the hair of the women seems never to have known cap or comb ; such clothes as they have appear never to be taken off, day or night ; they have no yards, and no back-door ; perhaps a pump is found in the little square, round which they have been built, but the supply of water is very scanty ; and five, six, or seven children will swarm in these closets of rooms, even in the day time. It is worse by night. A policeman, very recently, after due warning to the landlord of one such place (who persisted that only himself, his wife, and his son, slept in his house), broke in the door at two o'clock in the morning, and found sixteen persons in heaps upon the floor, of all ages, and in their midst a woman, with her new-born babe of scarce an hour old.

Into places like these did Marian penetrate; and into others so noxious, that a workhouse, which abuts upon them, is obliged to fumigate them over its walls. In some of these haunts of the fallen it was said, " What use is it to come with the Bible here? It is not for such as we are." But then she heard the answer, " Ah, let her come; I wish we were like her! "

Among the poor she perpetually found one or another who knew enough by hearsay, or by old remembrance of the Book of God, to welcome its messenger. It was not among the worst and the lowest that she found disrespect to the Bible—they knew nothing of its contents, but had a general notion that it was something intended to do them good. One " lady with lettuces " made her a courtesy in all reverence, and said it was because of the book she carried.

She found her way into places " where they knew no more of the BIBLE SOCIETY than they did of India ; " and when told of its object in thus sending the Scriptures to them, one person made answer,

" Well, I wonder what next will be done for us—it is time ; we have been left to ourselves long enough." Another, after looking at the copies, exclaimed, " Well, this cannot be for gain !" There appeared a general impression that the books could not be produced for the money asked as their cost price. Sometimes, where there was a determination to purchase, the penny was yet spared with difficulty, and with— " Ah ! you do not know, mistress, what a struggle I have for a livelihood." And she was able to answer, " Oh, yes, I do. I am quite as poor as you are. I know it all ; but get this book—it is the balm for all your sorrow—I bring it you, because I have found it so for myself."

At last she found her way into a court where she received vile usage : a bucket of filth was emptied upon her from an upper window. This, however, only elicited more sympathy from those who stood at their doors below. One woman took her in, and wiped her bonnet ; another brought water to wash her face, and on the whole her friends exceeded her foes, and from the date of this roughly commenced acquaintance she numbers several of her best friends.

" Do not go up that stair," said a City Missionary, who met her on her way in Church-lane. " The woman who lives there is not a woman—she is a fiend. It takes four men to carry her home when she is drunk."

"It is to such as her I go," said the quiet visitor, and passed one.

When she arrived at the stair-head she heard the voice of a fury, and, tapping at the door, immediately entered. The fierce woman, a drover's wife, standing six feet high, was accustomed to keep her neighbors at a distance, and stared in amazement at Marian. A boy of nine years old stood in the corner naked; his mother had just been beating him, after cutting his poor old trousers to ribbons, in search of a sixpence which she said he had stolen, having received it for sweeping a crossing.

"Do not beat him any more," said Marian; "I dare say he will remember this; but what will you do with his trousers? He cannot put them on again;" and, turning to the child, she added, "A lady gave me a pair of trousers this morning, but they were for a good boy, if I found him. Could you promise never to keep back the money any more from your mother if I brought them to *you*?"

The offer was so timely, and the voice of kindness so unusual in that apartment, that it melted the child, and even touched the mother. An influence began from that day alike over mother and children. This woman had been very violent to Marian in the first weeks of her new vocation, threatening "to trample her to pieces if she came canting into her court."

She now, however, began to subscribe for a Bible, to dress herself decently, and, with her two children, to be found in the gallery of the church of Old St. Giles's—the church in which she was married, but had never since set foot. Her good friend watched her, unseen, in her shadow of one of the pillars, and scarcely recognized, in the tidy matron, the ferocious virago. She did not tell her she had seen her, but the next morning, when paying her subscription, the woman said of her own accord, "that she felt so much more comfortable than when she had been to the gin-shop, that she should certainly go to church again." She became one of the "Bible-woman's" protectors in the notorious Church-lane.

It is interesting to recollect the fact that St. Giles's has been watered with the blood of martyrs, and of martyrs for READING THE BIBLE. The churches in the district, and the "Mission-hall" in the heart of it, have sprung up where a thicket or copse in St. Giles's Fields once afforded shelter at dead of night to perse-cuted Lollards. A company of these "Men of the Book" (at that time the MANUSCRIPT Book), which their leader Wicliff had translated, had met in St. Giles's Fields on the night of the 6th of January, 1414. From the hour that it was ordained in St. Paul's, by convocation, that no book of Wicliff's should be read either in public or private, his translation of the Bible became " the Book of the people."   Its precious words were treasured all the more for the prohibition, and in the dark cold winter's night, men and women came forth to listen to them.

Their enemies untruly informed King Henry V, then newly come to the throne, " that Lord Cobham (a favorer of the Lollards, and who had escaped from imprisonment in the Tower, and was really at that time taking shelter in Wales) was then in St. Giles's fields, at the head of 20,000 of his followers, meaning to seize the king's person, and make himself governor of the realm.

The young Prince believed the lie, and not being wanting in personal bravery, armed the soldiers about his palace, and instantly marched to the place. He attacked the few poor Lollards that were there assembled, killed twenty, and took sixty prisoners. He then pressed forwards, thinking he had only met with the advanced guard, but found that he had routed the whole body.

Thirty-six of those prisoners, including Sir Roger Acton and Beverley, one of their preachers, were hanged and burned, says the chronicle, near the spot where they were taken ; and three years afterwards Lord Cobham himself, being re-captured, was dragged ignominiously upon a hurdle, with insult and barbarity, to these same St. Giles's Fields, and there hung alive

2*

in chains upon a gallows, while a fire being kindled beneath, he was slowly roasted to death.

"Vengeance is mine, saith the Lord;" but "the blood of the martyrs is the seed of the Church;" and we believe the time is come when the Word of God, being "unbound"—the same good old Book for which their fathers suffered—and its "message from heaven" being freely delivered in St. Giles's, many a soul shall be saved on that spot, and many a brand shall be plucked from the burning.

It was very pleasant to the lady who sent this good woman into the dens and rookeries of St. Giles's— paying her by the kind aid of the British and Foreign Bible Society—to discover the result of former efforts made in this district. The decent poor—those who come to churches and chapels—were found very well supplied with the Scriptures, and the supply kept up. Mr. Thorold, the new Rector of St. Giles's, had, from the time he came into the parish, shown himself very anxious on this point. The sacred volume was given as a reward to the children in the schools, and a very deep interest manifested that every individual who came within his influence should possess it. The work commenced by the good Bishop of Ripon, as previous Rector, was being earnestly carried on by his successor. Marian lighted upon some large old Bibles which had been obtained by penny subscriptions. Some of them bearing the mark of BRITISH AND FOREIGN BIBLE SOCIETY had been well used, and must have been supplied by friends of this institution in former days ; and she was constantly told, "Oh, yes! I can get a Bible at the church if I go and pay the penny."

She, therefore, was advised that her errand was chiefly to those many thousands who never presented themselver either at church or chapel to seek the pearl of great price, and who were without the pale of all good agencies. In her own words, she found "enough for the labor of a lifetime *underneath all that.*"

The difficulty of finding access to the lower population of St. Giles's can only be realized by those who have attempted it. " Out, out, out," was the perpetual summer answer in room after room. Marian found them " such an unsettled set of people. They have no regular time for dinner. She supposed they did not often have a dinner. She was glad to perceive any sign that they were going to stay,—the little bit of curtain at the window, or the picture hung upon the wall ; but in their various avocations as watercress sellers, scavengers, road waterers, crossing-sweepers, &c., they are such a wandering folk."

In revisiting the rooms a second time, she found in them quite a new set of tenants ; and yet the others were said to be " coming back when haying is over ;" or " on the Saturday night ;" the present occupants remaining also. In several instances she found the message left for her from a subscriber, that their money should be paid on Saturday evening. From those who were at home she spoke of the reception as better and better every visit, but it required the devotion of far more than the five hours a day promised to the Society to meet the circumstances of the place, and the occupations of the people. In one house she had three subscribers, whose subscriptions must be sought at three different times. Each could only be found at a particular hour. One of them served milk ; she was a Welsh-woman, and seemed much in earnest to get a Bible, being no stranger to its value.

When the superintendent of this interesting work came to sum up the details of the first month's labor, seventy Bible subscribers were found on the books, two of them only being Romanists. The prevailing taste was for small copies, with gilt edges, and whatever had been the mixed character of the reception that " Marian " had met with, *she* at least had such a sense of the importance of her mission, that having made her way into recesses in the midst of which she had lived for more than a quarter of a century, without being aware of their existence, she said she could no longer leave them unvisited while strength remained, if haply out of those depths of misery she might bring one soul to Jesus.

These Bible visits, it will be perceived, were paid to a class of persons *below the decent poor*, and to those who compose that large underlying mass of humanity which never seeks to bring itself within the range of moral or spiritual effort for its own elevation. The one concern of these people—winter and summer, and year after year—is merely to live—and to thousands, the easiest and idlest mode to attain this end is by the vice and filth amidst which they were born and bred.

They crowd together in hundreds of courts and alleys like those above described, and, except in solitary cases, they are content to do so ; they have no wish to be raised—no feelings in common with the classes above them. They must eat, drink and sleep, and to-morrow, perhaps, die—knowing nothing of the revelation of a life beyond, and *not caring to know.* Few among those of the last generation can read, but the light breaking into the dark picture is found in the fact that many of the children can, and that a race is now springing up into men and women who have a great desire for reading. Many may be seen of an evening, sitting along the edges of the pavement, with penny periodicals in their hands, the character of which is of every varied shade of good and evil. The *London Journal* is one of the greatest favorites.

Of what unspeakable importance, then, was it to penetrate these regions with the Bible? Our next chapter will show what further knowledge was secured by these visits, concerning the habits and wants of the people. It was not the first aim to secure such knowledge. The enterprise was undertaken only with a deep sense that the message from God should be carried to every member of the human family. Its welcome from the lost and the fallen was somewhat unexpected ; and facts seemed very early to point to the supposition that the right agency, " the missing link," between them and those who wished to serve them, had perhaps by accident been found.

CHAPTER III.

THE second month of Bible visits had not passed away before a desire arose in the heart of the persevering visitor, and of the friend to whom she continually brought her reports, to do something to place these people *in a condition to profit by* the Book they were willing to buy. It was almost impossible to sit down to read the Bible to them in the midst of their dirt. "I should like, if you had no objection, ma'am," said Marian, "to ask a few of them to tea with me—my husband is in the country—and then I could have a little talk with them on their ways, and how to mend them."

The lady cordially entered into this proposal. She told Marian that any small expense to which the tea might put her should be met, and awaited the result. This, perhaps, is best given in the form of a conversation as it occurred between the parties.

"Well, Mrs. B., and did you have your tea-party of your most punctual Bible-subscribers, as you proposed ? How many did you invite?"

"Eight women, ma'am ; and they all came, and said they had never spent such a pleasant evening in their lives. After many visits to their homes to collect the pence, I had picked out those to whom I thought I might do some good ; and they had washed their poor gowns and caps, and came so tidy, I scarcely knew them for the same that I had seen in their ' dens.' Three of them brought babies in arms, which they could not leave."

" And how did you seat them ?"

" I had five chairs, and the rest sat on the bed-side. I asked my landlady, and she had no objection to the party."

" I suppose you knew who they were ?"

" Some were sellers of hare and rabbit skins, water-cresses, fruit, fish, and flowers ; but now they were all " going to the hops.' "

" What did their husbands do for a living ?"

" The same things, or some of them go out to cut turves for birds, and pay a trifle a quarter for the right to do so. But in one thing they were all agreed—they had all bad husbands."

" What did you say to that ?"

" I told them I felt I had a good one, and I thought they might have good husbands if they would, because a clean, kind, sober woman almost always makes a good husband ; but one who sits about dirty and idle, and never has a clean hearth or a nice cup of tea for him when he comes in from his work, need not wonder if he goes to the public house, and spends there in one night what would keep the family for a week."

"Now tell me about the tea. How much did you provide for your party?"

"I bought one ounce of the best tea, and half a pound of lump sugar, half a pound of butter, and a quartern loaf. I did think of two pennyworth of cream; but then, as I meant it for a pattern of a plain and comfortable tea, I thought they would not be used to that, so I did without."

"And what did it cost? You must tell me the items."

"The tea, 4½d.; sugar, 3½d.; butter, 8d.; bread, 8d.; in all, 2s. But not that really, because I had so much left."

"What did you talk about at tea-time?"

"They had all bought the same Holy Book, and had done so for the first time in their lives. So we talked about that; and I told them what it had done for me, and how *that* made me come and bring it to them; and they said they hoped, in time, it would make them as happy as I was."

"Were they all able to read?"

"No, indeed, very few of them; but their children could. I found that each had some dim knowledge of the facts of the New Testament, picked up from their children, who go to school."

"Did you talk about the children?"

"Yes; and I asked them to take some pride in their children. They have some lovely children; but they never seem to clean or comb them. They say, 'What use is it, for they have no clothes? It is as much as we can do to feed them.'"

"Did any of the eight attend public worship on the Sabbath?"

"I think one had been once or twice to Mr. Lee's cottage service on a Tuesday evening, and that some impression had been made on her. Another had been once to Bloomsbury Mission-hall, but the tale was the same—*No clothes to go in.* 'The people are so fine,' said one. 'Would you, Mrs. B., like to go and sit down with your poor old gown, and not a bit of a rag of a shawl on, by the side of a handsome cape, and a nice veil on a bonnet?' mentioning by name the wearers of such articles."

"'Yes,' I said, 'I know. *They are teetotalers.* The man earns but 15s. a week, and the woman works at the army clothing. You could dress just as well, perhaps, if you took the way they have taken, for some of you earn as much money as they do.' Then I told them how pleased I was to see them all now so clean and tidy, and that I felt so kind of them to pay me that respect. I had invited them only to try to do them good, and see if we could help each other to make a few more comfortable homes in St. Giles's. 'I know what you *could* do,' I said, ' because I have seen your places, and they would be as good as this if you liked. Now, if one of you gets new strong boots, another wants new strong boots; and new boots are the one thing you *will* have, it seems, whatever else you go without. If one of you would be clean, another would be clean.' Then they said they thought they would try."

"Thank God for that; we will help them to try. Were they all going now to the hops? Did they tell you about the hop-grounds? I suppose you have never seen them, for you told me you had spent the whole of your life in St. Giles's yourself, without going into the country till your husband's illness called you to G . . ."

"Oh, yes! all the rest of their talk was about the hops. I could quite fancy how beautiful they look; it is the time they reckon on all the year, like the gentry going out of town. Everybody goes—*i. e.*, of the lowest sort; but there are different places to which they go. Five of these women were going to Squire E.'s, of Town Maulding, and those who were going there were very happy and well off. He is a great hop-grower, who cares for his pickers, and has a set of barracks prepared on purpose for them; and his other

laborers go away to make them room.   But his people
are obliged to conform to his rules.   He rides on
horseback up and down the lines every morning to see
if things are all right.   A horn calls them to work;
they have a missionary to visit them; and he *will have*
the Sunday kept.   No washing, and no card-playing,
and no dancing; but he makes it quite pleasant to
them.   Their husbands are each binsmen, who take
down their own crew, partly their own families.
Generally speaking, the men seem to keep what they
earn, and the women what they earn, each to themselves."

"Were the rest going into Kent?"

"Yes; three were going to F——, where the farmers
care more for their horses than for men and women;
and they would take their own dirty beds and filthy
children, and sleep in barns or out of doors; but this
year is a very fine hop year, so it would not seem so
hard.   We had a little more talk about dirt, and I told
them all of the tickets so easily to be had for baths
and wash-houses, so that there is really no excuse for
being dirty in St. Giles's."

"And then, I suppose, you read a chapter to them.
What chapter did you read?"

"The 15th of St. Matthew, and they listened very
gladly; and then we knelt down, and I prayed as well
as I could that God would take them into his keeping

while they went to the hops, and they all said they did hope we should meet again when they came home. They will take their Bibles with them, and one of them took charge for me of a poor child, not nine years old, and carried her with her to nurse her baby. She has early been led into ways of sin, and was not old enough to be taken into a reformatory. I have heard from this woman, and I think she will keep the girl when she comes home."

As we are here relating facts in the order in which they occurred, it is at this period we must mention that the individual who had secured the services of " Marian," being the Editor of a cheap periodical entitled " The Book and its Missions," had given many of the foregoing particulars in its pages concerning the people in St. Giles's, under the head of the " Home Missions of the Bible."   One of its readers, an Irish lady, touched by the account of this poor woman's devotion to the welfare of *her* country people, had, unasked, sent £5 to promote the social improvements of which such need was indicated.   To this sum two or three kind friends at Cheltenham had added similar voluntary contributions, so that an unforeseen fund was placed in the hands of the Editor wherewith to promote such improvements.

A wish arose that God might, in His mercy, *multiply female agency like this* a hundredfold for neighbor hoods similar to St. Giles's; that He might raise up and train by His providence these native reformers of their own class; and that educated Christian ladies might find them out, and quietly help them in their work.

No lady, however self-denying, would have been able, by repeated visits, to seek the eight women above described in the haunts from which they came. Places like St. Giles's have their own pride and their own reserve. They need female agency *of their own*, co-operative with all present missionary work, and the right beginning and root of such agency is in the SERVICE OF THE WORD OF GOD.

A man colporter, with his bag of books, passing up and down the streets of St. Giles's, in the months of July, August, and September, especially when the people were gone to the hay, the harvest, and the hops, and acting according to the ordinary rules o. colportage, would probably have returned, saying he could make no sales, and that the people were supplied; yet, in the space of the same fourteen weeks, this experiment of female colportage, and weekly collection of pence *combined*, effected a sale of 174 copies—54 of them Bibles—and in the most unlikely quarters.

Our next purpose is to show how certain DOMESTIC reforms of necessity ensued from the continuance of the Bible visits. Domestic reforms!—how much needed! England is looked upon abroad as the country whose faith is founded on a Book which she wishes to give to all mankind. But while she goes forth to possess the field of the world, has she not too often forgotten her heathen at home—those who cluster round her in her capital city—pitiable beings, who live as if they had no God, no Bible, no hope, no thought of heaven—crowded together, often famishing, thriftless, naked, weary, drunken? We blush to utter the cry so frequently heard at the doors of their "dens," when a child has been asked for its mother; the answer is, "Mother's drunk!" No home, of course, for the father—none for the children. Do these people really belong to the nation that gives the Bible to the world?

CHAPTER IV.

" Now, Marian, and how stands the account between us, as to the sale of books, by this time ? You have been employed at the expense of the Bible Society for twenty weeks, and you do not seem weary of your work among your people."

"I do not know how I could be weary, ma'am, of that which gives me such true happiness. Indeed, every week's work seems happier and happier. I have sold 250 copies—130 Bibles and 120 Testaments—and mostly to a class of persons who would not have been likely to buy them of any one else. Wherever I have had a subscriber, I try and keep up the right of still paying a visit, so that, in 250 rooms, I mostly find an entrance and a welcome ; and, as one tells another, the number is always increasing."

"You seem to be much improved in health and strength yourself, since I persuaded you to leave off taking tea for your dinner, and gave you the iron saucepan to make nourishing soup instead. Do you

[48]

find that this notion spreads among the people? And to how many of them have you lent the saucepans and deep dishes, which our St. Giles's fund enabled us to buy?"

"To sixteen people, in different parts of my district. They have all bought the printed receipts* of the "soup that could be made for sixpence," with which you provided me, at one halfpenny each, and they valued them more than if they had been given away. Each woman, when she has made soup for herself, lends the saucepan to some one else, and she to another, so that they are serving about forty families. Everything is lent in St. Giles's, from a pair of bellows to a washing-tub. One article of each kind will serve a court. Indeed, they have seldom more than one among them of anything that can be borrowed."

"Is all your stock disposed of?"

"No. I am reserving two, which I had intended to give to Mrs. A. and Mrs. F. ; but I have heard a bad character of them, and have even seen Mrs. A. the worse for drink myself this week. So I thought I would ask you about it."

"Then I think we will *try* them, because it *is* by this soup, if they will make it, that, by degrees, they may, perhaps, be weaned from gin-taking. What is

* See Appendix for receipt.

3

it, do you think, that drives them so much to drinking ?"

"Oftentimes it is trouble. It was that just now with Mrs. A. Her husband drinks ; and one morning last week he came and took away their only bed, and pawned it for 2s., and drank the money. So then her neighbors pitied her, and said, ' Come, poor thing, we'll stand a drop to comfort you, and make you forget it.' I feared that if I lent them the saucepan he might take away that also."

"Suppose you give him a meal of your soup, and then tell him you will teach his wife to make it."

"Certainly I can. I bought three jugs, that I might always be ready to show them a pattern. They fly to drink because it is at hand, and warms them for a while, and ' makes them forget.' Their fathers and mothers did it before them, and no one has taught them any better. Yet they need not be so miserable, for they earn enough, if they only knew how to spend it. Sometimes, by selling in the streets, they earn three or four shillings a day between them."

"And how *do* they spend it ?"

"Well, they *will* have their supper. So they send out for a loaf of new bread and half a pound of cheese, and a pot of porter, which, altogether, costs 1s. 4d. The woman and the children get a little of the beer, and the man gets enough to make him want more, for which he goes to the public-house, and there stays, glad enough to get away from the comfortless room at home ; and then he drinks up the rest of the money, while that which they spent on their supper alone would make nourishing soup for half the week. The soup in the receipt is very good, and it takes with the people much more than if it had been said, ' make it of bones.' But I find for myself that if I buy a cow-heel, or a bone from which steaks have been cut off, for 4d., I can sell the bone for 2d., after I have stewed it ; and, with vegetables, the soup is, when cold, quite a jelly. Indeed, I have brought a basinful, ma'am, this morning, that you may judge for yourself."

" Thank you ; it is exceedingly good. I guessed that ' bones,' if mentioned in the receipt, would have been rejected : you can teach them further wisdom at discretion. I believe that soup-making *for themselves* would alone cause a reformation in St. Giles's, because the nourishment it would give would prevent the constant craving for stimulants, at which one scarcely wonders, amid the foul smells abounding, and the perpetual weakening of digestion by the hot cup of tea : and you cannot hope to raise them to think over the message from God, which you have carried to them, till some check is placed on their consumption of that which ruins them, body and soul. I wonder that the soup-kitchens, opened for them, have not long ago put them upon thinking of making it for themselves."

"They do not think much. They say their lives are passed in struggles for a living; and many of them answer me now with, 'I'm sure I never thought of this before, Mrs. B.,' when I am showing them what they might do, and how their places might look, if they would take a little trouble. 'We're willing to be taught,' they say, 'if you'll teach us.' And I do feel as if God were making them willing; for, when they speak to me, it is not as to gentlefolks, whom they could deceive. They know I know their ways; and how soup-tickets, and bread-tickets, and coal-tickets, and blankets, all are sold among them, like any other things, to get gin. I am more and more sure that gifts are of no use to them, except in some such way as the saucepans are lent—to make them try and help themselves."

"Have you found any other mode of doing this? What is there in that parcel you have brought with you this morning?"

"Some clothing for St. Giles's, ma'am, which again I find the people are ready and willing *to make for themselves*, if only put in the way. I have my eight women to tea now regularly two nights in the week, and not always the same eight. You dropped a hint one day when I was with you, a month ago, about a clothing club that you had known in Kent, where the poor women made the garment they were going afterwards to buy, the stuff being bought and cut out for them. So I thought it over, and laid out 1s. 11d., which bought this strong, unbleached shirting, and print for two pinafores, besides some calico. I cut out the shirt and pinafores, and fixed them, and had needles and cotton ready, and last night my party helped me to make them, and promised gladly to buy them when they were made. They said, ' Bring us plenty of these things, Mrs. B., and we will buy them, particularly if we save our money by the soup.' If I had taken them work to do for you, ma'am, they would have told me they had not time, or could not work ; but they will make time to do it *for themselves*. And what a change of life it will be to them from their lazy ways! I have been reckoning, but I scarcely like to ask for more money, though it is an outlay that would very soon be returned."

" Well, what is it you have been reckoning ?"

" I have been thinking that if I might provide scissors, bodkins, thimbles, and cotton (for not one woman that came to me had either), as well as material— shirting, calico, print for girls' frocks and pinafores, and jean for boys' blouses—I might cut out and fix garments, just such as the people say they should want, and, when I had fixed them, *they* would make them.

So the women would be taught to work while they were getting clothed ; and, at the same time, led to save their money from the gin-shop ; and then from decent clothing would follow the 'possibility of their going to places of worship, and their children to school ; while, again, this better dress would make them feel that they *must* have a clean room to sit down in. *All this good might come out of the Bible visits.*"

"I rejoice that you have discovered these things for yourself. You live in the midst of the human material that wants re-shaping, and you see its needs. You have been led to do this by God's kindling in your heart the earnest desire to carry to those homes HIS MESSAGE, HIS WORD ; and His power, not your own, has opened for you a door of entrance : *you must have had a message* to begin with. And amid all these schemes of usefulness, I should grieve if *you* personally ever swerve from this one aim of the circulation of the Scriptures as your sole employment for the five hours of the day specified. Are you willing now to under-take a fresh term for this special work, and (as God shall raise them up) to help to train others to go and do likewise ?"

"Oh, yes, indeed, I am ! I often feel that, paid or unpaid, I could never give up *that* work as long as I live, while God affords me health and strength to do it. In comparison with it the work for the body is of small importance ; but the one grows out of the other."

" I see it does. It always did, when the Bible work was properly done, even by ladies. You bear to the people the Book which says, ' Deal thy bread to the hungry ;' and which commands that ' when thou seest the naked, that thou cover him.' (Isa. lviii. 7.) And this is most effectually done, as experience has proved, by helping the poor to provide for their own necessities. I wish to know, that I may represent to others who believe that they wish, or are fitted for, this kind of employment, how you have followed out in detail the desire expressed in your letter to ' return in the evening to the homes where the aid of a friend-ly hand was needed to rectify disorder.' I should fear you would be too tired, on returning to your dinner at three o'clock, to make further effort."

" You know, ma'am, my district lies all near my own home ; and there is much that I can do while sitting still to rest. I can think and plan for individual cases ; I can cut out and fix the needle-work ; and see to my soup-making for the next day, for my fire is out while I am away from home ; and afterwards I very often find it needful to go and do the thing that I want to be done. If a poor woman is ill, I can make her bed and right her room for the night ; I can wash her children for her, and show her how bright their clean faces might be made ; and I can interest her now about being able to get clothes for them fit to go to school. The cover-all pinafore *first*, to hide rags (which I wash for her some day, perhaps, to show that they might at least be clean rags), and then that nice pinafore outside will soon bring the desire for the clean whole garments within. I have quite enough already to encourage me to persevere. And there is many a room where at first I found no furniture but an old table, with the tin beer-cans upon it, and perhaps a pack of cards, with two or three old baskets turned upside down for seats, and naked children sprawling round, that now begins to look very different. It does argue something good about them, when they are told I have 'a message from God' to them, so many are not unwilling to hear it ; and they may, by a continuance of this visiting, be persuaded to come forth and hear the message as explained by the ministers of His word. As I read a few verses to them sometimes, the words seem to drop like healing balm upon their sorrows, poor things ! for they almost all say that their husbands treat them badly and beat them. One learns to do so of another, and I believe it depends very much upon the women to alter it. They are certainly most thankful for a little kindness ; and one or two of them have said, after the saucepans were lent to them,

' Well, now, I am sure we can do no less, Tom, than go to church or to the Mission-hall (as it may be) next Sunday evening.'"

"I suppose they are settled now again into their winter quarters. How have they spent the money, in general, that they brought with them from the hop-grounds?"

"A few seem to have spent it wisely, and have bought excellent second-hand warm shawls and strong boots for themselves and their children. Many more have spent it very unwisely. St. Giles's was like a fair the first weeks in October. They met in ' factions,' and filled each other's rooms, and showed their new clothes, which, one by one, soon disappeared for drink. The clothes were very often unsuitable. I saw one woman wearing a flounced gown of all the colors of the rainbow, edged with black velvet, made in the height of fashion, but worn with uncombed hair and the boots that had served in the hop-ground. I believe two-thirds of this extraordinary earning by the hop-picking is gone in drink."

"That is sad, indeed ; but let us hope we have made a beginning that may lead to something better. In God's strength you are trying to lift the hand of the poor outcasts to lay hold on the advantages which are so abundantly placed before them in St. Giles's. The missionary friend from Burmah, Mrs. Ingolls, whom I

3*

brought to meet you in your district last week, was alike astonished and delighted with those noble Baths, Wash-houses, and Model Lodging-houses, which are the glory of the place. How she longed to have such institutions among her heathen abroad! What sympathy she felt for the detail of your work! You will never forget her prayer for you, and she will never forget St. Giles's. It will now be very desirable to think over the many ways in which ladies who desire to do so can render help to such persons as yourself. It seems that you feel there is room for three or four more agents of your own order in your immediate neighborhood. The Bible Society has signified its willingness to employ such when the right women can be found ; and as it is a position in which those who undertake it must be willing to ' endure hardness,' I should like each individual to go round with you for a week, to see if she can bear the rough with the smooth."

The last suggestion, practical though it might seem, and willing as " Marian " at first appeared to meet it, was not in practice found possible. The people expecting a quiet visit from the good woman in whom they had begun to place confidence, resented, she said, any perpetual introduction to strange faces, and asked "if they were going to be made a puppet-show of?" It was not, besides, a very extraordinary phase of

human nature, especially as self-educated, if Marian
liked to be " Marian " alone, and did not fancy that
any one could do her work in her way but herself.
The power of individual action, and that of training
others to the same, except as it may be by the force of
example, are not often found combined in the same
person.

Detailed reports of the work, therefore, such as the
above, in the Magazine—"The Book and its Missions"—
continued from month to month, were made chiefly
instrumental in planting similar agency in districts
beyond St. Giles's. To another such it is now time
that we introduce our readers.

CHAPTER V.

THE BIBLE-WOMAN AMONG THE DUST-HEAPS.

THE contents of every dust-bin in this vast London, a " province covered with houses," are carried periodically away to some great receptacle, and few of us even think what becomes of that which we call the " refuse" of our families. The dustman receives his small gratuity from each householder ; and collecting from as many dust-bins as will make him a load for his cart, he demands another shilling at the gate of the Paddington wharfs, as he deposits it within their precincts.

The monstrous heaps, when amassed, are to be sifted and disposed of, their contents sorted, and carried away in separate baskets. We can offer but a slight notion of the medley of which they are composed.

A dust-heap of this kind is often very valuable to the contractor, and a large one is said to be worth from four to five thousand pounds. Of course, its chief constituent element is cinders, mixed with bits of coal, from the carelessness or waste of thousands of

[60]

servants, which the searchers and sorters pick out of the heap, to be sold forthwith. The largest and best of the cinders also are selected for the use of laundresses and braziers, whose purposes they answer better than coke. The far greater remainder is called *breeze*, because it is the portion left after the wind has blown the cinder-dust from it, through large upright iron sieves, held and shaken, elbow high, by the women who stand in the heap, whilst men throw up the stuff into the sieves. The *breeze*, and ashes also, are sold to brick-makers, who will sometimes contract for 15,000 or 16,000 chaldrons of either in one order. The ashes are mixed with the clay of the bricks, and the *breeze* is used as fuel to burn between their layers.

But the heap is not all breeze and ashes; it includes likewise " software and hardware," the former comprising all vegetable and animal matters—everything that will decompose : these are carried off as soon as possible, to be employed for manure. Stale fish and dead cats come into this list ; the skins of the latter being stripped off by the women who sift, which they can sell for fourpence or sixpence, according to the color : white is the most in request.

But the " hardware" does not merely mean broken pottery, though of this there is abundance : some of it is matched and mended by the women who find it, and it then becomes their perquisite ; the rest, with oyster shells, is sold to make new roads. Hardware, how-ever, in the dust-heaps, means almost everything : rags, which go to the paper-makers ; bones, to the bone-boilers ; old iron, brass and lead, to salesmen of those metals ; broken glass, to old glass shops ; old carpets, old mattresses, old boxes, old pails, old baskets, broken tea-boards, candlesticks, fenders, old silk handker-chiefs, knives and salt-cellars, not forgetting the old shoes, which go away in bushels to the " translators," or people who turn old into new ones ; the dust-heaps, therefore, making work continually for our friends in St. Giles's. Everything that the householder has thought " not worth mending," and has decreed to " go along with the dust," besides many a wasteful addition that the mistress never knows, from mansions where extravagance and recklessness bear rule.

Rings, brooches, silver spoons, forks, and golden sovereigns, occasionally also get carted away with the dust.

But now to turn our attention to the human beings, and especially to the women, who are employed as sorters and sifters. Many a lady at her parlor win-dow had seen them pass, from their hours of toil to their ill-kept homes, in almost savage guise, with " dust and fine ashes filling up all the wrinkles of their faces "—with their apron full of cinders, perhaps on their heads, and their gown turned up so as to carry another heap of wood or paper, or whatever was their day's finding besides. Sometimes their feet encased in navvies' boots,—and hands and arms the color of ashes,—would scarcely be distinguishable from the grimy piece of carpet tied around their waist, which they wear as they stand in the heap, to protect them from the scraping of the cinders ; a man's old coat possibly completing the rest of the costume.

And what are the homes to which they wend their way ? Often " places like stables," where, with their children, ravenous for the evening meal, they sit down to partake of it with unwashen hands, and with no change of garments. The children's home during the day has been in the streets or on the stairs. These people, as a class, are very subject to fever, for they have an objection to open windows ; and their filthy walls are guiltless of whitewash, and seldom know the painting of the bright sunbeam.

They pay 3s. 6d. a week rent for their rooms. The perquisites they bring home with them are manifold. The kind city missionary of the district once went in to visit an old man, who, being bed-ridden, asked him to stir the saucepan on his fire ; and as he observed, in doing so, " that it was a savory mess," the reply was, " Well, mayhap you might not like to eat it, sir ; it is some bones well washed, and some potatoes and onions my wife picked off the heap. It's very well for me."

As their wages are only one shilling a day, they are very glad to find warmth from the supply of cinders and coals which they amass during the day. Paper and wood also belong to them, as much as they can carry, with corks of bottles, by which alone some will say " they find themselves in shoe-leather ;" pill-boxes and gallipots are also their lawful property, and a poor woman had once the pleasure of contributing a dozen of the latter as a gift to the Samaritan Hospital, where the poor often seek medicine or ointment, and have nothing in which to take it home. The finder of any jewelry or other small valuable is also very apt to pocket that which she may have discovered. A banker's cheque for a considerable sum was found in one of the dust-heaps—it was on Harris and Farquhar —in 1847.

There is a great difference among individuals even in this rough class of women. Some have a gay taste, and after being out all day on the heap, in the wet, will spend the evening in dancing and drinking. These frequently sleep away their Sabbath days, and are of the number who, on one or two holidays in the year, such as Whitsuntide, will be seen in flaunting ribbons and bright dresses, which, on their return from their frolics, will go to the pawnshop, to remain till a similar occasion shall call for their use. The husbands and wives have separate purses, and keep what they each earn, with the understanding that one shall find this, and the other that, in the housekeeping, such as it is, and miserable thereby is the lot of the poor children. The missionary says, when they become sober and thinking people, the woman is in general intrusted with all the money.

Many a lady at her parlor window, in the neighborhood of Hyde Park, had seen the dust-women pass, day by day, in their uncouth guise; but to the heart of one especially God had sent home a paper in the little periodical before mentioned, called "A Mission for Christian Ladies;" and this, in connection with the details of Marian's work in St. Giles's, caused her to seek personal communication with the editor, and to form the resolution to endeavor to elicit similar agency for Paddington. Her efforts were successful, and a "Martha" was ere long set to work among the dust-heaps. The incidents of the choice may be found interesting, and are given in connection with a report of the good woman's first month's labor in this new locality.

March 17th, 1858.

We know you are desirous to receive particulars of the commencement of our essay in Female Colportage. The difficulty of finding a suitable agent for this kind of work is greater than at first appears; and still I could not doubt that there must be some poor Christian person in this neighborhood who might, with careful training and direction bestowed upon her, prove very useful and valuable, and acquire increasing adaptation to her work as she pursued it.

My first consultations were held with Mr. Pearson, the excellent City Missionary of the district, whose twelve years' labor, superintended by the Rev. James Strattan, has borne admirable fruit, especially in connection with the chapel provided for canal boatmen, stablemen, carmen, dustmen, cabmen, coal-heavers, and wharf-laborers, who congregate in this locality, and make it specially a missionary station. A Sunday-school, a Penny Bank, a Sick and Provident Club, and a Reading-room are all now prospering under Mr. Pearson's fostering help; but he has long seen that some *womanly* teaching among the women, and especially as connected with *a Bible mission*, would be of great assistance to him with regard to his own work.

By the aid of his experience, therefore, the good woman, Martha P., was selected, as one who, though herself very poor, had, to the extent of her means, been always willing, at his suggestion, to clean a room or make a bed for a neighbor in sickness. He said he believed her to have been long one of the Lord's people, ready and willing to do the Lord's work.

Martha having, as you know, paid a visit to Marian in St. Giles's, also went round with the colporter, Mr.

Shaw, for a day or two, to observe his method of seeking subscribers for Bibles among the degraded classes who surrounded her own dwelling. Having long been their neighbor, she is not unacquainted with their habits and mode of life, so that they feel more ready to trust her with their pence than a stranger.

Martha's own full experience of poverty fits her to sympathize at once with her poorest neighbors. The missionary told me he could not forget the day he visited their home, when her husband was recovering from fever, which is abundantly prevalent in the district. The poor man, who by accident had injured his hands, and also his feet, in his calling as a plasterer, answered a kind word of congratulation with, "Yes, sir, I am much better; I am so hungry now, I could eat anything." "That is a mercy, is it not?" said the missionary; to which the reply was, "Yes; but I've nothing to eat—and yet God is very good," he continued. "Don't he hear prayer quick?" He went on to explain that they had been praying earnestly "that God would be pleased either to send them food, *or damp* the children's appetites; and all this morning," he added, "they have not once cried for bread."

The above incident occurred some seven years since. They are still poor, but their children are now more off their hands. In all their recent straits, they have, by close and self-denying management, been able generally to put by one penny a week in the savings-bank, to provide for still more pressing wants or sickness ; and many another good habit Martha can urge on others, by experience of its benefit to herself. I find her very active, punctual and good-tempered, with a clear head in keeping her account of the Bible money received ; so that, when the hour for my weekly superintendence arrives, I have never been delayed by mistakes. Another point which it especially gratifies me to observe is her humility and self-distrust. She is most willing to conform to anything that I suggest, and very simple and earnest in her dependence on God for any good result or blessing on her efforts. At present she cannot write, but takes her little boy with her to put down in a waste book sums received, which I copy for her in the collecting book. In needlework and the plain duties of housewifery she is a competent pattern. So much for the character of *my* " Marian." And now as to her mission work.

I asked her how she felt on the first morning she went alone to her district.

" All of a tremble," was the answer ; " but I just went to the Lord for strength."

" And how did the people, on the whole, receive you ?"

" Some shut the door in my face, and said, ' We want bread instead of Bibles ;' but it was not always so. I prayed as I went along, and the Lord heard. A great many of these rough people cannot read; but one of them bought a Bible, and said, ' Now she hoped her husband would not go so much to the beer-shop, but stay at home and read to her.' Another, with four children, had no Bible, and her husband, a tailor, no work, but she began to subscribe for a fourpenny Testament. Another woman, when I invited her to a place of public worship, said 'she had no clothes.' ' Oh,' I said, ' never mind your clothes. You have clothes enough to go out to buy your food, and you can come out in the evening to worship God. He will look at your heart's dress, and will never mind what you wear.' She asked me to sit down, and I read to her a part of the fourteenth chapter of St. John : ' Let not your heart be troubled, neither let it be afraid.' So in that there was strength for me too. She listened attentively, and began to subscribe for a tenpenny Bible which I showed her."

It was on the 25th of January, 1858—that day of general rejoicing on the marriage of our young princess—that Martha began to invite her poor neighbors to devote the pence too often squandered in gin to the purchase of the precious Word of God, which is the " water of life" to all who drink of its refreshing streams. For the first month, it was arranged that she should collect only three days a week,—five hours each day ; and in that first month she obtained forty-two subscribers for Bibles and Testaments, and paid me £1 13s. 2d. towards the purchase.

From the date of Monday, the 22d of February, she collected *every* day. She now obtained six additional subscribers among the poor women attending the Mothers' Meetings, held in the neighboring school-room ; and four were also found among the poor boys of the " Shoe-black Brigade," which institution is only one of many kindred schemes springing daily into extensive usefulness, from the active exertion and prayerful efforts of the managers of the Boatmen's Chapel.

Up to the date of my present letter more than ninety subscribers' names for Bibles and Testaments are on her book. The average sale increases every week.

On Wednesday, March 3d, I thought it time to propose the self-clothing club. The few hints dropped in the wharf district on the practicability of such a plan being carried into effect, were received with such marked approbation, that we thought it had better be organized at a little social tea-party, to which the *very* lowest and poorest were to be invited, and some pieces of material displayed. This party assembled in Martha's room ; and the good missionary looked in during the evening, and told me afterwards that the delight of these poor creatures, at such an opportunity of procuring warm and tidy clothing, was unbounded. Their expression of joy was so childish, the missionary seemed able to compare it to nothing but what he fancied a party of New Zealanders would exhibit before they were civilized by Christianity. Surely, there is something very affecting in this, when we remember the *numbers* there are in our great city in this state of semi-barbarism, and *living close around us* who bask in the full light of Gospel privileges.

Perhaps Shaw did not tell you of a little incident which occurred in his second round with Martha in the dust-wharf district. She said something to one woman, in a deplorable court, about the plan of collecting their pence for any garments they required ; and the woman immediately answered, " What a good thing that will be for us !" Whereupon, Shaw, fancying she might be anticipating some bonus, said, " But you know, mistress, you'll have to *pay* for what you receive, and to help to *make* it, too ;" to which the woman answered, " Ah ! that will be better still, for 'twill be teaching us to help ourselves." I thought this spontaneous expression of opinion very satisfactory. Each of the poor women, on Wednesday evening, became a willing depositor of money for clothes. One woman said she had once saved up two shillings towards buying a gown, but her children were crying for bread, and she was obliged to break into this little sum, and could never save it again. Martha was almost overcome by the friendliness and joy of her visitors. She had been rather tried by a feeling of fear and apprehension, lest, in seeking to help her neighbors, they should dislike her interference, and look upon her with distrust ; but it proves to be quite the contrary. She said to the missionary, "I thought they would be all against me, but you see here they are all for me. It is surely God's doing."

She is already made a great blessing to the sick persons on the district. There is a soothing influence in her cheerful smile and pleasant voice, which cannot fail to reach the heart. As a mother myself, I feel the charm of her winning way of speaking, even to an infant, and her sympathy is so practical. It is those who have lived in cellars, and been starved themselves, who truly know how to feel with persons in similar circumstances. May God shield her from every temptation to vanity and self-conceit! No one would call her a naturally superior woman, like " Marian ;" but it is in her real humility and entire dependence on her Saviour's strength and blessing that I so thankfully perceive her fitness for the work.

I cannot conclude this report without telling you of the great kindness and sympathy of feeling shown me by my personal friends, and the liberal response made to my appeal for pecuniary assistance to carry out this clothing plan, etc. Some of those at a distance have most generously aided me, and others are Christians with whom I have no personal acquaintance. May they all have the happiness of knowing that this effort for the help of their poor sisters prospers, under God's blessing, to the full extent that they could desire.

H. G.

4

CHAPTER VI.

THE plans which were being pursued in St. Giles's, of helping the people to help themselves, and which had arisen, step by step, out of the efforts to induce them to provide themselves with Bibles, took root also in the Dust-wharf district. A long list of subscriptions, all unasked, acknowledged on the cover of " The Book and its Missions," testified to the interest which was excited for the improvement of the condition of the poor in both localities. This money was subscribed, *not to pay for the Bible work, which, we must repeat, was done by the Bible Society*—but for addition of salary to the women, for the domestic part of their mission, and also to advance materials, whether for clothing of various kinds, or for cheap and clean BEDDING, of which the poor of London are so lamentably destitute.

A special inquiry into the latter particular was at this time suggested by a benevolent medical friend, Thos. Mackern, Esq., who had, in his professional visits

[74]

among the poor, been greatly moved to sympathy by witnessing their sufferings from cold at night. He offered from his own purse the first contribution towards an experimental supply of cheap beds, to be purchased by instalments. On investigation it was discovered that many of them slept on a heap of dirty rags—in the rags also of their day's clothing, and *never had slept in a bed*. They never rise refreshed and comforted from a night's rest, but begin the day with an early dram, often for the lack of that natural refreshment. Yet they could, it was evident, be induced to purchase a *good tick and flock bed for six shillings*, if they saw it, and that by sixpence at a time; and the receipt of *one* led to the desire for the purchase of two or three beds for each family, with their summer's earnings. Even the decent poor required the opportunity given them to do this; and the easy purchase of a Bible first showed them what else might be done in the same way towards the provision of their own family comforts. That which it was a habit to spend IN GIN, thus began to be turned into better channels.

The women of "Marian's" district presently commenced the purchase of fifty of these cheap beds. Her own account of the promise of this experiment was thus given soon after its commencement. She had been asked by her Superintendent, after ten months' labor,

what hope she saw for her people from her own in
creasing experience among them, and the following
was her answer :—

" There is hope for the hopeless, if their attention
should be first aroused by some one they know coming
to bring them God's Book. I should never despair of
any people, after what I have seen in St. Giles's. The
lowest poor have come to be what they are, by the
mistake of supposing they were too bad to be mended.
They drink to stupefy their misery ; and their money
will come out of the gin-shops, if other things are *not
only talked about but put before them*. I wondered at
the influence of the Loan Saucepans, and at the willingness of many persons to begin to purchase clothing,
with which numbers of persons in my district are become comfortably provided ; but now the cheap clean
BEDS seem as if they will surpass everything else in the
thoughts they will kindle, and the habits they will
alter. I have brought £2 15s. this morning, all in
sixpences, paid for beds only. I might have had more
than as much again ; but I have already taken 180
names, and am now come to ask if indeed another fifty
beds can be promised before more names are taken.
One woman said, as the money was being paid, ' Nine-
teen out of twenty of those sixpences would have gone
for gin ;' to which many around responded, ' Ay, that
they would !" Three hundred people came to the

Mission-hall last night, one after another, and from all parts,—Westminster, Mary-le-bone, Chelsea, Clerken-well. Mr. G. intends to have a board painted to say that no applicants can be received, except from St. Giles's."

"The hundred beds already gone out are all to persons you have known in your district, are they not?"

"Ninety of the number are to persons whom, having visited and watched through the winter, I myself knew to be without a bed. They have often spared the penny to purchase a Bible long before they knew that any temporal advantage would come after it. The rest I have allotted to some Irish, who were honest and desirous to improve their condition, which, you will remember, ma'am, you particularly wished, because you said £15 of the money sent for St. Giles's, and almost the foundation of the fund, came from an Irish lady, who delighted in the mission of the book to her people. I met the Romish canon of St. Giles's in one of the rooms this week, where a bed had been supplied, and he spoke very kindly to me, and said, 'You are about an excellent work in improving the condition of the people.' I said, 'You know, sir, they pay for the beds *themselves*, only in an easy way.' 'Yes,' he said, 'I am glad of it; and I am glad to perceive they have an opportunity to do so, without distinction of creed or country.'"

"Do the rooms become cleaner with the clean beds?"

"I can point to at least thirty rooms that are not like the same; and I should scarcely know the women for the same. Some of their floors were so thick with black mud, you could not tell there were boards underneath. A man, whose wife had subscribed for a bed, bought a birch-broom to give his floor the first cleansing, and then came the hard scrubbing and red-sanding. When they do take to be clean, they can be very clean in St. Giles's, and they like to have the floor like a gravel walk; and then, when they get the bed, you should hear them say, 'Oh, we never knew what a night's rest was before!' It does me good to hear the mothers exclaim, 'We cannot find it in our hearts to put our children to sleep on the rags we had before. When we have paid for this, oh! if we may but have another, and another—but then we shall want two rooms!'"

"Well, thank God, we have shown them what it is in their own power to do for themselves; and may His blessing rest upon the extension of such an agency far and wide. Are any of them buying bedsteads?"

"Yes; I have heard of half a dozen; and very many more will certainly do so, as their summer earnings from the flowers and fruit increase."

And now it is the 10th of June—a sultry morning in London and everywhere else. Perhaps, after all, no region is much cooler than the shady side of our broad, well-watered streets, before the sun attains his strength, and pours his fervid rays centrally down on the tide of human life, which stays not for heat or cold.

The early cries of St. Giles's and its fraternity salute our ears, and presently " Marian," with whom its name will now be identified to our readers, steps into the parlor, where this day year she went forth with her first Bible for the " dens." The sum of her account sold is now 1004 copies—413 Bibles and 591 Testaments, purchased in St. Giles's in twelve months, oy the penny subscriptions of " the lowest of the low," each penny called for once, twice, and sometimes thrice, by the patient and earnest NATIVE AGENT, chosen from among themselves.

Few would imagine the labor that it has cost to collect the £24 returned for their Bibles from " the wandering folk," whose life is mercifully spent out of doors, for how could they exist otherwise in the heart of our great city at this season ? A year ago " Marian" knew little of the circumstances of her neighbors beyond the precincts of her own court. *Now* she has seen their ways, their means, and their miseries, through the vagrant summer and the pinching winter ; she has become a MOTHER OF CHARITY, by various methods, to many who felt they never had one before ; and in carrying them the MESSAGE FROM GOD, she has watched week by week their want of water, and space, and pure air ; their want of cleanliness, of clothing, and of bedding.

She has reported simply and faithfully to her Superintendent, who has again reported to the lovers of the Book and of the poor, the discoveries made by this its HOME MISSION. The Lord has disposed kind hearts from far and near, not to cast *gifts* as into the slough of despond, which would never have mended it, but to advance the means to help the mothers of St. Giles's to help themselves.; they repaying, with an honesty and a punctuality which have done credit to their English, yes, and to their Irish hearts, with the earnings of the summer, to a very considerable extent, the advances of the winter ; so that the benefits of a temporal kind they have received are becoming *purchases of their own (like the Bibles)*, for which, nevertheless, they express tenfold the gratitude they have ever bestowed for pure gifts.

Marian's Clothing and Bedding Clubs for these " lowest of the low " were not fully organized till the late autumn and the winter of 1857, since which 'the people have paid to her £35 by instalments, towards an outlay of £63 for the provision of 250 beds, and £15 for garments of various kinds, making a total of about £50 saved during the first half-year's experiment of turning aside this money from the gin-shop, into whose current of liquid fire it would otherwise certainly have flowed. Yes, and not only this money, but much more, for the person who has begun to save *for a bed*, when that has been obtained, has almost invariably tried to save for something else—for a bedstead, for sheets, and for a little crockery, and even for a picture on the wall. One woman left off beer for a month that she might get the bed, and " in that month I have learned," she said, " to do without it ; and if I can do so now, in this roasting weather, I can do so always."

But, oh ! the revelations from St. Giles's during this time of almost torrid sunshine. The beds have done wonders to induce the keeping clean of many rooms, but in numbers of others the inmates can never lie down *to sleep ;* and after trying to do so, the close " den " is forsaken during the live-long night for the pavement and the door-step, and this even by respectable artisans. Nothing but pulling down many of the houses would exterminate the vermin. These, and the foul odors, are alike the almost invincible hinderances at this time in the way of the Colporters, and of all who visit the London poor at this season of the year. The smells cannot be forgotten when once imbibed, and they are indeed deadly poison. We have long made grand streets, and built princely public

4*

offices ; but we are only just beginning to think of England's Public Fountains, and well-drained and ventilated dwellings for the poorer classes of our great cities. Marian's continued report concerning her people is, that they do not want *relief*, but *provision* for their rightful and natural wants, of which, as a money-earning and industrious race, they will be willing to take advantage. The industrious in every class can, in general, earn sufficient for their own support ; and the only true aid that can be rendered to them is that which *helps them to help themselves*, though the doors of sickness, sorrow, and extraordinary need are always standing open in a world of sin, through which the bounty of the upper classes may wisely and legitimately find entrance.

CHAPTER VII.

A MIDSUMMER FETE IN ST. GILES'S.

" Marian " has a tea-party to-night, the 7th of July,
but it is not one of her old kind ; not half a dozen
women from the " dens," who had washed their gowns
and caps to pay a visit, perhaps for the first time in
their lives, to a quiet, clean room, where they were to
learn to work, and to listen to her reading from the
Book.

Still, it is the Book that brings them together. It
is a party given to the Bible subscribers by the subscribers to the St. Giles's Fund, who have been the readers
of " The Book and its Missions " during the last
twelve months. Out of the 1004 persons to whom
" Marian " had in that space of time delivered " the
Holy Word of God," she, in conjunction with her
superintending lady, had invited about forty to partake of a somewhat more bountiful repast in one of
the large rooms at the Broad street Ragged School
and Refuge, which was kindly and gratuitously lent
for the purpose.

Six o'clock was the hour named. and as the clock

struck, the guests began to arrive and seat themselves quietly on both sides of the long tables covered with white cloths, placed up each side of the room. They had themselves previously brought a voluntary contri-bution to embellish the feast—which, though there are no gardens in St. Giles's, it was in their power to do, as a flower-selling people—jugs of stocks, roses, pinks, and pansies, which took our hearts out to country cottage doors; and two glass vases of Marian's own were filled with regal white lilies, which might, among the Romanists, have done honor to "Our Lady."

On the high window-ledges sparkled balsams, ger-aniums, and fuchsias, which were gladly lent for the occasion also by the partakers of the treat; and more lovely still, as a product of the spontaneous gratitude of the Seven Dials, on a small table which connected the two long ones, lay half a dozen *bouquets*, which might have been the envy of Covent Garden, and which, we were told, were " for the ladies who had been so kind to them." When one thought of " Church Lane," and Marian told us these had been made *there*, and that no one would say who had made them—" it was the offering from all "—our hearts were touched ; and considering ourselves but as the local representa-tives of a far wider circle, we offer to our subscribers this testimony from the heart.

We wish they could have seen the looks of pleasure from the givers as these bouquets were taken up and admired. Water-lilies or choice white roses formed the centre, encircled by scarlet geraniums, heliotropes, mignonette, calceolarias, and all delicate and sweet-smelling additions, surrounded by a bordering of lace paper.

The flowers will not live forever, but the feeling that brought them shall not be forgotten till " Church Lane," *as it is*, is swept from the earth ; till its rags overhead no more darken the sunshine ; till on the site of its gloomy dens rise wholesome dwellings ; till the fountain adorns its entrance, and the Book of God is the guide of every home.

There is not a room there now into which the Bible-woman cannot find access; and many a reformed woman she has brought out of that locality to find lodging elsewhere.

Look around now at our guests ; they are an out-door folk. We only gave them three days' notice of our tea-meeting, so they have had no time for special preparation. You see them as they are : women who seem as if they had known rough usage ; whose faces look as if they had once been in the school of the fist and the stick, and who, perhaps, have often deserved it, but who are now desirous of leading a new life—who have heard of something better. They have brought their twenty babies who could not be left at home, and we have seventy or eighty, rather than forty mothers; but our provision is on an elastic scale. They always approve of Marian's arrangements, and she "likes to provide things of the best."

So they turn contentedly to their tea and cake, and "plenty of bread and butter," and tell us "they are so very happy; it is so nice to be waited upon by ladies." Before they began, they were led by Mr. Lee to sing a prayer for blessing, which they did very nicely :

> "Be present at our table, Lord."

And at the close,—

> "We thank thee, Lord, for this our food."

All being fully satisfied, the tables and tea-things were quickly cleared away by the aid of three or four handy girls; the forms were turned; and, almost before they knew it, these women, many of them so lately fierce, wild scolds, were seen willingly seated with their babies, to listen to the lively addresses of various friends belonging to different congregations of Christians in the neighborhood, and to some from afar. It was the first time that it had been found possible to gather them in any numbers, and to seat them in order, as their habit had been to pass in and out on the Clothing Club night, not seeming to think it worth while to sit down.

The Rev. James Wilson, from Aberdeen, was there. He and his lady have for seven years past been accomplishing, with the aid of other friends, and in the strength of God, similar transformations in the North, and he was quite at home with our women of St. Giles's. Professor Martin, who accompanied him, expressed himself much struck with THE FIRST ELEMENT in the present reform—that "of beginning with the Bible." He said "he meant to carry that idea to Scotland."

The Rev. Thomas Phillips, late Jubilee Secretary of the Bible Society, next told some stories, which were listened to with interest, about the scarcity, in past time, of the Bible in Wales. One, of a poor woman, who walked forty miles to get the Book, and then paid for it all she had—two shillings, and six pairs of stockings of her own knitting ; and the contrast to this scarcity was easily depicted in referring to the cheap Bibles, for which the whole assembly had subscribed, and which could not be sold at the price except by a Bible Society. Mr. Phillips being Welsh, and a Bible agent especially for the Welsh, attracted some sympathy from his compatriots in the company, two of whom, as he left the room, bade him "*nos dawch*" (good night), with much fervor, in their own tongue.

Thereafter followed several friends (and each, as it

seemed, met with individual welcome), who described to the eager audience the large colored diagrams or pictures on the walls, which are published by the Educational Union, in illustration of the "Book and its Story," and to which all eyes were directed with pleased inquiry :—"The Ancient Scribe writing the Manuscript Copy of the Book;" "Wiclif declaring before the Archbishop that 'its truth should prevail;'" "The Bible Chained to the Church Pillar;" "Luther finding it in the Erfurt Library;" "The search for the New Testaments under the floor at Cambridge;" "Jehoiakim burning the Roll—the first destroyer of Holy Scripture;" and the "Burning of Bibles," at a later day, "at St. Paul's Cross." Time failed to explain them all.

J. Hampden Fordham, Esq., one of the parent committee of the Bible Society, and well known in connection with Ragged Schools, added some welcome words on the Bible being the Book for *all*, and a precious Book to the poor—the word of Him who said, "The Spirit of the Lord hath anointed me to preach the Gospel to the poor."

And thus, by aid of various kind helpers, the time passed swiftly away, till, true to his promise, the Rev. Anthony Thorold, the beloved Rector of the parish, came in to close the evening with a few words of exhortation, as he had opened it by prayer. It was his first introduction to many faces there, though he recognized others present as having recently accompanied him for a day's fresh air, among four hundred of his parishioners, to Erith. His most appropriate and simple, yet spirited address won every heart, and showed how thoroughly he had identified himself with this Bible Mission to the lowest of his parishioners— not so much ecclesiastically, as he did as a Christian man. He told the people how he sympathized with the effort made to help them to help themselves, whether to obtain the Bible or clean clothes and beds—how he desired to encourage them still further to do this— how he delighted in whatever brought them to know and love the BOOK—and how he should now look to see many of them at his Monday evening service, held in their own precincts, especially *for the poor*, when he should rejoice to tell them of the love of Christ, who died for them.

He said he had seen the providing of BEDS, though apparently a common-place idea, to be nevertheless so important that he had himself provided a second depôt for those articles, and had sold a great many, and that in the winter he intended to " open a shop," &c., for blankets and sheets, to be procured by instalments—a statement which elicited great applause. He wished them never to forget that the Bible had brought us together, and that now, as women's work among women had secured this communication, he trusted they would all join him again in an earnest prayer that the Holy Spirit of God might come and fill every heart, and accomplish in us what is far beyond the power of man or woman to do, viz., "take of the things of Christ, and show them unto us," to the redemption of our souls.

The meeting then broke up, and, as the people retired, they expressed universal satisfaction, and several of them said they should accept Mr. Thorold's invitation to his Monday evening service.

It was a very pleasing feature of the evening, that as many of the Female Bible Missionaries as it was possible to assemble were included in the party, and helped to make the tea. Owing to the short notice they were not *all* there ; the representatives of Spitalfields, Clerkenwell, and Paddington, were missing ; but Westminster, Somer's Town, Gray's Inn Lane, and Islington sent their " Esther," and " Charlotte," and " Lydia," and " Anna," to assist " Marian " at her Midsummer Fête.

CHAPTER VIII.

THE close of our last chapter pointed to new stations for Female Bible Missions—vast fields of crowded humanity.

Six hundred years ago that portion of London's heart now called CLERKENWELL was a green and pleasant country spot, famed for numerous springs and wells, which were places of resort on holidays. When Clerkenwell-green was really a green, instead of a stony triangle, the Priory of St. John of Jerusalem arose in that age on its south side, and the Nunnery of St. Mary on the north. A fine open country spread around the rising ground on which these monastic establishments were built, on all sides but the south, where lay the city. The landscape was varied with vineyards and meadows; springs and rivulets descended from wooded hills and uplands, and watered vales of luxuriant verdure. Now that the country has been swallowed up of the town, it is refreshing to escape, if only in thought, from the dust and smoke of the "million-peopled city," and to remember the olden time.

The rural passed, by degrees, into the suburban, and in 1617 a number of fine houses had been built in the district, which were inhabited by persons of rank and fashion. In another century, fashion took its deparure further west; and in yet another, the neighborhood became celebrated as the peculiar abode of WATCHMAKERS; and that wondrous little machine, which passes through more than one hundred hands to its completion, bade "its escapement makers, engine turners, fusee cutters, springers, finishers, face and dial makers," and all its train of contributors, find their homes in each other's vicinity—in this same Clerkenwell.

The population of this district was, in 1852, more than 64,000 persons, and of these between 9000 and 10,000 were employed in the watch, clock, and jewelry trade. The attendance at public worship on the census Sunday, in 1851, was proportionally *smaller* in Clerkenwell than in any of the other thirty-six districts into which London was divided for the purposes of the census; and we regretted to hear, at the Bible House, that there had been *no Bible Society Auxiliary* in Clerkenwell since the year 1850. An auxiliary had been established in 1835, which, during the fifteen years of its existence, accomplished a sale of 4808 copies; but this, in 1849, dwindled down to merely seventeen in the year. The institution was soon afterwards pronounced "defunct," which leaves the inference to be drawn, without doubt, that whatever may have been the distribution made from any sources of private benevolence—or, more recently, at St. James's Church, by the zeal of the Rev. R. Maguire, the new Incumbent—a large Bible work, and one much needed, has at once to be recommenced in Clerkenwell.

Encouraged by the successful exertions of the female Bible missionary in St. Giles's during the last ten months, the British and Foreign Bible Society have been willing to authorize the careful selection and superintendence, by suitable ladies, of more such missionaries as *paid agents* in other low parts of London. Mr. Maguire, who has been so successful in an open-air mission to the working classes, and has thereby attracted them to a Tuesday evening service within his church, thus speaks of the commencement of a Female Bible Mission in his parish, in his pastoral letter to his congregation :—

"Within the first three weeks of the operation of this agency, as many as seventy-three subscribers for Bibles were obtained in some of our poorest streets. They are to be paid for by small weekly instalments, and much spiritual and domestic good may be expected.

with God's blessing, to result from this organization."

And what is the description of many of these poorest streets, in this now dense mass of human habitations? The Report of the City Mission has thus painted them: "Dingy, swarming alleys, crowded with tattered women, and unwashed, lazy men, clustering round the doors of low-browed public-houses, or seated in unwindowed shops, frouzy with piles of rubbish, or displaying coarse and greasy food." This is the neighborhood in which Mr. Vanderkiste, who was for six years a City Missionary, made "Notes and Narratives of a Mission to the Dens of London"— those dens which, up rickety staircases, and through fever and dirt, still want exploring day by day, with the Bible in hand. Has the Bible Society scarcely sent forth 5000 Bibles and Testaments in twenty years among so many? If St. Giles's wanted a "Marian," and Paddington a "Martha," Clerkenwell needed its "Sarah"—a devoted, vigorous, motherly "Sarah."

We will therefore follow her in a few of her first Bible walks, not so much into a district of costermongers, as amid the homes of poor *artisans*, out of work, or in half work; and, in contrast to the many forms of misery she has found among these, the daily-paid out-door laborer in St. Giles's seems rich. Even those women who would be called respectable, if their husbands were in work, excuse their filthy and untidy habits by saying the men earn little or nothing now ; and with numbers health has failed. "Sarah" meets the worn and jaded cabinet-maker, who has walked with the chair or chest of drawers he has made till he is ready to drop, and is obliged, at last, to sell it for little more than the material has cost him, because "they are starving at home." She is one who herself slept last winter without a blanket, for the sake of others. She is sometimes almost desperate on behalf of the misery she sees. God help her in her efforts, and the people in their misery !

In commencing with Bible work as "Marian" did, she thereby investigates the habits and customs of the people.

"*April* 1*st.*—Called on an Irishwoman ; solicited her name as a subscriber for a Bible. She gladly promised a penny a week, saying she had long wished for one.

"Called on a man in C—— street. His answer was, 'No, missus, I do not want a Bible. I have one in my box, and it is one hundred and two years old.' I replied, 'I should like to see it.' He took it out, and I was obliged to say, 'It looks as if every page condemned its several owners.' 'How so, missus ?' 'It has always been kept in the box, and not a leaf is soiled.' 'Yes,' said he; 'but I cannot see to read it, my eyesight is so bad.' 'Then you want one that you *can* see to read, and that can lie open on the table, to teach you the way of salvation through the blood of a crucified Saviour.' 'Well,' was the reply, 'you can put my name down, and be sure it is a good print.'"

The people of Clerkenwell are artificers, dressmakers, flower and fan-makers, comb, brush, and box sellers, smiths, farriers, and wheelwrights—persons who in good times can earn from 13s. to 14s. a week, but who now say that supply overpasses the demand for their work. Numbers seem wretchedly off for decent clothing, and especially for beds; and, having heard of the supply in St. Giles's, they are become eagerly anxious to obtain them in Clerkenwell also by instalments, which is a principle understood among them for other purposes. If at all possible, it is their habit to pay, by degrees, towards a trip into the country in the pleasure vans—most often made on the Sabbath—and for which the charge is 3s. a-piece, and half-price for children; and for this day a fine dress must somehow or other be obtained, if only to go to the pawnshop on the morrow. Tally-shops abound in Clerkenwell, which provide this, at twice its cost price, on credit, and which usually summon the husband for the payment, leaving the wife and children destitute of necessary clothing or comforts, *for that one day's sake*, to the end of the year.

These women all want teaching, just as much as in St. Giles's, to prefer to this soon past and expensive pleasure the neat print dress, which may be *their own* for 3s.; and also to make the cheap soup, or savory dish, that shall invite the husband to his home, and nourish themselves and the children.

"If I have but ¾d. I only spend ½d., says Sarah to her people; "and when I have but 1d., I never go on trust for 2d." This is what they want teaching in Clerkenwell.

"*May 3d.*—Visited forty subscribers; found many out, but the penny left for me at the neighbor's.

"This day I met with a fellow-missionary—a Scripture-reader to his neighbors *on his own account*. Not knowing this, I asked him, among others, if he wanted a Bible. 'Yes,' said he, 'I do; but I have not a penny till I have been out to sell my fish, and then I will leave it for you. I want a Bible very much, for look here at these few leaves of the Gospel of St. John. When I come home at night I have my tea, and wash myself, and then I go out to read these to my neighbors.' His wife testified that this was true. She gave me the first penny an hour afterwards."

This is the kind of man to make a future colporter!

"'Here, you Bible-woman,' called out a young man

who had paid a penny for a Bible last week—'here's your penny for the Book, but you never told me you sold shirts. Don't you see, I've no mother, and I want a shirt—the Bible won't clothe me.'

"But,' I said, ' it will teach you to clothe yourself. However, I do not sell shirts at this time ; I only sell Bibles. If you want a shirt, you can have one ; it is ready made for you—a good strong working shirt ; you must send your sixpence by some woman you know, to my clothing-club room on Wednesday nights, and you may get a shirt for 1s. 6d., but I cannot take your money now.'

" 'I think,' said an old man, one of his fellow-workmen, 'you might as well take mine. I was going in for a glass of gin, but I'll give you this twopence for a shirt. I would not give it you for a book.' 'I hope you will some day,' I said, ' when you hear more about the Book ; but I suppose I must take it for the shirt, to save it from the gin-shop, only it is not my rule. I do one thing at a time.'

" *May 5th and 6th.*—After collecting yesterday my Bible subscriptions, which constantly increase, I went this morning to mention that the club was now open for the receipt of subscriptions for bedding ; for which the people appeared very thankful, and numbers promised to subscribe as soon as they got employment, as they now slept on the floor and on dirty rags.

"*7th.*—Visited Fryingpan-alley, Row-alley, and Turk's-head Yard.   Here I found costermongers, coal-sack makers, beggars, tinkers, and a few water-cress girls. Part of the houses are fallen down, giving a little more air than otherwise would be obtained.   Up one of the yards, the whole of the ground floors are turned into sheds for the carts and wagons of cowkeepers, stable-men, and wheelrights.   This is one of the vilest places in London.   In the gateway stood many girls, from fourteen to eighteen, for whom my heart ached, and I must surely try to carry the Book among *them.*

"I have sold all our ready-made clothes.   The people think it is ' one of the best ways that has been thought of to help them.'   One woman said ' she had lived fifty years in the parish, and that this new plan of subscribing for clothing and beds would certainly be one of the greatest blessings that ever happened for Clerkenwell.   Old clothing of all sorts is eagerly asked for.

"After collecting for my Bibles on Thursday, I went on Friday, and called on twenty families in Turnmill street, all of whom were pleased to hear of the club for clothing and beds, for they possessed no beds.   *As they had been induced to have a bit of print and calico of some tally-shop, they could not now put down their names to me, although they would pay 7½d for print no better than mine at 4d a yard.*

" *May 24th— Whit-Monday.*—Left home at 8 A. M., to be in time for some of my subscribers who were going to make holiday. Reached Compton street, Clerkenwell, which presented a scene not easily to be forgotten,—nine vans filled with people, young and old, with children of all ages. One very old woman told she would read a tract I gave her on her journey. Left that bustling scene, and passed to Allen street, where a great many persons had been cheated by a man who had for many weeks been collecting their pence to take them a trip in the country by van, and had decamped with the whole sum, amounting to between three and four pounds. These poor creatures had saved their pence out of a hard day's washing or cleaning for this trip, some paying 2s. 11d., others 3s., others 1s. 6d. One woman, my subscriber, had paid 1s. 6d., and was going to pay the man a shilling more if he had come. ' Well,' she said, ' after all, it is better to buy a Bible ; so here, missus, take this shilling. Let me have my large Bible, for that will pay it up ; and instead of drinking anything, I will read it.'

" *May 25th.*—Made thirty calls ; succeeded pretty well, they having left my pennies for me.

" One of the Sunday school teachers had given an old man a Bible ; and as he never would lend it to his wife, when I called to ask them to subscribe, the following conversation ensued:

"OLD WOMAN (above seventy) : 'Now, dear, see what a nice Testament; only fourpence! I can see *that* print; do buy it for me—you never bought me a book in your life—and then I shall be able to read nicely. Hear how well I can spell !'

"MAN : 'What do you want with it? You have got two or three !"

"WOMAN : 'But they are so dirty, I can't see to read them ; and look, what a beautiful book for only fourpence! When I took my boy to school (he's now forty) I used to ask the mistress to tell me a letter or two, and so by that means I learnt the little words ; and now, you know, I can spell big ones.'

"I then sat down and read a short portion to them ; and by degrees he drew the fourpence out of his pocket, and bought the Testament.

"The following week the son gave me his name for a Bible, and paid twopence, his own being too old-fashioned to take to church ; and his mother told me, with her hands uplifted and streaming eyes, 'that her son had been a cruel drunkard, and had often helped his father to beat *her* and turn her out of doors ; but now, since Mr. Maguire had come to the parish, he kept himself clean and sober, going regularly to the Institute for Working Men every evening, and to church on Sunday.'

"Two evenings afterwards, this woman came to my

house at half-past nine, with twopence from a neighbor who lived opposite, to whom she had shown 'her beautiful Testament,' asking for a card to prove to her she had *paid* the twopence, and requesting me, as the Bible-woman, to call next week, as they wanted a 2s. 6d. Bible, she having seen what a splendid book I could sell for that price; and 'I mean,' she said, 'to show my book to everybody, and get as many customers for you as I can.'

" *May 26th.*—Called on a poor man for his subscription, who said, 'I am very sorry, but work has been so bad that I cannot get my little money together to take us into the country when master sends for us for the hay-making; so I am afraid I shall be obliged to make my part-of-a-Bible do till I come back.'

"'Let us see the part you talk of," said I.

"'Here it is.'

"'It looks well used; but how came you to have it in this cut state?'

"'You see, when my mother died, I and my brother both wanted it, so we cut it in half, and he had the New Testament and I the Old. I take it with me almost every year to read in the hay-fields to my comrades.'

"I called the next morning, and left my own Bible with this man as a gift. I hope both the brothers are Christian people.

" Called on a poor man to ask him to become a sub-scriber.

" ' That's all you religious people think about—if you can thrust a Bible or a tract down our throats, it will do as well as food. Now, I have five children and a wife, and no work.'

" ' My good man, you quite mistake me if you think I want you to live on the Bible. I only want you to live by its precepts, that you may be led to call on Him who careth for you in all things, and died to save you, that by His stripes you may be healed.'

" To my surprise he said, ' Well, then, put down my name ; I'll have a Bible.'

" *June 7th.*—Going out this morning, met two of my subscribers coming with their pence for me before they left home for a day's work. Called on a poor man ; showed him one of my large Bibles. ' Well,' said he, ' this is a fine book for only 2s. 6d. ; it is just like a gift, it is so cheap. Now, if you will keep this very one for me, I will give you twopence.'

" ' I cannot promise that very book, but you shall have one of the same sort.'

" ' That won't do for me, for I must have this very book, it is such a beautiful type ; so I shall put my name and address in it, to prevent the sale.' "

An old man, who became a Bible subscriber from the commencement of this mission, explained, as he procured first one shilling Bible and then another, that he wished them to give away with his own hand. Sometimes he paid a halfpenny, sometimes a penny, sometimes more, till he had purchased no less than three, and was subscribing for a fourth; when one day, being very ill with severe rheumatism, he was compelled to bid the Bible-woman enter his room for the first time, and, to her surprise, she found only tokens of extreme penury and personal want. He had always put his card and money out at the door, and had paid so regularly, that she little thought to see a room so unkept, and with nothing for a bed but some sacks in the corner. She asked him how he had been able to give to others, if himself so bare of necessaries. He said, " He liked to give to God, and the small sum he had spared would not have made much difference to his own supply."

He appeared to be a man of some education, having been intended for a teacher, but he had become a whip-handle maker; and just then, having no power to work, was consequently in distress. When asked whether he had not better, while ill, go into the work-house, " No," he said, " time has been when I have received my own dividends; I would rather be carried out of this room—starved!"

When Sarah saw her superintendent in the evening, and found that some ready-made linen, for the use of the Missions, had been sent by a clergyman's lady at Woodbridge, she asked for a couple of shirts for this man, who had cared so little for himself, and been so little cared for, that he had only worn rags these last six months. They were very gladly so bestowed, it being ascertained that drink had not been the vice that had brought him to this low estate ; and as she was about to make a fresh supply of beds for her subscribers, she was ordered to add one to the list, with a cover to keep it clean, and a blanket and rug, purchased with the Mission funds which had been kindly sent for Sarah's use. He had slept for months with only a sack under him, and three above him ; and, in fact, when the Bible-woman penetrated into his room, he said he had laid him down, as he thought, to die. The message was sent with the gifts, "that as he had loved to spread God's word, the Lord had unexpectedly restored him fourfold." He seemed most thankful, and made answer, "Not fourfold, but a hundredfold, He has, all my life long." Comforted by the help given, he had his room cleaned, and began to work again.

Various tokens of sympathy have since reached us for this poor man from country friends. One kind hand sent him his Christmas dinner ; another, "six shillings, because he had denied himself for Christ." He is just one of those friendless waifs upon the wilderness of life, needing the help of a female missionary to raise and cheer him. There are many such who pass unobserved, except by the All-seeing Eye, from time into eternity. They retire hopelessly into the depths of their poverty. How blessed a work it is to seek out and succor them!

CHAPTER IX.

BIBLE-SELLING IN SPITALFIELDS.

HAVING now introduced our readers to three distinct neighborhoods in London—St. Giles's, in its west central division, Paddington in its north-west, and Clerkenwell in its northern portion—we shall invite them to traverse the north-eastern districts of the million-peopled city, the densely-populated vicinities of Spitalfields, Bethnal Green, and Shoreditch, which are remote as the poles, comparatively, from the aristocratic localities of Grosvenor and Belgrave Squares in the west.

The population of London alone is supposed nearly to equal that of the whole island of Madagascar, or that of all Norway and Sweden ; and as the habitations of the rich and noble become scattered towards the extremities of the circle, they leave the working bees thronging together at the centre of the old hive.

London is a wonderful place ; it has within its borders whole colonies of populations NOT NATIVE, which represent foreign nations and communities. There is a cluster of God's ancient people at its heart, the once mighty sons of Abraham, known amongst us at present but as the " offscourings of all things," yet one day to be gathered (can we doubt it?) with all their exiled brethren of the wide, wide world, and reinstated as the lords of their own land.

Strangely blended, too, in this very district, with a fragment of the JEWISH nation and church, are to be found the vestiges, as distinctly visible, of an old HUGUENOT colony—the French nation and the French church (which came over at the Massacre of St. Bartholomew in 1568, and which was greatly increased in number by the revocation of the Edict of Nantes in 1681), itself an offset from the yet older VAUDOIS church in the valleys of Piedmont, the uninterrupted descendant of that primitive CHURCH IN ROME, which dates from the persecution of the pagan emperors. Here, then, in our island metropolis, we have the types and remnants, defaced and blurred it is true, but the unmistakable types of the TRUE churches of the EAST and WEST, " persecuted, but not forsaken ; cast down, but not destroyed." They await their recovery and manifestation at the time when they shall anew receive that Divine Word which at first gave them birth. Their fathers were the treasurers of the OLD AND NEW TESTAMENTS. These precious records those fathers first brought to the Anglo-Saxons, whose priceless privilege it is now to distribute them by millions of copies all over the earth, and to those " beloved for the fathers' sakes." It is a work that seraphs might envy, to restore these title deeds to the children.

With this knowledge, let us suppose ourselves standing in the centre of Spitalfields, and the district naturally falls into three main divisions. Each division, indeed, has its own *proportion* of the ordinary laboring English population ; but each has its very marked and distinctive character. To the south-west is a densely-populated district, containing between 4000 and 5000 JEWS, many courts and streets being entirely inhabited by them. In this section is a great part of the well-known Petticoat-lane—" The Lane," as it is commonly called by the many buyers and sellers of second and third-hand goods by whom it is frequented, just as Covent Garden is by the St. Giles's people called " The Garden."

To the south-east is an almost equally distinct part, consisting of the very lowest of the London poor, and containing about sixty lodging-houses of various descriptions, and some courts and alleys almost wholly given over to the fallen and the vicious.

The third part of the parish, lying to the north and west, has its large proportion of persons engaged in the silk trade. They are Weavers and Silk-winders ; and of these there are many thousands. The French

Refugees taught the English improved modes of weaving, and brought with them models of the looms of Tours and Lyons. The manufacture of silk has ever since continued to be the staple trade of this locality.

If we first explore the JEWISH quarter, we shall find in the neighborhood of Petticoat-lane four markets for the sale of old clothes. The oldest and most respectable is called "The City Clothes Exchange." This is inscribed over the entrance. A little to the north of it, perhaps about fifty or sixty yards, are *three* markets joining each other, yet distinct. One of these is called "The Exhibition Exchange," from the circumstance that it was built principally with material belonging to the Great Exhibition of 1851, in Hyde-Park. This market is covered with part of the glass of the Crystal Palace, and the roof supported by columns which stood in that building. That which was once the admiration of the world, and the shade of all that was exquisite in art and manufactures, covers, not the beautiful contributions of distant empires, but the refuse and cast-off personal apparel of our London population. In this " Exhibition Exchange " there are stalls rented to persons who regularly occupy them.

Another of these markets is an oblong square, uncovered to the sky : for each day's leave to sell there the people pay twopence, or one shilling per week.

This may be regarded as a medium market between the " Exhibition 'Change " and " Halfpenny 'Change," of which we have yet to speak.

" The Halfpenny 'Change," which is, after all, the most popular, is so called because every person .entering it, either for the purpose of buying or selling, has to pay one halfpenny toll. Into this market crowd hawkers and buyers from all quarters, and the nature of the traffic it would be impossible to delineate ; it must be witnessed to be understood.　You have here the refuse of everything in the way of old hats, boots, shoes, coats, vests, gowns, shawls, bonnets, &c., &c., all the results of the importunate demand made at so many stores and doors during the day, " Any old rubbish in the way ? We pay you well for it." Hundreds of people pour in about the hour of one or two, with all such rubbish, into the 'Change, and then order is lost ; it is a perpetual scramble going on between multitudes of living beings, every one appearing to be *turning over* and making selections from heaps of old articles, which cover the whole place. It is chiefly from this source that all the other markets and shops are supplied ; for out of the selected boots and shoes, coats and trousers, the " translators," by mending and scouring, stuffing and dyeing, produce their salable wares ; and in all this much skill and deception are practised, so that what is sold in this latter market at a groat, when metamorphosed, brings a goodly price, by which the JEW becomes proverbially rich.

The site on which these three markets stand was covered with small houses some fifteen years ago. The owner of the estate, an improvident young man, let them fall into decay; the ground was purchased, and a privilege obtained to open markets, as it was thought likely that such accommodation would improve the condition of the place. Every part around it is densely inhabited, and thousands daily pass and repass through all the avenues of this dirty but golden highway. On our Christian Sabbath-day it is crowded more than ever with the Jew salesmen, who scream and shout in recommendation of their goods; and as a crowd of ten or twelve thousand persons assemble there, the place is called RAG FAIR.

Some members of the Open-Air Mission resolved, one Sunday in June, 1858, with about twenty of their friends, to make a regular visitation of every lane, alley and booth in this extraordinary place. They gave away some thousand tracts, and made numerous addresses, which seemed listened to with interest. The Bible Society had kindly granted them a supply of Testaments, and these were used when any expressed a desire for the book to read at home; but the greatest acceptance was found for SCRIPTURE CARDS, containing five or six verses, printed in red and blue letters. In only two instances were these cards refused, and nearly 1500 were distributed. The journal of a colporter in Spitalfields, and of his visits paid chiefly in the Jewish quarter, will here prove interesting.

JOURNAL OF A BIBLE COLPORTER IN SPITALFIELDS.

On Tuesday, October 5th, 1858, I visited about 130 families in the Tenter-ground, near Petticoat-lane. Forty years ago this square was an open space, appropriated to the stretching of dyed cloth on timber frames by hooks, from which the place derives its name of "Tenter-ground." One of the old inhabitants remembers the ground being so employed, when not a house was built, but it was filled with cloth of divers colors. It is now covered with houses, inhabited principally by Dutch and German Jews, speaking their own languages, from which circumstance it is often called "Dutch Ireland."

The Jews in this neighborhood are of a very poor class. I met with but few *men* at home, as might be expected, they having to get their living abroad by various kinds of traffic. The women are not communicative with an English-speaking visitor; they understood my inquiries but little, and I as little their replies; yet some interpreted for others, and the common answer I received was, "My husband is not at home." They are in general poorly lodged, but others arc fond of display alike in their persons and houses. The large floating ribbons for the head attire appear indispensable as a rest-day's ornament, both for young and old. I believe they bestow much care on their children ; I have been often pleased with the appearance and vivacity of the little ones, and thought of the promise, "And the streets of the city shall be full of boys and girls playing in the streets thereof." Were these beautiful little figures brought up on the " mountains of Israel," with " timbrel and dance," &c., instead of being doomed to a sedentary life in the low districts of London, as most of them are, what a contrast would they form in riper years to the heavy business-loving matron of Petticoat-lane and its vicinity !

I consider it due to the people of this quarter to say that in no instance have I received an uncivil reception, nor had the door slammed in my face without an answer, as is too frequently the case elsewhere. This has been the effect of Christian missions amongst them, as once no Gentile was admitted into the house of a Jew.

Few of these people can read the Bible in English. All appear to stand in doubt of the book. One asked, " Is the name of Christ in it ? " and, when answered in the affirmative, replied, " Then I can have nothing to do with it." Many have asked, " Is the New Testament in it?" and when I said, "Yes, it is," the same answer followed. I had, consequently, little success this day, but having obtained one Jew as a subscriber I also obtained seven subscribers who were not Jews.

A City Missionary, who has been laboring here for some years, told me that he has circulated, by gift, about 400 copies of the Scriptures in the Dutch and German languages amongst the Jews of this locality. I met also a Jew who is an old inhabitant of this place, who assured me that he has distributed about 1000 copies of the *Old Testament*, in the English language, amongst his countrymen. Some of these I have seen; they are copies of the authorized version as read in our churches, having a little difference in the separation of the verses; the reading is more continuous, like the reading of other books. It is but just to the name of MISS HOOPER to say that all these Bibles were supplied by her: she was, as I have learned, a Gentile Christian lady, most kind to the Jews of this vicinity.

The person who circulated these Bibles for her amongst his brethren informed me that thousands of pounds had also passed through his hands, as her almoner, in the way of needful gifts to the poor Jews. Another, who showed me a Bible he received from her, told me that she was in the habit of making collections for them when she travelled from home. One

of the most respectable and intelligent females I met with said that she frequently visited the Jewesses, and that she would sit and read to them out of the Old Testament, but never say a word to hurt their feelings by talking about " Christ." Now that Miss Hooper has been removed to her reward, her memory is respected by all the Jews. This recalled to my mind that the elders of the Jews had said to our Lord, concerning a certain Gentile, " That he was worthy, for he loveth our nation."

The Jews of this neighborhood are also supplied from their synagogue with the Old Testament Scriptures, both in the Hebrew and English languages. In several of their rooms I saw a picture of Moses holding the two tables of the Law, which was written in Hebrew on each table. An elderly Jew told me, as well as he could, that he had travelled over the East, and practised as a physician when abroad ; he was now " translating" old shoes. He pointed to a table whereon were pots, cups, plasters, &c. He said he made people good (well) without asking any money. He ran over the different languages that he could speak, but said that he could not speak either English or French well. His wife had to explain to me what he was saying.

In another room I met a venerable Jew, ninety years of age, at work at tailoring ; his daughter, who was quite grey, sat by his side. He told me that he subscribed for a long time to societies which had for their object the relief of poor aged widows, without any distinction as to sect or nation. These people had the Bible, and appeared to be comfortable in circumstances.

Perhaps the most interesting interview I had was with a Jewess, who I saw was very intelligent, and she told me that if I *gave* my Bibles to the Jews they would, the next moment, sell them, for they cared nothing about them, and would not read them. I was to tell my friends that she, a Dutch Jewess, told me so in kindness. The Jews knew that they had the truth, and were not like ignorant Christians, bowing down to images of wood and stone, and kissing them, &c. I attempted an explanation, but I fear she knew not how to distinguish between those professing the name of Christ, and those who worship Him in spirit and in truth without such symbols. I insinuated nothing concerning the past history of her people; but I thought of the Scripture : "From all *your idols* will I cleanse you," &c. She, too, spoke of Miss Hooper as never offending their prejudices. "The Jews," said she, "despise the Lord Jesus." She did not herself believe that Jesus Christ, *the poor fellow,* ever declared that he was the Son of God. The ignorant people about him said so, but *he* never said that God said to him, "Sit thou on my right hand." She repeated that the Jews had the truth, and were good people, but not good enough for the Messiah to come yet : when they were good enough then He would come, &c.

The next house I entered I had reason to think what I heard from the Dutch Jewess was true. It was a chandler's shop, as well as a coal and rag shop. The owner told me that he was often grieved to see Bibles sold for waste paper. "A Jew named Levi said he had brought me a large Bible to sell for four or five shillings. I said, 'Levi, you are surely not going to sell that Bible?' He said, 'I am.' 'Well, I could give you no more than twopence per pound for it.' He went out, and in a few minutes returned, and flung the large Bible out of his bag like a bundle of rags into the scales—it weighed 14 lbs. It was an Oxford edition of the Scriptures, and I sent it," said the shopkeeper, "as a present to my daughter-in-law into the country."

The lady I have referred to as Miss Hooper had studied the Hebrew language. She had apartments, where she used to meet the poor Jewesses two or three times a week, in classes of about fifteen, and read and expound to them the Scriptures of the Old Testament. It was her custom to give them each a bowl of tea and a cake on these occasions, which she handed herself. She visited the sick amongst the Jews, and made their welfare, both spiritual and temporal, her greatest care. The title-page of the Bible she distributed reads as follows :

" The Paragraph Old Testament. The Old Testament, translated out of the Original Hebrew, diligently compared and revised with the former Translations, arranged in Paragraphs and Parallelisms. London : Printed by G. E. Eyre and William Spottiswoode. 1852."

THE BIBLE-WOMAN IN SPITALFIELDS.

HANNAH, the Bible-woman, commenced her work in Spitalfields, says Mrs. Patteson, her lady superintendent, in the month of August, 1858. The character of the people she visits differs materially from that either of St. Giles's, Clerkenwell, or Paddington ; but yet, in a population of 21,000, not 1,000 families are of a class above receiving her visits.

She has not had very much success among the Jews, owing to the many Bibles previously sold in their quarter by a city missionary. She has, however, sold four Bibles among them, three of which were said to be wanted to compare with their Hebrew Old Testaments. She says the Jews, on the whole, treated her with more courtesy than the Gentiles.

Many of her visits have been paid among the weavers. There is something peculiarly sad to see in the contrast between these miserable, half-clad work·people, and the rich and beautiful textures, on the creation of which they are employed. The weavers always live at the top of the house, for the sake of the extra light, and their attics may be distinguished down the length of several streets and courts by the windows extending along the whole side of the room. They occupy, indeed, the two highest stories. They are an independent race, but not inaccessible. The silk trade employs many of the women and children. Fringe-making, tassel-making, button-knitting (as they call the work over fancy silk buttons), and winding the silk on reels before weaving it, are their prevailing occupations; while the children are useful in winding the *quills*, which form a part of the actual shuttle: both men and women are employed at the loom.

How useful a Female Bible and Domestic Missionary may be to numbers of the poor overworked mothers, by giving a kind word or practical hint, need not be told. In her direct work, in Bible distribution, she has an ample field before her. Many years ago a strenuous effort was made throughout the north-east part of London for the further distribution of the Scriptures, since which no direct Bible work to any extent appears to have been undertaken in Spitalfields.

Hannah's visits have hitherto invariably been well received. Her labor must be earnest, as she will often have to call once and again for the expected penny, finding the poor weaver with an empty loom and an empty purse. At the same time there is much that evinces a good feeling among the people; they show great pleasure in inspecting the Bibles, and in many cases, we may hope, a real desire to possess the Word of God, able to make them wise unto salvation.

Her reception was very encouraging from a poor woman, who ran for her husband, saying, "Oh, James, we've got this precious Book come to us—just as we can pay for it—a little at a time." In another family the woman was a Roman Catholic, the man a Protestant. She has begun to pay for a Bible. When Hannah called he was sitting with his wife and a neighbor. He said to his wife, "Now fetch out 6d. for the book." "Don't you do any such thing," said the neighbor; "if I were you I'd never let him have it. My husband bought 'that book' in Ireland, and it's changed him so, I've never had a bit of a dance or fun with him since. I sold it once for half a pint of whiskey; but when he came home from his work his first words were, 'Where's the book?' and I was obliged to get it back as I could. Now, mind me, and don't you let him get this book, or he will be quite changed." The man, however, is persevering, and the woman has promised to join a "Mothers' Meeting" held in the neighborhood.

5

"Hannah" in Spitalfields, as the result of six months' labor, has sold 151 Bibles and 57 Testaments. She afterwards undertook, for a short time, the charge of a Refuge, but is now desirous to return to Bible selling. She left in the hands of her successor 88 subscribers, a number since increased to 122, while the number sold in all amounts to 256 copies. When the larger books have been obtained as "Family Bibles," many have joyfully brought them to the "Superintendent," begging her to inscribe their names. A poor convict, with weak sight, had repeatedly written home, asking his relatives to send him a large-print Bible. His last letter urging, "Pray don't forget the book," stirred them up to resolve to send their own small dirty old one, when they were told of the "Bible-woman," and most gladly secured good type for him by instalments.

An ignorant woman, gaining a living by fortune-telling, became a purchaser of a Bible, and she told Hannah, "Well, I'm getting it a' into my head, but I can't get it into my heart."

In a short report from this agent herself, she says :

"In looking over my six months' labor, though I have often been very tired, I have much to praise God for. His Holy Word has been sown in much weakness, but He has watered it oftentimes with the dew of His Holy

Spirit. One little boy who was ill with fever when I first called, has, I humbly hope, been led lately to seek the right path. He followed me out of the room when I left my district, and, flinging his arms round my neck, said, 'I never forget to pray morning and night.' His mother said he was now a good, obedient boy. His trade is a very dirty and unwholesome one—polishing umbrella handles, and he wants to be a carpenter.

"A women, with a very drunken husband, was helped to a little tidy clothing, and has ever since attended a place of worship, and bought a Bible. She says she thanks God I ever called at her door. In some parts of my district I met with rather a rough reception. In F—— street they had a pelt at my head three times ; but the people in general say, 'The Bible is a useful book, and it ought to be in every house.' " In the Domestic Mission work, " Hannah " secured twenty-six subscribers for clothing and beds.

It really surprises those engaged in this work to hear the gratitude expressed for what, after all, is not gift, for it is purchased by the people with their own money, though at a much better market than they could secure. This kind of female agent for the lowest neighborhoods of cities and large towns finds access by means of her one message to every room, to an immense class unreached by District Visitors or Scripture-readers—to those who have never been brought within the circles of the benevolent agency which emanates from places of public worship. These degraded ones never worship. They know not God, and they are often sunk below the instincts of brute animals. Their welcome to the Bible-woman, we must repeat, is surprising.

CHAPTER X.

THE district of BETHNAL GREEN is inhabited chiefly by silk weavers, and the very name of that locality will recall to mind immediate associations, with donations implored by its clergy, on behalf of the pitiful sufferings of their poor in the inclement days of winter. They would speak parochially, of a population of upwards of 90,000, and of a proportionate amount of wretchedness far larger than in most other neighborhoods.

On the census Sunday of 1851 there were forty-one places of worship in this locality, thirteen of which belonged to the established church, and twenty-eight to other denominations. On that Sunday the congregations in all these places *unitedly* amounted to something like 12,000 in the morning, and 10,000 in the afternoon and evening. Assuming that fifty-eight persons in every one hundred might and ought to have been present, the congregations should have consisted of 52,000. The absentees, therefore, numbered at least

40,000, a number equal to the population of a large town, not inclusive of children.

Whatever change for the better may have taken place since the census Sunday, it is still the opinion of those who know the neighborhood, that to these " absentees" a Female Bible Mission will certainly not be out of place.

We may add that " not more than one-half of the surface of the parish is, or ever has been, under visitation by the City Missionaries ;" yet their number is *thirteen*, and the committee of the London City Mission (not reckoning their special receipts from Christian friends for the purpose) annually expend £400 of their General Fund here.

So many good stones having been thrown into this " Slough of Despond" with a view of mending it, and the place yet remaining " almost as bad as before," let us try if, with the true *foundation stone* for all future evangelistic labor, we can find the bottom, and to this end endeavor to make acquaintance with the people. It has been said—we are not yet certain how truly—that not more than one in thirty persons is at present in possession of a Bible.

In company with our friend the curate, we have entered one of their rooms, ascending to it by a dark, narrow, winding, and broken stair, without any landing-place. There is scarcely space to stand, for the chamber is filled up by three looms and a bedstead ; its long casement window at either end makes it suitable for weaving.

The father is moving about among the looms amid two or three children engaged in winding quills, and, in the interval of attending to the handsome piece of fringe he is making himself, he is giving assistance to his son, a lad of thirteen, in the corner, who is weaving a fringe of mixed colors. That fringe will adorn the gay dress of some wearer, who will probably never think where it was made. The boy cannot read, but says he would like to come to school ; he has been hindered from so doing by this early work for his bread. Must he not find time to get food for his soul ?

The mother of the family has just returned from the doctor's with her little child ill of inflammation ; it droops and wheezes on her arm, and it has been ordered to " be kept very quiet," which is a thing impossible here ; the rest of the household cannot stay their work for the poor baby. They must earn their few pence for that which the mercer will turn into many shillings, or the " pot au feu" will not be kept boiling. It is a token of their old descent from French ancestors that this utensil is so often seen among the weavers.

This family have attended no place of worship " for want of clothes." They are " subscribing a penny a week for a large-print Bible, to replace the old torn copy which they showed us. They were delighted to hear of the possibility of getting a six-shilling bed by instalments, and garments in the same way. It is very certain they will welcome the Bible-woman and her simple apparatus of helping them to help themselves.

Now let us take another street, and explore another stair. We find ourselves in a room smelling strongly of whelks, of which a fresh heap is thrown upon the floor, from market, thence to be dispensed by street sale. In this room are two bedsteads and one loom, and a similar long window. We are here introduced to the mysteries of both " broad " and " narrow " weaving. The man sits by the fire paring potatoes; he is just recovering from a fever. Here also on the fire is the soup-kettle. The woman's dark eyes and expression of countenance bespeak her French origin : she is weaving rich black satin, for which she will get eightpence a yard—it will sell for more than eight shillings. She listens with an intelligent look to allusions to the history of her forefathers, the Huguenots, the Men of the Book which their children have forgotten. She will welcome the Bible-woman, she says, and the man listens with some earnestness to the offer of a six-shilling bed. In this room the holes in the ceiling were pasted up with newspapers, and the good matronly Englishwoman, who accompanied us to see if she

thought she could undertake the district, was of opinion that " the husband looked the more able of the two
to take his seat at the loom, and leave the wife to set
her place to rights." It will be a favorite idea of our
own, however, to find for this district a " Native
Agent," already well acquainted with the ways and
habits of the people, and who, under good direction,
might improve them. For another part of Bethnal
Green, the Victoria Park District, this kind of agent,
as will be seen, appears to have arisen.

Descending the stair, we arrive in another room, in
which there is much to observe. In the first place,
there is nothing clean but the cat, whose white fur con-
trasts with all around. On the table is a pile of cups
and saucers, which a little girl of fifteen is washing up
at one o'clock in the day. She looks slatternly, but
as though she might be easily transformed into a nice,
neat, modest maiden ; her brother of twelve is squat-
ting, with his face towards us (a face like Murillo's
peasant boy, without its good humor), sulkily on a broken chair before the fire ; his knees peep through his
dilapidated and filthy trousers, and we ask him if he
would not be happier at school than sitting there
idle.

His sister answers for him : " He is a bad boy,
ma'am. He's always running away from his work,
though he can weave as well as mother, if he likes ; so

6*

father's cut away his trousers, and now he can't run—he must stop at home."

A comfortless home it looked to stop in, and the boy ready for all mischief. A novel lay upon the table. The mother then came in—a hard-working woman, who seemed open to conviction that better clothes and more comfort, a certain portion of work, and an opening for school instruction, would be a benefit to herself and her children. She said the boy was a famous hand at figures when he pleased. Here, too, was scope for the friendly visits of the Female Bible Missionary.

A more recent report from Bethnal Green gives us details of the settlement of an "Alice" and a "Sophy" in these districts, and of the work of each their lady superintendent already gives a favorable account. Alice has forty-seven Bible subscribers, and has sold twenty-six copies, besides bringing more than fifty women to the Clothing and Mending Club, in a most dirty and destitute district. "It is truly marvellous," it is said, " to watch the amount gathered weekly at these meetings, from people whose appearance would bespeak them the very dregs of society, but who will soon be so no longer. It is money evidently snatched from the gin palace. Many a filthy chamber is already much cleaner. 'Alice' lately took me into a room which I had known to be most revolting from its stench and dirty condition, and my delight was great to find its mistress, brush in hand, on bended knee, with pail beside, scrubbing heartily. She said 'she was sorry to see us while it was wet.' She is now attending a place of worship. 'Alice' had asked a sweep what was his reason for not coming to the school-room service. He replied, 'The people complained of the sooty smell of his clothes, and none would sit by him.' 'Oh,' said she, 'come and sit by me; I shall not mind.' On the following Sabbath she placed him close to the wall, and sat the other side of him herself.

" I suppose you would be pleased to hear more of the 'Murillo' boy. The next time I called with the Bible woman his dress was by no means improved; he looked more dilapidated than ever, and the room was the picture of wretchedness. His mother said to us, 'Oh dear! if you could but save that boy, you might be the making of us. He drives his father to drink, and he had that broomstick broken over his back on Saturday; and such a wretched day we had, but it only hardens him.'

" ' Now, Jim,' said I, 'do look me in the face. Are you not tired of all this? If I lend you new trousers and jacket, will you come to my Sunday school? It will be better than having a stick broken in beating you.' He looked as if he thought he would. 'Alice' therefore brought him, with scrubbed face and brushed hair, next day ; and the equipping him in fresh clothes has led to a complete reformation. Mr. S. says no boy behaves better in the school, and he now steadily works with his father besides. His sister, also, who in ' Alice's' journal is described as being 'blunt, as if she was brought up in a wood,' has joined my Bible class, and is making great efforts to improve herself.

"We asked an intelligent, half-naked lad, lounging at one of the doors, what he did with himself all day long in the streets. 'I don't know what to do,' he replied ; 'my mother has not a penny to send me to school, and they won't even take me to a Sunday school.' 'Alice' brought him to me next day in the wildest state, his hair standing on end, but reduced by her visits into decent order : he sits by Jim at school, like the man rescued from the tombs, clothed, and in his right mind. The Domestic Mission in Bethnal Green is positively essential to prepare the way for the Bible."

"Sophy," under Mrs. ———, in a kindred district, has thirty-five Bible subscribers, and again a Clothing Club has been immediately found most welcome. The very shopkeepers of the locality perceive the necessity of receiving payments from the poor by instalments, of course for their own benefit. *The people seem so powerless to save their money unless it is taken from them ;* and as to their selection of articles, so reckless are they of suitabilities, that a woman whose ragged shawl will not look worth a shilling, will actually have scraped together ten shillings, and paid it off a four guinea silk gown.

"Many families are now being visited who were almost starving. none of whom could attend any school or place of worship for want of clothes. When it has been dark before we left, in order that we might go safely down the crooked and dangerous flights of stairs, a girl has preceded us with two or three lucifer matches, one of which she lighted as the other went out, until we found our way into the scarcely better lighted street."

SCRIPTURE READING IN A COURT OF BETHNAL GREEN.

(The witness of a City Missionary.)

I met with a chimney-sweeper, named B——, and several others of the same calling, assembled in a house to-day, all of whom gave me a rough but hearty welcome.

After my sooty friend had informed them that I was "the kind gemmun what comes to talk to them poor people about summut better," he turned to one of his company whom he called "Buster," saying, "I should like you to hear the old buffer, Buster, 'cause you knows a thing or two—it's regular stunning, it is; and, what's more, it's cutting, too. Come, Mister, oblige me by giving these gents a stave: let's hear summut about that young rascal that bolted away from his poor old father—that's a regular good thing, that is, Buster;" and I regret to state that an oath was appended in confirmation. "Come, my infant," he added, addressing a tall muscular man, about six feet in height, "hand over the cushion." The man spoken to did as he was desired, giving me the only chair of which the room could boast.

On taking possession, I observed, "Our friend here requests me to explain a portion of the Scriptures to you. He tells me he should like to hear about the Prodigal Son. Now, I shall be most happy to do as he desires, if you are all willing to listen, and I shall be glad to answer any questions you may ask upon the subject." They promised compliance, and lighted their pipes when they heard I had no objection to their smoking. They listened most attentively to the reading and exposition of the sacred narrative. My friend's eyes glistened when anything was advanced that touched his feelings. I remained with them for nearly half an hour, once or twice inquiring whether they were tired, and receiving for reply, "Go on." They were very quiet and orderly while I implored a blessing on the interview. A few promised to attend the service at Prince's Place on Tuesday evening, but all made objection to Sunday.

P—— Court, —— Row. — This place is still the abode of the more vicious and depraved portion of the residents of my district. The visitation of such families is anything but agreeable, and seldom results in profit. Most of the occupants of these houses have a resemblance to each other in dirt and nakedness and vice, so that one would be a specimen of the rest. I will take No.——, being the nearest to the schools, and the first visited. The lower room, into which one enters from the court, is about seven feet square. The boards are so covered with dirt, that they would be undistinguishable from the ground, were it not that a hole here and there serves to indicate a lower depth. The cupboards are all open, the doors having been broken off for fire-wood by former occupants. In the windows, paper supplies the deficiency of glass. The furniture consists of two or three rickety stools and a kind of tub, which, being reversed, answers the purpose of a table.

There is another room above, somewhat less in dimensions than the lower one, which is used as a dormitory, but no bedstead has been seen there in the "memory of the oldest inhabitant," and not one of the last five tenants has possessed a bed. The sole furniture is a curtain to the window, which is a shirt undivested of sleeves. Five children here exist, amid dirt and wretchedness beyond description, one being an infant in a state of nudity : their outward defilement is a symbol of the waste within.

"Do you ever say your prayers?" I asked. "What! don't you even know 'Our Father?' Do you know who God is? Did you ever hear of Jesus?" Each inquiry was met but by the vacant stare of amazement and an unmeaning laugh. In a short time the mother came in, in whose countenance might be traced marks of depravity and excess. "Your children don't go to school, they tell me," I observed to the woman. "La! bless you, master, how can poor critturs the likes of us send children to school? Why, we can't get wittles for 'em to eat, let alone things to kiver 'em. You people an't got no feeling for the poor, or you would never ask such a thing." After a little conversation, I found that she indulged in "a bit of bacca"— "the only comfort poor people had ; " also "a drop of beer," and sometimes "a *little* gin," which, she observed, "don't hurt nobody." I am led to conclude she is not married to the man she lives with. The Word of God read *here* appeared to make but little impression. *Truly it is the female visit that is needed to follow, or even to precede mine, and place these poor creatures in a position to listen to the truth.*

On the 12th of December, 1858, the Bishop of London again visited Bethnal Green parish, being the third time within a fortnight. He preached at St. Peter's Church, on the occasion of reöpening that edifice for Divine service. His attention seems to be especially drawn to the want of religious knowledge and conviction in the East end of London.

The Rev. J. H. Wilson, who has been so successful in the evangelization of certain low districts of Aberdeen, had a recent interview with the Bishop of London, at his lordship's invitation, at London House. This portion of the metropolis was the immediate subject of conversation, and the bishop strongly advised the employment of female colporters, to sell Bibles there without delay.

The Missionary of the Truth must wait before the pass of Khyber long and patiently, at the portals of Central Asia, to acquire languages, and to find the men of courage and peculiar fitness, who shall carry the treasures of the Scriptures with him to the five millions of Afghanistan ; but there is no such bar to entering into the streets and lanes of our one vast city, comprising in itself three millions of souls. May the efforts of the church militant, in all its sections—the efforts of great and small, young and old, of paid and unpaid agents—*all* be brought to bear upon the advancement of the kingdom of God by the spread of His Word ! And yet it is not enough to go forth to these masses with the Bible, the tract, or the Gospel alone.   If we do, they may well answer, as they have long done by their virtual rejection of the message, " We are not in a state to listen to you.   We have bodies as well as souls.   Look at our food, our clothing, our lodging, and see where we take cold rest from our labor on bare boards or rags !   Do you wonder that we try to lose the sense of our misery in gin ? Teach us better habits, and pluck us from the hand of those who grind our poverty.   Show us how we may become self-reliant, and lift us up to listen to your Book out of our depths of woe."   How many have actually said to these women, " We understand this new plan ; we think this is really caring about us ; it is going the way to teach us to care for ourselves ! "

CHAPTER XI.

IT is now twenty years ago since a minister of Christ, one Sabbath evening, delivered an address to silk-weavers in Mile-end New Town, from the words, " Consider what I say, and the Lord give you understanding in all things."

Having announced his text to a congregation largely composed of these artisans, he proceeded to give them a very interesting history of themselves and their forefathers—those French refugees who came to England to escape the persecutions that followed on the revocation of the edict of Nantes, in 1685. At that time it was decreed that Protestantism must flee out of France within fifteen days ; and, while 400,000 persons left the kingdom, as many more perished of famine or fatigue, in prison, in the galleys, and on the scaffold, while a million seeming converts to the superstitions of Rome maintained in secret, amid tears and desolation, the faith of their ancestors.

History has preserved to us a *tableau vivant* of the

expression given by our Queen Elizabeth to her grief and indignation at the previous massacre of St. Bartholomew in 1568. She refused for several days to give audience to La Mothe Fénélon, the French ambassador ; when at last she consented to admit him to her presence, she received him in her privy chamber, which had the gloomy aspect of a tomb. She was surrounded by the lords of her council and the ladies of her court, all attired in deep mourning. The ambassador passed through the silent throng, while every eye was averted from him in anger, and approached the queen, who demanded how he could justify his master from that odious crime. England had, for more than a hundred years, supported the Protestant party in France, by arms and by negotiation.

The French colony in London, at that time, consisted of but 422 persons. After the massacre, the French church was no longer able to provide aid for those who arrived in a state of destitution. The queen commended the refugees to the charity of the Archbishop of Canterbury, who relieved their misery. She afterwards protected them against the animosity of the city apprentices, and of the shopkeepers, who were jealous of the new-comers, and even clamored for their expulsion from England. More than 20,000 of them took up their abode in Long Acre, Seven Dials, Soho, and Spitalfields.

Thirty years after this massacre, in the year 1598, the edict of Nantes was promulgated by Henri Quatre, which guaranteed liberty of conscience to the Protestants, and marked for France the end of the middle ages. It was sealed with the great seal of green wax, which testified that it was irrevocable. Nevertheless, in 1684, under the government of Louis Quatorze, all things were tending towards its revocation. It was in Poitou that the king first essayed the terrible means of conversion to the Catholic faith, afterwards known by the name of *dragonnades.*

" This was a military mission, by which dragoons were sent to those towns in Poitou which contained most Huguenots. They were quartered in the poorest houses, and even in those of the widows. In many places the priests followed them in the streets, calling out, ' Courage, gentlemen ; it is the king's intention that these dogs of Huguenots should be pillaged and sacked.' The soldiers entered the houses with uplifted swords, sometimes crying, ' Kill, kill,' to frighten the women and children. As long as the inhabitants had wherewithal to satisfy them they were only pillaged ; but when the price of their furniture was spent, and their clothes and ornaments sold, they were seized by the hair to be dragged to church, or tortured in their houses to convert them ! The feet and hands of some were burned at a slow fire ; the ribs and limbs of others broken with blows of sticks. Several had their lips burned with red-hot irons; and others were thrown into damp dungeons, to be left to die.

"The newspapers of the Hague and Amsterdam informed Protestant Europe of those odious acts, and one long cry of indignation arose in Holland, England, and Germany; but the French Gazette was filled with lists of 'converts,' and the court was dazzled by such marvellous success. 'I think there will be no Protestants left in Poitu but our own relations,' wrote Madame de Maintenon to her brother. 'It seems to me that everybody is becoming converted.' These horrors, and worse than these, extended to other provinces; and the constancy of many sufferers yielded to the prolonged rigor of their torments. Vast numbers fled their country; and at last, on the 22d of October, 1685, the revocation of the Edict was signed. 'The temples of the Protestants were to be demolished, and all exercise of their worship to cease; their schools were to be closed, and all their children to be baptized into the Church of Rome, while the property of those who fled was to be confiscated.'

"And this was fulfilled to the letter. On the very day of the revocation began the demolition of the great temple at Charenton, built to contain 14,000 persons, and in five days no trace of the structure remained. Cheyron delivered a farewell sermon in the celebrated temple of Nismes, and exhorted his flock to be steadfast even unto death. Their temple was soon but a heap of ruins, in the midst of which was long remarked a stone, which had surmounted the over-thrown portico, with this inscription — '*This is the house of God, this the gate of heaven.*' The Protestants beheld the destruction of their 800 places of worship, and the Roman Church declared that heresy was no more."

About 80,000 refugees, according to the registers of the French Church in London, appear to have established themselves in the kingdom of Great Britain during the ten years that preceded or followed the revocation of the Edict, and at least one-third of these settled in the metropolis.

From the year 1686 to 1688 the French Consistory in London met once every week, being occupied almost entirely in receiving the marks of repentance from those persons who, after abjuring their faith to avoid death, had escaped from their persecutors, and resumed in a more tolerant country the religion they preferred to their native land. The ministers examined their testimony, heard the narrative of their sufferings, and received them back into communion with their brethren. In 1687, during the month of May alone, 497 persons were thus re-admitted into the church they had appeared to abandon.

Their return for their hospitable reception in England, and for benefits then received, was fourfold. They imparted to our trade and manufactures an immense impulse, the effects of which are felt to the present day. English paper was, up to that period, of inferior quality, and of a greyish color. These exiles brought with them the secrets of a finer manufacture in this article, as well as in silks, velvets, and light tissues of linen and wool. They also understood the superior fabrication of glass, hardware, cutlery, clocks, and watches, so that such articles were no longer sought from the Continent; and the French ambassador was known to have made brilliant offers to certain distinguished artisans to return to France for this reason. But it was too late: the secrets were divulged. Religious persecution had driven more than half her weavers from her bosom. In 1698 the looms of Lyons had decreased from 18,000 to 4000; and out of 20,000 workmen who manufactured fine linen at Laval, more than 14,000 had quitted the kingdom.

It was not in trade and manufactures alone that the refugees enriched England. The French church in Threadneedle street for five years had for its pastor the eloquent JACQUES SAURIN, before he was called to the Hague; and, as far as the difference of language permitted, great must have been the private influence of those who, as a body, were sufferers for the truth.

One of them, *Graverol of Nismes*, wrote a book, which contains an affecting narrative of the sufferings of the Protestants of Languedoc. "We," says he, "who are in a country so remote from ours *only for the sake of God's Word*, and for the testimony of Jesus Christ,—let us study to render our confession and our faith glorious by discreet and modest conduct, by an exemplary life, and by an entire devotion to the service of God. Let us ever bear in mind that we are the sons and the fathers of martyrs. Let us never forget this glory, but strive to transmit it to our posterity."

During the reign of Louis XIV, and long afterwards, many of these emigrants did not give up the hope of returning to their country ; but their petitions and aims to do so were in vain. Temperate in habits, and accustomed to toil, most of them gradually worked their way to competency, and some even to wealth. They became able to relieve their suffering brethren, still languishing in galleys and dungeons for their faith ; and the Vaudois had their shade of this fraternal charity.

Many thousands of these exiles had settled in Spitalfields, then, like its neighboring district of Bethnal Green, an open space of ground without the city walls, belonging to the Hospital or 'Spital of St. Austin. These spaces did not, till the beginning of the eighteenth century, become fully covered with houses as the seat of the silk manufacture. The starving French refugees were at first relieved by a parliamentary vote of £15,000 a year ; but God prospering their industry, the silk trade had in 1713 attained such importance, that upwards of 300,000 persons were maintained by it in England.

For a long time the population of these districts continued to be exclusively French ; that language was universally spoken ; and, within the memory of persons now living, worship was performed in French in the chapels erected by the pious refugees. Here were to be found French coffee-houses ; French songs were sung in the streets, French manners prevailed, and the houses were many of them built in the old French style, with porticoes and seats at the doors, where the weavers on summer evenings enjoyed their pipes, and chatted in their own tongue.

During the eighteenth and nineteenth centuries their descendants have been, however, gradually blending with English families, and even changing their names by translation. The *Lemaitres* have become Masters ; the *Leroys*, Kings ; the *Tonneliers*, Coopers ; the *Lejeunes*, Youngs ; the *Leblancs*, Whites ; and *Lenoirs*, Blacks. The chief vestiges of the old French colony are now to be found in Bethnal Green.

"In the last hundred years," said the preacher to his congregation, "very great changes have taken place.

The French language is no more spoken among you. You have many of you translated your very names into English. The Lord greatly blessed your fathers in this place; but you, their children, have forsaken their altars—their temples of worship are deserted shut up, or sold. You are a poor and wretched people. Because you have departed from the God of your fathers, you are being chastised for your sins; and your troubles are only beginning to set in upon you, from which you will not be delivered unless you repent and return." He then pointed them, with affectionate earnestness, to the Saviour of sinners.

The service ended, and the audience dispersed. Among them were some of the leading men of the silk trade; but by them the summons seemed to pass unheeded, and the troubles of the artisan portion of the listeners continued to increase.

One of these latter, however, a poor and humble individual, had heard that night a history he never heard before, and it made an impression on him that was never forgotten. He had been apprenticed as a weaver, and was looked upon by the masters as an intelligent man, having much influence with his fellow-workmen. Shortly after he heard this sermon he was laid aside by sickness, and for a year and a half was in a hospital, during which season of rest the thought grew in his mind that he would try and find fifty Christian weavers who might prove the first lay evangelists of their class in Bethnal Green.

He recovered, and the resolve was fulfilled, slowly and surely. He found first ten Christian weavers, then twenty, thirty, forty, amid a mass of careless, thoughtless, depraved infidels; and these formed themselves into what they called a " Christian Society of Operative Silk Weavers," which has many honored names attached to it as a committee of reference.

This is a little seed of what may be a large and glorious future. The society has published seventeen annual reports. They have one place of worship at Thorold-square, Bethnal Green Road, with various Schools, Charitable Associations, and Missions attached to it—one especially to Victoria Park, the great outlet for this part of the population on the Lord's day.

On the 26th of October, 1858, the Rev. A. T. Marzials, minister of the French church at St. Martin's-le-Grand, with his family, complied with an invitation sent them by this poor and humble little flock to a tea-meeting, at which about sixty persons were present, and everything was conducted in very plain and simple style. In the room where the meeting was held was observed a tablet, bearing the following inscription :—

THE

CHRISTIAN SOCIETY OF OPERATIVE SILK WEAVERS.

Jehovah=Jireh.

———◆◆◆———

THIS TABLET

WAS ERECTED BY THE MEMBERS OF THE
SOCIETY,

ON WEDNESDAY, JULY 16TH, 1845,

AS A PUBLIC DECLARATION OF THEIR
FAITH,

THAT OF LATE YEARS THE SUFFERINGS OF THE SILK WEAVERS HAVE

BEEN GREATLY AGGRAVATED

THROUGH A DEPARTURE FROM THOSE PRINCIPLES OF PIETY

WHICH ENABLED THEIR FOREFATHERS,

THE FRENCH REFUGEES,

WHO PLANTED THE SILK TRADE IN

SPITALFIELDS,

TO ENDURE THE LOSS OF ALL THINGS;—

ALSO TO RECORD THEIR INTENTION TO ERECT A HOUSE FOR GOD

AS A PUBLIC EXPRESSION OF THEIR DESIRE

TO RETURN TO HIM, AND A MEAN TO RECOVER THE DIVINE BLESSING.

~~~~~~~~~~~

</div>

" Thus saith the Lord of hosts ; Consider your ways. Go up to the mountain, and bring wood, and build the house ; and I will take pleasure in it, and I will be glorified, saith the Lord. Ye looked for much, and, lo, it came to little ; and when ye brought it home, I did blow upon it. Why? saith the Lord of hosts. Because of mine house that is waste, and ye run every man unto his own house."—*Haggai* i, 7–9.

In the course of the evening many interesting statements were made by parties present, amongst whom
were the Rev. G. Huelins (the last minister among the
~~~~~~~~~~~

French refugees, but now a minister of the Church of England), and the Rev. Mr. Tacchella, from Piedmont. It was noticed that many men who had attained eminence in different branches of practical science had come out of Spitalfields. The well-known Dollond, senior, the improver of the telescope, was at one time a weaver. Simpson and Edwards, the lights of the mathematical world, were taken by government from their looms to teach the cadets at Woolwich and Chatham. Simpson came down from the loom in a green baize apron to the gentleman who was in search of him. "I want to see the Mr. Simpson who wrote the work on fluxions," said the inquirer. "I am that Mr. Simpson," was the reply ; and perceiving that his visitor looked incredulous, he added, "If you will come up stairs I will show you the manuscript at the loom." The new engagement took place, and on being asked when he would fulfil it, he replied, " When I have finished the piece in the frame."

In contrast to the mathematical, historical, and floricultural societies existing in this district in a past generation, were brought forward many proofs of the religious and moral degeneracy of the people, and of the heathenism prevailing in these districts at present. Sketches were especially given of the Sabbath-breaking in Brick-lane and Club-row, together with accounts of the want of education among the children of the French refugees, arising from the necessity that the parents feel to make something by the labor of their children, to eke out their scanty means of living, now that such low prices are paid for their work.

The resolution was made at this meeting that monthly services, especially for the descendants of the French refugees, should be held in the different chapels in the weaving districts, once belonging to them. This took effect on the 21st of November, when a sermon was preached at La Patente Chapel, Brown's-lane, Spitalfields, the first temple built by the exiles, at which 800 or 900 persons were present; and on the 19th of December, at the fine old "French Temple," called Spitalfield's Chapel, which has been repaired and occupied by the Wesleyans since the year 1819.

The good and humble man, who has for so many years lived by faith, in the course of finding his fifty Christian friends, thus sees the desire of his heart perhaps beginning to be accomplished. Among the operations on a small scale sustained by his Society, Open Air Missions, Tract Distribution, Maternity Charity, Provident Fund, Temperance Lectures, and all other good things seem included, though, perhaps, the one foundation work with which our St. Giles's experience teaches us that evangelical labor should begin, remains to be carried out on a larger scale. A certain number of Bibles have, however, been sold at half-price, and now the offer made that a Mission to the Mothers of the district, by one of themselves, with the offer of the Word of God, should be at once commenced, was hailed with extreme delight.

On ascertaining the above particulars, a suitable Female Agent appeared at once to arise in the wife of the above-mentioned individual, who has been most truly and long his helpmeet in his work of faith and labor of love. Her countenance bespeaks her of French descent. She is the "Mary" of Victoria Park district, the northern portion of Bethnal Green, and we would solicit for her the helping hand of all who love the memory of the old Huguenots.

She commenced her labors on the 13th of December, 1858, and has since that time sold eighty-one copies of the Scriptures, and found fifty-seven subscribers for clothing and beds. The Christian people among the weavers, with whom she is particularly associated, held a special prayer-meeting to ask that God would prepare her heart for the work, and the hearts of the people to receive her ; and the answer to this prayer is found in many instances of an encouraging nature. One person, who is a professed infidel, is nevertheless subscribing to her for a Bible, and she is extremely well received generally. She has a helper in her work in a "turner on," one who is reckoned an "upper-class man" among the weavers. He has to place the silk on the roller for each artisan ; and as they bring him their silk, he speaks to them of the Bible and the Bible-woman, and has already obtained for her several sub-scribers, himself and his wife becoming the first pur-chasers. The people generally give the Bible-woman a kind welcome, begging her to "turn in and rest," or to "eat and drink with them." Oh, that a large out-pouring of the Holy Spirit's influence might bear wit-ness with the Written Word to these descendants of a godly race of old, to whom England owes so much ! They have richly repaid to her the refuge she afforded them in their evil day. The gates of France have now for sixty years been thrown open to the posterity of Protestant exiles ; but, though some have returned to the country of their ancestors, many children of the fugitives still rest with us ; and why, but that we may seek to restore them to the faith and the Book for which their fathers suffered ?

CHAPTER XII.

BEFORE we leave the North-east London District, comprising all that lies above the White-chapel road, we must take some note of the need of the poor in Shoreditch and Hackney, especially that part of Hackney bordering on Bethnal Green.

Here also are found many weavers. A lady living in this direction had heard of the employment of a "Bible-woman" in Exeter, and that such an agency had arisen from the perusal of articles in the "Book and its Missions." She ascertained particulars by correspondence, and being already a member of a Ladies' Bible Association, and well acquainted with Bible work, soon selected a woman, whose fitness was well known to her, for her own locality, and, obtaining a small grant from the Bible Society, so filled her hands with Bible work, in the lower parts of the Haggerstone district, that she brought in £3 a month to the Committee. Meanwhile the lady became acquainted with the superadded domestic aims of the mission, and obtained from friends £2 towards their commencement.

She then came into personal communication with the Treasurer, and £5 were gladly offered from our General Fund for the prosecution of her design, with a promise of more as needed. Shoreditch was added to the field of labor, and after the following fashion the work began.

"I spent Wednesday with our 'Rebecca,'" says the Superintending Lady, " in visiting the miserable courts and alleys. I had never been there before, and I think more dismal human dwellings could hardly be seen. I could not ascertain that there was any Christian visitation whatever. We went to B—— Buildings, D—— Court, H—— Court, and C—— Gardens, hoping to find a suitable room for Mission purposes ; but the houses all seemed woefully overcrowded. Many of the women were out selling in the street ; the children informed us, ' Mother is at the stall.' I was very much pleased with our reception. As we entered one court a woman ran across to make our coming known, and then there was quite a group to hear if the room was taken. I had no idea we should find it so difficult to procure a suitable place. A furnished parlor in U—— street seemed the only one to be met with at all within our means, and for that we are to give 2s. per week, and have the use of it whenever we like. There was one I preferred in D—— Court, but it was 3s., and perhaps U—— street is more central for all.

I suppose that it will be better to take a room entirely for Mission use when we can meet with one. We have purchased, as you recommended, calico, print, flannel, &c., but have not yet visited Spitalfields about the beds and bedding.

"We invited some into the room on Wednesday, to commence paying in; and thirteen made their first small payments, and a few others came to see, and will begin next time. One poor man said, 'My wife, from her bed, where she has long been confined with rheumatism, overheard you telling about it, and I have brought a penny for a sheet.' Another woman said, 'My girl is going to the *Christian* Palace with her school, and I should like her to have a new pinafore.'

"I had no idea that this opportunity of getting clothes by their own payments would be regarded as such a proof that they were really cared for."

In another week it is added :—

"We have found a Mission-room which has two doors; one opens into U—— Buildings, the other into H—— Court. The second time, the same people came, and brought others. They entered by the front door, and we sent them out by the back to say what was doing; and still more came running in with, 'We never see the likes of you in these parts.' We have now forty subscribers for clothing and bedding. Into what scenes of life are we penetrating! The drunken men are outnumbered by the drunken women! I inclose a morsel of journal. 'Rebecca' proposes to meet in her room whoever will come on Sabbath afternoons, as well as in the week. This is the response :—

"One poor woman who sells water-cresses declares that her husband must go her rounds and his own too on Sundays; 'for,' she added, 'I s'pose you mean to read summut to us out of your Book. There's a good many of us who can't read, and this makes us more consarned that the young 'uns should. When they comes from school, and tells us what they larn, we wishes we could read for ourselves.' 'I wish,' said a man, 'the great 'uns had a thought of this plan afore; we should a seen fewer pipes in the young 'uns mouths, and heard fewer oaths out of 'em.'"

After this Sunday reading meeting came a little tea-meeting, or what was to have been one. "On Wednesday," Rebecca says, "I fear I have wasted both tea and time; for at five o'clock none of the persons that promised on Sunday afternoon made their appearance. I fear they were off, as I was told, 'on the fly.'

"At last a knock came, and I opened the door to one of the lads who had come to me on Sunday. 'I'm one of the club, ma'am,' he said; 'mayn't I come to the tea-meeting?' Seeing me hesitate, he added, 'It's all right, ma'am; you ax the old woman' (meaning his mother), 'and she'll tell you how I gives her a penny every blessed week since you told her on it. You sees I want some togs ; ' and truly he was a bundle of rags, and withal looked so cold and hungry, that I could not resist the impulse to let him come in and warm his hands, and bid him eat.

" While I was cutting him some bread and butter he showed his delight by repeating what he had heard on the Sunday. Suddenly he broke out with, ' Oh, I say, ma'am ! you shouldn't have took it so quiet when that cove at No. 5 in our court went on so at you for asking his wife to come to tea. I suld have. liked to have gi'en him his own, and summut to boot, only you looked smiling like at him, and I thought you wouldn't be pleased. But I say, ma'am, would you have let *he* come to tea?'

" ' Perhaps I might,' said I. ' But did you not hear him say we had a purpose in getting the people in here ? '

" ' And have you ? ' he asked.

" ' Of course I have,' I replied. ' Cannot you guess what it is ? '

" He paused a few moments, and then bringing the basin he had in his hand down on to the tea-tray with a bang, he said, inquiringly, ' Is it to read to them out of your book'—pointing to a Bible that lay on the table—' and to talk as you did last Sunday about *Jesus*, and *the great white throne* that will be in the clouds ?'

"'Yes,' said I, 'that is my purpose. I have much to tell you about Jesus; and then I want to show those who do not know, how to make the things they buy of me.'

"He opened his eyes to their full extent, gulped down a great mouthful of bread and butter, and then added, 'Do you mean to say as if I had bought the stuff for a jacket you'd show the old woman how to make it?'

"'Yes,' said I.

"'Well, then, you are a stunner! I shall like you, I know, and I'll bring 'em;' and so ended my first intended tea-meeting."

A large clothing club has arisen out of "REBECCA'S" earnest commencement. After three months' labor the lady again writes:—"The great demand which the sale of clothing makes upon my time has led me too often to neglect the duty of recording our work. How to lessen what we may call our *shopkeeping* responsibilities I do not know, and yet I feel desirous to secure leisure for things still more important.

"Hardly a week passes without our receiving fresh applicants desirous to subscribe for calicoes, flannels, and prints; and the usual remark is, 'Ah! my poor children would not have been seen in rags if this had begun before.' Our first duty, or the one that immediately follows on the offer of the Word of God for their own purchase, is to give these poor creatures the opportunity of providing themselves with decent clothing.   Our aim in doing so is fully appreciated, and brings us into friendly contact with the people at once.

" The division of the SHOREDITCH and HAGGERSTONE districts, which now afford quite work enough for two women, has taken up much time. ' REBECCA' has introduced ' DOROTHY' to her new vocation. In their first call they met a City Missionary, who was also paying his earliest visit on the district, and as it was at the house of a Christian woman, they knelt together to seek a blessing, recognizing in this accidental meeting the voice of God calling them to united prayer as the commencement of new duties.

" The Haggerstone district will henceforth have ' Rebecca's' undivided attention, but she is not content to lose sight of the warm-hearted Shoreditch boy formerly mentioned, who has quite adopted her as a new kind of mother to *him*. A kind friend sent him some clothing through her means, and she likewise obtained work for him at a type-foundry. She has reason to believe he will receive yet more lasting blessing, and never cease to thank God that he was the Bible-woman's first friend at the tea-meeting. ' Rebecca' has a very long list of Bible subscribers, and many sick persons expect a frequent and helpful visit from her.

" One of her earliest calls was made on a poor young woman lying in intense suffering, whose rough, ungodly husband, increased by his profaneness the misery of her lot. He hardly ever spoke without an oath. The hand of God, however, pressed heavily upon him, and his favorite child was taken from him. REBECCA continued her visits and conversation with his wife, and although he had not attended either church or chapel for years, when his wife recovered, instead of opposing her wish to go, to her great surprise he accompanied her to a place of worship, seeming, however, to sleep during the service.

" How different now is his appearance in the house of prayer! Eyes, ears and mouth wide open, as if he would drink in the Gospel Message. He has been visited by a dream in the night, and, from the great present change in his life and conversation, we cannot doubt that it came from God. 'I thought I was in torment,' he says, 'and the Saviour tried to save me, but it was too late, and I was lost.' He woke trembling with terror, and crying out, 'What must I do to be saved?' He has found peace in Jesus, and speaks with delight of being 'a new creature.' His wife says that all his old discontent has passed away, and that a heart happy in Christ makes a happy home. He embraces all opportunities of attending Bible-classes and meetings (for he cannot read), and evidently most earnestly desires religious teaching ; and that which he receives he communicates. He tells his fellow-workmen, 'My lads, ye think yer better scholars than I am ; but I think the Lord thinks I am the best, for now I know his will, I'll try and do it.' It is very interesting to hear him narrate his conversations at the lime-works ; his companions certainly hear startling truth from him, and must wonder at the change. O that more such witnesses may be raised up, and that the faithful words, 'Know the Lord,' may be heard by every ear!"

"Rebecca" passed over to "Dorothy" the new Bible-woman for this district, the names of twenty subscribers ; and the first week "Dorothy" went alone she obtained ten more. She is always received with civility, and by many of the people is warmly welcomed.

"Some years ago she was engaged in a ragged-school in this very district, and relinquished its duties on account of the long-continued illness of her husband. She has met with two or three of the parents of her former pupils, and with one of her early scholars, now a young woman, who confessed, with tears, that she had so far forgotten the instructions received in childhood as to be unable to read. 'Dorothy' told her that nothing would give her more pleasure than to be again her teacher, and thus to place in her hand the key to the treasures of God's holy Word.

" I send you," says her lady friend, " a short extract from her journal :—

" ' Called on an old man, and when I told him my errand he burst into a flood of tears, and said he hoped it was not too late for him to begin to read the Bible. I told him it was not, and strove to point him to a Saviour. He seems to have been for some time under convictions of sin, but has had no one to take him by the hand and direct him to Christ. He began to pay for a half-crown Bible, and promised to send his daughter to a Sunday-school.

" ' Collected in B—— Row, &c. Called on a poor widow who keeps a little shop, which she has closed every Sunday for some months, in consequence of something she heard said in a service she attended, conducted by a City Missionary. She says she has lost a great deal of custom by the change, but that she shall never open again on the Sabbath. Last week she was robbed by a lodger of the greatest part of her bedding, so that to her the news of the clothing and bedding to be paid for by instalments was very welcome.' "

To both the last-mentioned individuals how welcome proved the call of the good visitor of their own class— one to whom they could express their sorrows, and who " knew how to feel for them !" A poor woman, with the " Message from God " in her hand, is found the most sympathizing and suitable instrument to obtain admission to their miserable abodes ; and, while fulfilling her first errand to sell the book, she leads them, meanwhile, no longer to seek mere relief from the rich (which, when obtained, is most often squandered), but to depend upon themselves for all the necessary comforts that shall reform their homes : thus she secures their rise BY THEIR OWN EFFORTS out of their depths of filth and degradation.

CHAPTER XIII.

INTO all that lies below the Whitechapel Road, and between that boundary and the river, we are only beginning to make research. We know that many a faithful laborer has gone before us, and that each true agency has brought home some wandering souls. We find, however, enough work left.

In LIMEHOUSE FIELDS we have a steady, persevering "Priscilla," who gets on admirably. Her district was pointed out for her by the Secretary of the Ladies' Bible Association of the district, the voluntary work of which is described to be "in rather a low state." "Priscilla," therefore, entered upon it, and with the help of a colporter, carrying his box of the Bible Society Bibles, has obtained in the first month one hundred and fourteen subscribers for Bibles, and fifty-four for clothing. Her superintendent says, "It is a most densely populated district. She has visited one hundred and eighty-four houses in one street, and found two families in almost all. Those who have never visited the East End of London can form no idea of the narrow streets and teeming population. My heart sinks at the thought.

" The people are very poor ; they are coal-whippers, costermongers, and dock-men ; and when winds are contrary, so that the shipping cannot get up, the latter can find no employment. The women are chiefly employed in needlework, and are miserably paid. ' Priscilla' has been well received among them, and the poor creatures express themselves pleased that any one cares for them. I should think this district needs even more aid to help itself than Bethnal Green or Whitechapel, concerning which more sympathy has been already excited. Any provision of ready-made useful clothing to sell cheaply to them would be much welcomed. Many go to a place of worship in the dark winter evenings, who say ' they must hide themselves now that the evenings are lighter.' Talk about heroism ! If you want to see it in many an unrecorded form, you must go amongst these poor ; but ah, how many of their true tales make one's heart ache ! "

The following is a letter from the same superintending lady of more recent date :—

" *June* 10*th*, 1859.

" It is now three months since the commencement of a Female Bible Mission in Limehouse Fields, during which interval our 'Priscilla' has paid upwards of 1300 visits, and has had 200 subscribers for Bibles and Testaments. She still retains on her books the names of 79 persons, and has delivered 121 copies. Every week she extends her district, and there is yet much ground for her to explore. Having received for the above number of Bibles the sum of £7 18s. 3d., this amount has been paid in by me to the Stepney Auxiliary Bible Society. 'Priscilla's' salary from the treasurer of the grant from the Jubilee Fund for Female Colportage has been £5 7s. 3d. in the above space of time.

"She has found many persons in possession of a small Bible, who have told her that they would gladly pay for a larger one, but their husbands have been so much out of work that they have not the pence to spare.

"Others, owing to their intemperate habits (O that I had it not to write!) and want of Bible principles, have brought themselves down to such a state of poverty, that their souls are kept without knowledge, and their bodies without decent clothing. This class, however, must not be left unheeded, and all who desire the spread of the Bible, especially in places where ladies could not *persevere* in visiting, must and ought to lift up their hearts in gratitude to God for having put it into the minds of His people to devise this fresh effort for carrying to the poorest the only effectual remedy for their miseries, and by means so likely, with God's blessing, to answer the end—the poor woman going with the Bible to the poor.

"I trust that Christians will be moved to aid, by their prayers and their money, in multiplying such agents in the dark places of the east of London, which may be truly said to be 'full of cruelty.' God is certainly stirring up the minds of many, for I am often asked the question, 'Could we not have a Bible-woman in Shadwell? could we not have one in Ratcliffe?' and can but answer, 'The silver and the gold, as well as all hearts, are in the hands of the Lord. You must pray that ways and means may be found, and help will surely come.'

"But to return to my own district. The moral degradation of the people is very great, and many do not seem to know it is wrong (to use their own words) 'to mend their children's rags' on the Sabbath morning, and were surprised when the Bible-woman remonstrated with them for it, saying that their week days were taken up in earning their bread ; and what were they to do if they did not work on the Sunday? It is not many days since a man stabbed his wife in the face in the street, nearly opposite 'Priscilla's' residence. When we enter the close rooms in which the people live so many together, and with so little to employ or interest them when their hours of work are over, or in the days when they are out of work, we are scarcely surprised to find them quarrelsome.

"I should inflict much pain on my readers were I to record all the details which I am obliged to hear; yet they would even then acquire but a faint idea of the manners of the people amongst whom we have to work. They are quite capable of being taught, and many among them are sighing to escape to a better state of things, and I have often thought that could they but be transported to some district in China or India, how great would be the desire evinced to send Bibles and teachers among them; and though I would not abate one jot of interest in the far-off heathen, surely those at our own doors should not have been so long neglected.

"It is a ray of light in our picture that in so short a space of time 'Priscilla' has sold 121 Bibles and Testaments. While accomplishing this important work, she is received as a friend among these poor, degraded ones. They tell her their tales of sorrow; they ask her advice, *but never beg of her*. One woman had sunk so low that she was literally covered with vermin and filth; yet being struck by the repeated calls of the Bible-woman, and with the fact of any one taking an interest in *her*, she subscribed for a 2s. 6d. Bible, and since then has kept herself much cleaner;

has had her windows mended ; scrubbed her room ; and told 'Priscilla' that she 'meant to get a piece of muslin to make a short blind for her window, to be a little decent.' She is now doing some needle-work for the Clothing Mission, and she puts by the money earned for clothing for herself and children, except when she is without bread, when she will ask for a few pence of it to buy a loaf. She is not a drinking woman, but broken-spirited through poverty. The neighbors have marked the change, and have said to 'Priscilla,' 'Well, we never saw Mrs. T—— so clean till you came to her ; you have certainly done her good.' She said herself, with tears in her eyes, 'I could not see any way of getting on till you came to me. Your constant calling made me ashamed, and now I am determined to try and keep myself and the children clean.' She lives in a wretched place ; there are four other families in the dwelling ; the filth of a slaughter-house runs before her door, and the stench is so abominable that no visitor can remain many minutes in her room without a feeling of sickness ; and it is swarming with rats besides. Yet I am told that, had I seen it three months back, and could compare its past and present state, I should be astonished at the improvement.

"'Well,' said a subscriber, when she had obtained her Bible, 'this is the first book I have ever had that

I could call my own. I shall read it, and, as you say it is a good book, I hope it will do me good.' 'Priscilla' happened to call on one of her subscribers, who was paying for a 2s. 6d. Bible, while the husband was at dinner. On seeing the 3s. copy, the wife said she must wait another week, and have one of those. The man immediately came forward, and gave the extra 6d., adding that 'he had long felt he should like to have a Bible, and now he meant to read it.'

" 'Do you know,' said another, ' I never thought I could save money till you came to visit me. Now I have paid for my Bible, I will pay for some clothes,' which she continues to do. I think it a most cheering feature of the work, that most of those who have had Bibles are now paying for clothes, and some talk of leaving their dirty rooms. Many have said to ' Priscilla,' ' It is so kind of ladies to send you among us. Here we were quarrelling, and drinking, and abusing each other, no one seeming to care for us ; but we like to see you, and are very pleased that you have come to live near us.' The fact is, that, though a gentle little creature, she often parts them in the midst of a fight.

" She has been the means of recommending two girls, who were anxious to go to service, but had no clothes, to a society with which her superintendent is connected, by whose means they will be supplied with an outfit suitable to enter a respectable family. In several cases, when the people have been spoken to on the sin of Sabbath-breaking, they have promised that they will not work on that day, and many of them have tried to keep their word. Her constant quiet presence among them works in so many ways for good ; and, though it may seem but little that she does, when we think of what is to be done, yet, if we bear in mind the value of one soul, we cannot feel that the work is unimportant. I could multiply facts of the Bible being well received, but I must say a few words about our Clothing Mission. In this department 'Priscilla' is very useful, as she can cut out garments, arrange and fit them, and, as she is herself a good needlewoman, she endeavors to teach the women the best way of doing things. She has obtained seventy-six subscribers in this department of her work, most of whom have paid previously for Bibles, and has brought in from them, up to the 10th of June, £10 16s. 8½d., all which money would otherwise, probably, have been spent in drink.

" The women come to the Mission-room every Monday evening, to bring their pence, and to choose the articles they would like ; they appear satisfied and pleased with what is purchased for them, and particularly so with READY-MADE clothing, one parcel of which we received from the treasurer, one from a lady at Stoke Newington, and a few second-hand articles from a lady at Shadwell ; also some pieces of print from a friend at Stepney Green, which were made into pinafores and little frocks. One evening every week they meet also for work, when an excellent lady, accustomed to conduct Mothers' Meetings, presides. She reads a portion of Scripture, explains it, and, after offering prayer, reads aloud to them some useful book, such as the ' First and Last Day of the Week,' with which the women are much delighted : some have told ' Priscilla ' it is like heaven on earth to them.

" We have had a tea-meeting, at which twenty-two were present, some so very poor that they scarcely ever buy fresh tea, milk, or butter. One poor woman came that had just lost her baby. It had pined away almost from starvation ; she had nursed it while living only on stewed tea-leaves and dry bread, and while making two shirts a day, for which she received 4d. She has a husband at sea, a very bad man, and she has not an article of furniture, one of her poor neighbors allowing her to share her bed. ' Priscilla ' believes her to be a hopeful character, and thinks that, with instruction, her trials may be made useful to her.

" Many of our poor guests said that it was years since they had spent such a happy evening. I do not expect to get the most depraved to our meetings at first. They must be sought out and sought after : those who know anything of the human heart can understand the force of our Saviour's complaint when He was on earth, ' Ye will not come unto me that ye might have life, because your deeds are evil.' When light arises in a dark place, ' every one that doeth evil hateth the light ; neither cometh to the light, lest his deeds should be reproved.' But we have first the poor weary wife and mother, who needs cheering, teaching, and encouraging to do right—who is willing to be advised to better plans of management ; and this class will imperceptibly influence others around them. Several of the women asked if we could let them have something to take home to read to their husbands. On hearing this, I wrote to Mr. H. F. Barclay, who kindly responded to my appeal by sending five hundred copies of ' The Band of Hope' and 'The British Workman,' which are freely distributed among them.

" The people need civilizing almost as much as savages abroad. At some of the houses at which ' Priscilla' calls, it is no uncommon thing, at the end of the week, to see the very young children running about the room quite naked, and the elder ones with merely a rag pinned round them, the mothers saying, when spoken to about it, that they must take their clothes off once a week to wash them, or else ' to keep them out of the streets ;' but the truth is, they have no second suits. Several of these are now paying for more clothes, and many of the women that are wearing the clothes that they have subscribed for, are accosted by their neighbors with, ' Why, you look so nice, I hardly knew you. I shall try and get some clothing too.' The good Bible-woman is herself cheered by a visible alteration in the inmates of many rooms ; and the increased comforts of the people, earned by their own efforts, are strongly associated in their minds with the BLESSED BOOK which contains the history of the Saviour of sinners, at whose feet many of them will now, we hope, be brought to sit, ' clothed and in their right mind.' "

SUSAN IN WHITECHAPEL.

" SUSAN," in WHITECHAPEL, has already fifty Bible subscribers. She had the advantage of going round . first with the Bible Society's colporter, and they visited the Jewish, the German, and the Rag Fair districts, in company. Owing to the Christianizing efforts which have been long at work in the district, they found the Gentile population, on the whole, well furnished with small Bibles. Yet the very names of the streets, notwithstanding all effort hitherto, have still a dreadful renown as the abodes of want, and sin, and misery. It now, therefore, remained to present and recommend the cheap *large* prints, which are at this time calling the attention of the ignorant so much more vigorously to the holy volume of inspired truth.

Many who could not read expressed great thankfulness that a Bible-woman would come and read to them, that they might learn the way of salvation.

"Sometimes," says the Colporter, "a dozen boys and girls swarmed around us in the courts, and one or two would even herald our approach. An elder lad gave us his name, Jim James, and invited "Susan" to come and see where he lived, that he might subscribe; it proved ' all right,' and he gave her a penny. When we knock at the door of a Romanist, we often encounter the lowering look and a downcast and sullen demeanor. They belong to the church which does not allow the Bible. How different the expression of the faces where the light of the Gospel has fallen; how cheerful the reply, whether they are supplied or are desiring a larger type! One cordial smile of welcome compensates for a large measure of refusal and rebuke.

" From the Jews we met with civility, though they generally told us they had their own creed, and their own Old Testament. We sometimes heard of a Christian residing in their midst: one, a tailor by trade, when we reached him on a narrow flight of stairs, said, ' The Bible was the very thing he *did* want.' We met with another who had been a Bible subscriber twenty-four years ago, when residing in the self same court. If they were not all Jews in the other courts, she told us, they were Roman Catholics, some of whom, it appears, act as 'Shuboth-guys,' or servants, on Saturdays, to these descendants of the noble Abraham." The exiled remnant of the original depositaries of the law of God, they still so minutely observe it " to the title," that they refuse to snuff a candle or poke the fire, but impatiently call, " Shuboth-guy—Shuboth-guy," as the stoker passes from room to room for the purpose. Wonderful witnesses to the utterances of Sinai, which they have " made void by their traditions."

It is well known by many persons in this neighborhood that George Yard, Whitechapel, and its immediate vicinity, was once considered one of the vilest places in the whole of Middlesex. Some remember the time when people were allured down there to some den of infamy, where they were drugged, and the contents of their pockets taken ; and in bygone days many so trepanned were never seen to emerge from those depths again. Day, evening, and Sunday schools are now established, and open-air services are held in New Court, an outlet of George Yard, on Sabbath evenings. The congregation is often thus gathered together :

The school children are appointed to meet at a certain place, and, when assembled, they walk through the back streets of the neighborhood, singing a hymn to a

8*

cheerful tune. Crowds, composed chiefly of the lowest characters, soon gather round, and march back with the children.

It is a motley congregation. The vilest have the gospel preached to them there. In the crowd we might recognize ticket-of-leave men ; on the low wall are seated groups of poor pickpockets with upturned faces, hearing, perhaps for the first time, that Jesus Christ came to save and die *for them*. Blind beggars, led by the hands of their friends, come and seat themselves, to listen to the message of mercy, and at all the dingy windows round may be seen anxious persons, who probably would never have heard of the way to heaven but for such an opportunity, and who seem surprised that any are come down to sympathize with them in their degradation. These are often also aged and afflicted people, who can seldom leave their dark and miserable homes.

To such it may be conceived how welcome will be the visit of the kindly BIBLE-WOMAN, bringing to the door of every room the Book of which the minister has spoken, and from which he uttered that story of comfort and peace. It is towards these " dark places of the earth," in the heart of our Christian city, which have been " full of cruelty," that the purifying waters of the stream of life must be turned in fresh and abundant rills, and that NOT BY GIFTS, which would be made away with, but by continual presentation of the Divine Message for easy purchase.

Whitechapel, with its 213 streets and 5000 inhabited houses, is a world we must further explore. The Rev. W. W. Champneys and the Rev. Hugh Allen have been faithful laborers there for many years, and their unceasing efforts, combined with those of others, to preach the Gospel to these poor, cannot but have effected much. Mr. Champneys says, " There were but sixteen communicants the first day I entered the parish church, in 1838, and then there existed but one church for 30,000 persons ; now there are four, and the congregations in all are overflowing." He adds, " If Whitechapel *is* what it still *is*, what must it have been twenty years ago?" A communicant of Mr. Allen's church has been found to undertake the Female Bible Agency, which will penetrate into every room, and thus fruit already borne shall peradventure lead to the bringing forth of more fruit; for " to him that hath shall be given, and he shall have abundantly," is a record in the harvest field of souls.

Cheap clothing is here very much needed. People are crowded together, many of them having been reduced from former respectability, rather than born to the bitterness of poverty. The men saunter down to the docks, and often get no work ; the women sell in the streets. They welcome the opportunity of ob-

tainiug large Bibles at a cheap rate, and will probably
do so more and more.

THE BIBLE-WOMAN IN SHADWELL.

Through the efforts of the Lady who so success-
fully superintends Priscilla, a new mission has now
taken rise at Shadwell. She had her attention called
to a person of suitable age and appearance—a tried
Christian woman of great moral courage and intelligence, and much kindliness of heart, who solicited
the work, and was not unwilling to be appointed to
Shadwell, where the population is of a most low and
debased character. We cannot enter into all particulars, but its main thoroughfares are streets through
which a respectable person cannot walk without deep
concern ; and thoughtful men have been heard to say
concerning it, that " as there are incurable diseases in
the physical world over which the skilful physician
cares not to spend his time or exert his talents, so it is
with places like this in the moral world—they cannot
be mended."

Such, however, is not the resolve of our earnest-
minded sister worker. She desires to see what the
Bible will do even here, and she has already some encouragement.   " I feel," she says," as if I had opened
a pestilential cave, the vapors of which have so overcome me that I must shut it up a while to recover my-

self. We have penetrated into the regions where the inmates, sitting in darkness and despair, say 'Nobody cares for us. Our destroyers are still caressed and welcomed in society, but our portion is scorn and shame for ever. If we leave our present life we must starve. Drink—we *must* drink, or we should drown ourselves.'"

That among these wretched ones it is a WOMAN's special mission to go, and with God's Word in her hand, we believe that succeeding months will prove.

Perhaps three-fourths of the population are Romanists. Some of the people told "BARBABA" they had their crucifixes ; and they would rather have them than the Bible. Others said " *They* never prayed to God, but if she did, they wished her luck ; they should be glad to see her, and would treat her civilly if she did not interfere with their religion ; for, as theirs was the oldest and the best, she would never change it. They meant to stick to it." Some inquired if she was a Puseyite, as they had plenty of that sort about there, and they hated those who were neither one thing nor the other.

Many poor Protestants said they were glad some one was coming among them. They had a Missionary once, but it was a long time now since any one had cared for them.

In a house up one of the alleys, which she entered

to write a name, the man noticed her hand trembling. He said, " Missus, you need not be frightened.   We shall all be civil to you if you say nothing against our religion."   One woman added, " I will come to your clothing meeting; but I won't stop to your reading nor your prayers."   " BARBARA " has already sold several Testaments and some Bibles.

We have need to go forth with her, supporting her with the prayer of faith, as she penetrates up those dark alleys.   Sailors of every clime and color elbow her at each step as they crowd towards the gin-palaces.   Many, doubtless, have been on board ships that took out Missionaries to. the HEATHEN.   What must they think of this port of entrance to the land of Bibles?

The American is there, with his slouched hat, his sheathed bowie-knife, and his tobacco-pouch ; and the dark, tall, bearded Lascar, in his blue check shirt; the African, with his woolly hair ; the Chinese, with his long-tailed head-gear ; each chattering in his own tongue to his companions, or lounging against a wall smoking, or joking with the girls, dressed in shabby finery.   Abominable smells abound, and heaps of cin-ders and garbage fill up the way.   The women often fight like raging furies; the children of six years old look like fifty, with their hunger-bitten faces ; they are not at play—they sit gazing out of the dark courts ;

and boys of twelve, smoking short pipes, lie outside the doors.

The Bible-woman seems especially fitted to deal with the unfortunate class. They are very civil to her, gather round her to hear her read a chapter, and ask her to come again.

In one alley there was a filthy family, and the next time she called she found both mother and children washed, as they were expecting her. One woman said, " I tell you what it is. Poverty is a curse—a curse! It works all the good qualities out of you, and you ponder, ponder : it takes all your thoughts to know how you are to get bread."

In entering upon a new district we would never be understood to suppose that nothing has been accomplished previously to our own efforts. In God's book of record is inscribed every genuine and self-sacrificing effort to save souls. He knows the history of all kinds of evangelism and their results, and he marks successively each true laborer as he sows his seed ; but that the seed of the Word is still to be sown in all these wide deserts of sin and shame, and to be carried especially by woman to women, is a fact which none can deny.

Oh, what a voice is uttered from such depths in testimony against under-paid needlework !—a voice most surely heard by the Judge of all the earth. " The hire of the laborers kept back by fraud crieth, and the cries are entered into the ears of the Lord of Sabaoth." There are white slaves in England that yet need their Wilberforces, and there is an army of watchers to do evil, waiting for the unwary, sleepless at their posts, whom we have scarcely yet begun to meet by our Mothers of Charity watching for good. It must be sad and secret service; but there are some at whose hand the Lord requires it, and to whom He would render in its performance a rich reward.

CHAPTER XIV.

RETURNING again by the spacious old road of White-chapel, which was in former times, as the one "high-way into Essex, skirted by numerous inns, with their ancient galleried yards," we make a bend round Houndsditch, and come within the antique limits of the old City Wall. There are associations with the words "London Wall" that carry us back to the days of Theodosius, the Roman Governor of Britain ; nay, to old Londinium, with its earliest fosse and rampart cast up to protect its "considerable depôt of merchan-dize before the days of Cæsar." A town is known to have existed on this spot for well-nigh two thousand years. When it became the Roman *Colonia* of Augusta, the Prætorium and its adjuncts, with their tesselated pavements, are supposed to have occupied the present site of the Poultry and Cornhill.

Suetonius built its wall of " hewn stone commingled with brick," beginning at a fort occupying the present site of the Tower of London, and carried northward

[185]

through the Minories to Aldgate, crossing Bishopsgate to Cripplegate, thence to Aldersgate and Ludgate, inclosing an area of somewhat more than three miles, and leaving one side open to the river. The wall is said to have been guarded by fifteen towers, and to have described a figure like a bent bow, of which the Thames was the cord.

The names of the old gates remain, and so still do a few scattered fragments of the antique wall in the churchyard of St. Giles's, Cripplegate; and in its venerated decay it still gives its name to the district. London " within the walls" made a rapid expansion into the adjacent fields. It has been for eighteen centuries the seat of a busy and ever-increasing population, and has a history coëval with the Christian Era. Soon the number of buildings " without the walls" began to exceed those within, and left them as a mere kernel in the midst of the mass; while the ever-multiplying dwellings of the city have since overtaken the villages of Southwark, Westminster and Lambeth, and, indeed, have now absorbed every adjacent village on every side within ten miles round.

It is, therefore, a matter of some interest to go back to the " kernel" of this "province covered with houses." London within the walls is divided into ninety-eight parishes for ecclesiastical purposes, and into twenty-six wards for municipal purposes. It was once very thickly populated, and is still the centre of business to the world, but the opulent have long since removed their private residences to the western suburbs. The Earls of Oxford and of Essex, De Veres, Dudleys, and Cromwells, have left St. Swithin's Lane, and Bishopsgate and Throgmorton Streets, and the Bishops of London have forsaken their palace in Aldersgate.

An act for improving and paving the city passed in 1532, which describes the streets as "very foul and full of pits and sloughs, very perilous and noyous for all the king's subjects on horseback, on foot, or in carriages." Narrow, crooked streets were gloomy by day, and left in total darkness at night. The vilest by-lanes, alleys, and courts, to which public attention is being pointed now, are scarcely worse than was the general London of the Olden Time. Thatched roofs covered the plaster and timber dwellings, densely inhabited and badly ventilated, so that pestilence was a constant visitor, and a destructive fire a great blessing. Such happened in 764, 798, 801, 1077, 1135, and 1212. The great plague of 1665 was followed by the five days' fire of 1666, which destroyed thirteen thousand houses and ten millions of property. "Heaven be praised," says Malcolm, "old London was burnt!"

Still, however, the "Broad street ward" is associated with the name of London Wall;" and still, no less than ever before, is this to be considered as the most wealthy locality in the world, comprising within its boundary the Bank of England, the Stock Exchange, and the Royal Exchange. The city of London proper occupies a surface of more than six hundred acres, and this ward is the twentieth part of it, comprising thirty acres. It contains so many public halls and offices, with the premises of so many private banks, clubs, and companies, that its income tax was lately rated at more than two millions and a half; and yet in close proximity to these—in their very midst—are wretched courts and alleys, in which, according to the recent statistics of the City Mission, are to be found six hundred and fifty families who were accessible to missionary visitation.

The church above mentioned, "St. Giles's, Cripplegate, or St. Giles's *without* the walls," is rich in another relic besides the remains of the Old Wall of London. The ashes of John Milton there repose in his father's grave—" the man whose name is his monument—the poet to whom England has done justice, and whose renown equals his merits." Is not this partly from the sympathy of all mankind with his glorious subject— the tale the Bible tells of their own human history?

Another interesting feature of this district is, that the parish register of the church of St. Bartholomew, be. hind the Royal Exchange, proves that Miles Coverdale was buried in its chancel. He is well known as the translator and editor of the first complete copy of the English Bible, which was ordained by the capricious Henry VIII to lie open in every church in England, though its parts had been prohibited in detail. Coverdale was buried in 1658. The great fire occurred in 1666, in which that church was destroyed, and the Sun Fire Office now stands upon its site.

The poor population of the city within the walls have, in early life, resided in rural districts, and have been accustomed to attend public worship; but "coming to London has been," they say, "their ruin." They have found their way here as office-keepers, porters, stablemen, laborers, carpenters, shoemakers, and tailors; and the wives are occupied in shoe-binding, needlework for shops, washing, and charing. The City Missionary writes, "More than one-half of the working men are habitually more or less given to drink." Among 1200 individuals, in 307 families, in one of the wards, one only was found to be a communicant; and the man or woman who would maintain a Christian walk or conversation in these courts must be a Christian of the same order as would, if called upon, martyr for his faith upon the scaffold.

Of the ninety-seven churches standing within the walls of the city before the great fire of London, sixty-three was reërected, besides St. Paul's Cathedral, by Sir Christopher Wren, and to these churches are now added many chapels for Dissenters. There is a provision of nearly 51,000 sittings for about 55,000 persons, which is a most remarkable amount of ecclesiastical accommodation. A minister for every 500 people! The city ought, therefore, to be a model of a religious community.

It is certain, however, that, with few exceptions, both churches and chapels are very badly attended. Oftentimes scarcely a dozen people are present, inclusive of the official persons engaged in the service. On the Sunday before Christmas, the largest congregations may be expected, in anticipation of the customary gifts at that season; but according to an estimate made, even on such days the united attendance is hardly 13,000, and of these not 1300 are poor persons in the free seats. The abuse of Christmas gifts throughout London is patent to all those who have opportunity for observation.

In the spring of last year this subject came under the notice of a gentleman well known in the city—Mr. W. Coles—one of the committee for administering the benevolent funds of the Broad street ward. Exploring by the aid of a City Missionary, and also with his own eyes, the interiors in Sadlers' Place, White Lyon Court, Leathersellers' Buildings, Carpenters' Buildings, Peahen Court, &c., he found the character of the neighborhood to be such as it generally is when the poor

are accustomed to receive abundant help from the rich
without much investigation.   The well-meant and frequently repeated dole of charity, so called, only renders the receivers improvident hypocrites and ungrate-
ful rogues.   Dirt, drunkenness, and beggary are the result of sovereigns indiscriminately showered over those
who are happiest if they receive shillings, *and work
for them.*

Still no man or woman can actually go to visit the
dens of London, and not see that there is a great deal
to be done for their inmates ; and, of course, Mr. Coles
saw this. By his aid, and that of other gentlemen, courts
were cleansed, and dwellings, where pestiferous filth
had oozed through the floor, were placed under a
proper system of drainage and water supply.   During
the hot weather of last summer, when the missionary
had urged them to wash their floors, he had received
for answer, "We have not even water to wash our
skins, or to boil our vegetables.   It is only laid on for
half an hour a day, for two houses and ten families.
How are we to wash our floors?"

These things only needed to be made known to the
authorities, and in this case they were soon altered.
Could not the rich men of every neighborhood deter-
mine to have them altered, and, like those who, in the
third chapter of Nehemiah, repaired the wall of Jerusalem, work each man " over against the door of his

own house?" The building of that wall was accomplished in fifty-two days—a noticeable fact in sacred city history.

On this amended sanitary state of the courts and alleys of the Broad street ward, another agency was also brought to bear. The British and Foreign Bible Society (of the parent committee of which Mr. Coles is a member) sent two or three colporters to penetrate into every room of the district, and to obtain the names of subscribers for Bibles and Testaments. They did not find the people destitute of the Scriptures, but some of the copies they possessed were small, and most of them were old ; and they obtained many promissory names for lady collectors, besides selling two hundred and forty-nine copies by immediate purchase.

It happened that there was resident in this district an excellent lady, superintendent of the ward school, who, long before the city missionary commenced his researches, had taken an interest in, and had visited and advised, the poor of the neighborhood. She had even been instrumental in persuading them to purchase, from time to time, one hundred Bibles. She hailed these new movements, and, under her inspection, "Sarah," formerly of Clerkenwell, has now commenced a Female Bible and Domestic Mission in the Broad street ward. We will give a few life sketches of the state in which she finds the people. She begins, of course, *with Bible work*, limited to a given district, selected as the worst of the locality. Her journal will be a source of perpetual interest to those who care for the poor.

Dec. 10th.—Visited twenty-six families; obtained seven subscribers. One man, a bootmaker, said to me, " Yes, I have a Bible, but, you see, the truth is, I am such a drunkard that I quite hate myself; and, if I had had the pluck, I really should have cut my throat this morning." " You say you have a Bible, but you certainly never read it, for there you will find that no drunkards shall inherit the kingdom of God." (1 Cor. vi, 10.) " But I always pray that I may not die drunk." " How do you know that you may not die so, if so you live? We may die at any moment. You might enter this, your own room, and never leave it alive. I shall give you another word from my book, and it is the word of the Lord Jesus Himself : ' Except ye repent ye shall perish ;' and another, ' Believe on the Lord Jesus Christ, and thou shalt be saved, and thy house ;' saved from your sin and from your misery. These are the words of God's book." " Well," said the man, " put down my name for a 2s. 6d. Bible, and then I shall see you again ; it will do me good to be talked to."

Sold a three shilling Reference Bible to a French gentleman.

Carried a 6s. bed to a poor woman, who had been subscribing sixpences for it ever since she heard I was coming to the district. Surely my various kind of work is needed in this dark corner of London. No one seems to me to think that they have a soul to be saved.

Dec. 22*d.*—Visited eleven families, and obtained three new subscribers. Met with one man, who answered, " Why, we've five Bibles in the house, and not one of them can I see to read." " Look at this," replied I, presenting him with the clear, large type, issued at 2s. 6d. to the poor. " Any one who can see at all may see this," he cried out ; I can read it beautifully. This shall be my Christmas choice."

Dec. 26*th.*—Made fourteen calls, but found only one subscriber, and this was a poor woman who gets her own living, and helps to support an aged husband, by making parasols, for which she receives a penny farthing each. She gave me a penny for a 2s. 6d. Bible.

Dec. 31*st.*—This has been a terrible week in this district. Large gifts have been distributed, and often in money. Some old inhabitants have received as much as three sovereigns ; and the scenes of drunkenness have been past description. The people have sent their boys and girls for gin, which they drink on their way back ; and the depraved habits of the young hereabouts surpass any I ever before met with. I was jostled by boys, of ages varying from eleven to fourteen, with clay pipes in their mouths, a bottle sticking out of each pocket, and spilling beer from pots in each hand besides : other children were so far gone that they could not stand.

There are people in the heart of this city who, generation after generation, never think of bringing their children to be baptized, or train them with any knowledge that there is a God in heaven, or that the Sabbath is anything more than a day for drinking and riotous living. I went into one place where an old woman was dying, covered with vermin, while her two daughters were hanging over the bed drunk. I went into another, which, upon inquiry, I found had not been cleaned for sixteen years. The day before Christmas-day I met two men distributing almanacs, with the prices of liquor attached to them. As they saw me with my Bibles they said, " Well, mistress, you *will* keep pace with us." This place used to be called " Otaheite," and truly many a savage yet dwells in it, but not one beyond the power of the grace of God. May it please Him to give the spirit of wisdom and forbearance, with meekness and loving-kindness, to all those who are engaged in visiting amongst these home heathens, so that some of them may speedily be led to the Cross of Christ!

The poor bootmaker whom I first visited has been very ill, and is supposed to be dying. He has met with much kindness in his distress from Christian friends, and appears to have been brought to a review of his past life, and to a deep repentance for it. He told me this morning that he was resting on the finished work of Jesus for pardon. His shivering wife and child are now supplied with garments to make for their own wear; and being then paid for the work, they will with this payment buy the articles they have made, and be able to go out to get employment. They are thus placed in a condition to help themselves.

March.—Called to-day on sixteen families. I only collected eight pence for Bibles. One rough man, a sweep, has from time to time told me that he wished I would keep out of his house, for, said he, " I'm no chapel-goer, and I don't want to be pestered about your book. You see, if I've my pot and my pipe it's all I care for, and I've no time to look at the Bible."

I asked him if he had ever thought he *must* find time *to die*, and told him he knew not how soon that time might come—that perhaps already the grave was open, and the worms were waiting for his poor body, while he had a soul that could be miserable forever. " You had better," I said, " give me a penny a week to buy this book, which will lead you into all truth." "If you don't get out I'll kick you out," was his answer. I departed, telling him I should pray that he might think differently.

I went again another week to the door of this poor sweep, and he then called down stairs to me, " Come up, missus; I want you. I'm a rum chap; but, after all, I dare say what you said was true. I don't care anything about myself, but I should like a Bible for my boy. Here is sixpence, and you may call every week, for perhaps a little of your talk may do me good."

May, 1859.—I have found some fresh Bible work in *Moor Lane*, and have already secured twelve subscribers; and when a Mission-room is opened in this neighborhood subscribers for clothing and beds will abound. The place is a kind of maze of houses, with windings and turnings that remind one of that at Hampton Court. It is called the ' Horseride,' because, according to one of the oldest inhabitants, Dick Turpin, the highwayman, used to ride through it to escape the officers who were after him, and who were invariably lost in its turns. There is, in many cases, no light to the staircases but from a trap-door above, and in some houses this gleam falls through iron stairs full of holes. I have to grope my way up to one subscriber at the top of such a house. In one room I found two old people who welcomed me, their hearts being softened by the recent loss of a son of twenty years of age, and, "of course," said the mother, "he had a soul to be saved."

"How do you dare venture here?" said a woman to Sarah. "Don't you know that the policemen are afraid to come even two together?" "No," answered our good woman, "I am not afraid. You will do *me* no harm, and I am come to do *you* good. I am come to bring you God's Book, and you little know what that can do for you." Another Bible-woman, who accompanied Sarah here one evening, shrank from this district, and said " the people seemed like tigers," so given to fighting. A Mission-room has been opened there, and about a dozen people attend.

Many of the poor within these boundaries can support themselves by working three days in the week; and they will only work three days, and drink what they earn the other four. Drink occasions their fearful quarrels. Numbers of the women are employed as office cleaners at six or seven in the morning, and from six till ten in the evening. These spend the day in drink, and may be seen intoxicated and black as sweeps in their interim of idleness. They manage to get sober by the evening to earn more wages, to be wasted in the same way. It must be evident that they need the daily watching of a female missionary, who offers them SOMETHING ELSE TO DO WITH THEIR MONEY. "I know what you say is very true," is often the reply made. "I will turn over a new leaf. I will come to your meeting and buy a bit of calico, and make my man a shirt, and then I can bring him with me, and you can talk to him." "Sarah" is particularly well off in the arrangements made by her kind and liberal friends and superintendent of her Mission for the weekly meetings of her subscribers ; and these meetings, attended by both men and women, have continued to be crowded even through the hot weather. A larger room is now being provided, and much fruit seems springing up to the glory of God. The aspect of many of the poor is quite changed, and there never before was so little drunkenness known at Whitsuntide in the city.

" The sweep and the bootmaker, referred to at pp. 193, 197, have been watched with much interest. They now regularly attend our weekly gathering for prayer, and maintain a consistent walk at other times. The sweep has not been drunk for two months. He used to be the pest of the place ; now he cries out, ' I am a sinner,' and seems to be seeking pardon.

"In the same district a City Missionary has for some time labored, and a room is kindly appropriated for his meeting, in a poor locality, by the proprietor of the houses, showing how much such a light in a dark corner is valued ; but in consequence of the ill health of the Missionary it was proposed to close the room for a time, much to the regret of all, especially of our friend the bootmaker, who requested the little congregation might still be allowed to meet for united prayer.

"This was readily complied with, and deemed a favorable result of missionary labor ; and our friend has proved, by his earnestness in prayer and zealous endeavors to lead others to Christ, that his soul was convinced and converted from the error of its way. He has for some time taken the Bible to read to his neighbors, testifying what God had done for him, no doubt much to the astonishment of those who well knew his former habits of life."

"I found a girl," says Sarah, "in Peahen Court, to whom I was sent by the City Missionary, as she wished to be taught to read. All the family were living and sleeping in one room. Being invited to a Sunday-school, she replied, 'She must go to 'Change that day,' which ' 'Change' is the market for old clothes described at page 110. This girl goes in the morning at half-past seven, and stays till half-past three, and is then so tired that she sleeps for the rest of the day ; but she earns more money then than she does all the rest of the week. Drunken wives are glad to go to this 'Change to get a clean shirt or a pair of mended stockings for their husbands, when, as they have been drinking all the week, their own are not ready."

———

It is delightful to find that the Female Mission work, in the heart of the City of London, should thus begin to take root and flourish. Sarah already brings to her Superintendent a pound a week for clothing, as subscriptions from the people. A store of bedticks await the completion of their purchase, by sixpence or one shilling a week, ere they are filled with flock, and sent forth to make known to many, *for the first time in their lives*, the comfort of a clean warm bed ; while blankets, indelibly marked, are lent to the most destitute, for the three or four winter months, on condition that during that period, by small subscriptions (which the opportunity shall be given them to earn), they make a similar article *their own* before the time comes for the return of the loan. Soup is prepared in the winter at one penny a quart for those whose avocations prevent their making it ; and it is indeed to be wished that in every district in this vast metropolis might arise the possessor or the collector of £100, to carry out these simple reforms in the social science of practical benevolence. By £100 so bestowed, and ever more or less reproducing itself, more will be done than by £1000 bestowed in undiscerning gifts. The

9*

Bible Missionary must live among those she serves, and should not, *in general*, be of a condition in life above doing so. Like can teach like with a hitherto unsuspected power. It does it in evil things—it can do it in good things.

In a few weeks the very presence of a good woman amongst them is a testimony, *and the people hear it.* Her face, her dress, her manners, are a leaf out of a new volume to them. Will not the Christians of London set themselves to find out such women and employ them?

CHAPTER XV.

MARIAN and her superintendent one day paid a
visit to some model lodging-houses in Portpool-lane,
to observe the nature of the bedding there supplied,
when necessary, to the lodgers. In penetrating to the
top rooms of the building they found, in one tidy
room, a mother and two daughters, at work at shoe-
binding. The family could scarcely support themselves by their utmost industry at their trade. The
mother, however, voluntarily took care of the city
missionary's room in the lodging-house, and this, with
other circumstances which came to light, led both
visitors at the same time to think that they had met
with a steady, quiet, matronly body, who desired to
do good to her neighbors, and might train into, a useful missionary.

She soon afterwards commenced work in her own
neighborhood, under the guidance of Thomas Shaw, a
colporter, who had sold many thousand Bibles in the

remote hills and dales of Yorkshire, as well as in such large towns as Bradford and Leeds.

He was now employed by the Bible Society for a time in London, and was remarkably successful in obtaining subscribers, not because he professed to pay his thousand calls a week, but because he did not leave the people in garret, den, or cellar, till he had found a way to interest them severally in the " message from heaven," which he presented to them. He, perhaps, first gained their sympathy by talking on quite other subjects ; but, whatever the subject was, it always came round to " The Book," and the promise of subscription for it, in small sums, so often followed, as to amaze many a well-intentioned lady collector at the result in her own district, which she thought " thoroughly supplied," and where, after a fresh course of visits with this valuable pioneer, she found a multitude of doors opened which had been hitherto closed, and opportunities for usefulness thence arising, such as she had never supposed would be met with in the crowded city.

One secret of Shaw's success, worthy of notice by the uninitiated, is, that he did not give the people too much of what they called " preaching," which the majority turn from with disgust. He carried the " Voice" which was to be heard above his own voice ; and his object was to make the people desire and listen to *that*.

A walk with Shaw through a few of the streets in the west central districts of London will show his mode of gaining the names of subscribers, whether to be taken up by lady collectors or by the Bible-woman. . He says :

The poor people in London are more difficult of access than those in the country. They make you wait a long while at the door, and, in truth, the house being let in separate rooms, belongs equally to so many tenants, that one of them will not answer for another. I have found Bloomsbury and St. Pancras by no means destitute of small Bibles, supplied from the Sunday-schools, many of them, however, old and in bad condition ; and the proof that more are wanted is, that I have obtained so many subscribers for large-print Bibles in the course of a few weeks.

I have met with a great deal of poverty, and wretchedness, and dirt : the people seem to waste so much money in drink. I am very frequently told, " It is of no use bringing the Bible here. What we want is, something to eat and drink." One man told me, " If the parsons lived as *we* live, they would not think so much of the Bible;" and I answered, "If you thought as much of the Bible as they do, perhaps you would not live as *you* do, for the Bible is the poor man's friend. If you learn to live as it would teach

you, you would not really *want* ' any good thing.'
Godliness hath the promise even of the life that now
is, and also that which is to come.   See, here it is written in the Book : 1 Tim. iv, 8.   Have you, sir," said
I, " a Bible of your own ?"

" Yes, I have," he answered ; " butit is in pledge."

" You must have been very poor to pledge your
Bible.   Can you not get it back ?"

" No ; it would cost me less to have a new one than
to get that back."

" Well, you can get one by paying a penny a week.
A lady will collect the pence, and call upon you every
week for them."   After some more conversation on
the state of trade, he gave his name as a subscriber,
for a Bible at 2s. 6d.

The neighbors of this man were chiefly Irish.   I
could not do much with them.   They say they have
their own Bible, and are not allowed to read any Protestant books.

In the Colonnade to-day I saw a man who said he
had long wanted a Bible in large type.   He had a
New Testament, but he should like to have the Old
Book too.   He said the chastening hand of God had
taught him the emptiness of all worldly pleasure.   He
had a family of little children, and was glad of the
opportunity of small subscriptions, as he could not pay
the money for a Bible at once.   Another woman said

" Now I shall get a large Bible, which I never could before."

Cromer street.—To do any amount of work here I must spend three or four days in the street. The people would only answer, " No," if I began by asking them whether they wanted a Bible. The Romanists often tell me they have their own Bible, but when I get to see it, it is only a Roman Catholic prayer book.

January 28th.—I met to-day with some curious people. One man said, " Religion is very cheap, now ; we can have it for fourpence."

"Having a Testament," said I, "does not make a man religious. There are many people who have whole Bibles and are not religious ; but the time will come when they will wish they had been religious. Do you ever think, sir, of that time ? "

"Sometimes I do when I cannot help it."

" I believe that is a true statement. Have you any books besides the Bible ? "

" I have a song book, but no Bible. I had one once, and I lost it through drink."

" Oh, that drink ! it is the ruin of thousands. Will you be a subscriber for a Bible at one penny per week ? "

" No, mister, I won't. I have such a wretched hole of a home that I should not like any one to come and see it to get the subscriptions."

"But if you had a Bible, and heeded its directions, your home would soon improve. Do let me have your name as a subscriber."

."No ; but I will buy one of these Testaments."

"I am glad of that. I hope you will read it, and that you will pray for the teaching of God's Holy Spirit that you may understand it. He can lead you ' into the way of all truth.'"

Calls to-day, sixty ; subscribers, seven.

I have been employed this week in the poorest districts belonging to the Brunswick Square Association. In some of the houses there are six and even eight families, and sometimes two families in a room. I found that in one house thirty-seven persons were living. It takes a long time to canvass such places. The ladies hitherto have merely called at the front doors, and been told, "We do not want any Bibles." But I do not like to omit any family, because every one *ought* to have a Bible.

February 3*d.*—Attended the Ladies' Committee : the reports were much more encouraging than last time. They have taken up two hundred of the subscribers I have obtained, and I have been round with several new collectors to introduce them to the subscribers ; also, with four persons desirous of undertaking the work of colportage, under the Bible Society's auspices, in other districts.

Employed in the afternoon in —— street. Saw an aged woman, who, when I inquired if she would buy a Bible, replied, "No, thank you, sir; I have one. I should not like to live in a house where there was not a Bible."

"I suppose you have had one a long time?"

"Yes, sir. The Bible was the first thing I bought after I was married, and it has been the guide of my life from that time until now."

At the next house at which I called, a man said, "Curse you and your Bible," and shut the door in my face.

4th.—A man in —— street said, "He did not think it was right for the parsons to endeavor to shut up people's shops on Sunday, when they earn their own living by preaching on that day."

"Have you, sir, a Bible?"

"No; and I don't want one. I have something else to do besides reading the Bible; and if people who go to churches and chapels would read less and work more, and pay their way, the times would mend."

"Sir, I should like to have a little talk with you about the times. I will call again this afternoon when you have had your dinner."

"All right, my good man; if you call after dinner I shall have more time."

I did call, and before I left him I had his name as a subscriber for a Bible at 6s. 6d.

6th.—I canvassed —— Place. It has not a respectable name. I walked round it two or three times, looking at the shop windows, and noticing the children at play. The question was asked more than once, "What's that man after?" I spoke to a person who was standing about, and he happened to be the collector of the rents of most of the rooms. From him I learned that there were thirty-six houses in the place, and that about three hundred families lived in them—one family in each room, and sometimes two, and that I could pass from room to room without asking leave at the front door. Then I went to work, praying for the Divine blessing.

Some of the people are very poor, and these rooms have scarcely any furniture. When they move, which they often do, there is scarcely anything to take away. Many had no bedstead. Something that served for a bed—apparently for all the family—was rolled up in the corner of the room. I went into one, where the man, a shoemaker, was at his work. His wife was washing, and a child on the floor squalling. I took up the child, spoke to it kindly, and hushed it with a peppermint lozenge. Afterwards I turned to the man and looked at his work.

"Do you want any thing to-day, master?" said he.

"I was thinking," said I, "if you knew of any remedy for cold feet: the people keep me standing so long at their doors. Yet I have pretty strong shoes already." "I should think," said he, "you had better wear horsehair soles in your shoes." Meantime I had unstrapped my box, and displayed to him the large print 2s. 6d. Bible.

Now," said I, "you have done me a service, I think I shall do you one if I offer you this book from the Bible Society at 2s. 6d., and by the payment of a penny a week you can get it. I don't see any Bible here."

"Well," said the man, "'tis a fine type. Sally, look here."

Now I thought that Sally, as she came forward with her hands in the suds, might say, "No, we've no money to spare." So while the man read a verse or two I said to her, "Mistress, I fear you won't get those clothes dry to-night." She looked up at me, and said, "Yes, I shall; I've a hundred of coals all ready, and I shall soon get them dry."

"I am very happy to hear, mistress, that you have a hundred of coals while times are so hard with many. I think you will be able to spare a penny a week to get this nice Bible. Your master here must drink a pennyworth less beer."

"Ah, master," said the man, "I'm of your mind on that already, for I am a teetotaler."

"Well, then, mistress," said I, turning to the woman, "you must have the book by a little pinch in the tea and sugar—it won't be much."

So the man gave me his name as a subscriber. When I visit these people with the lady collector we must have a little further talk on the priceless value of the book they are going to buy. I obtained that morning twenty-one subscribers, and I think, if I were to go through the place again, I might obtain twelve or fifteen more.

Many more days were devoted by Shaw to exploring the "cork-screw" courts on the left hand side of Gray's Inn Lane, where he has obtained the names of forty subscribers. We must let him tell his own tale—

If ever a female missionary was wanted to follow up my footsteps, he says, it is there. I have been into courts also out of Chancery Lane, so narrow that, though there is a sky above them, the people never feel the sun. I have been into old houses that seem ready to fall, and up staircase after staircase, into rooms where I could not get my breath for the smoke and the thick foul air. I was going up to the top of one house, when a woman called me back and said, "Master, you need not go up there ; there is a dead man there." "Well," said I, "my message is to the living, and not to the dead. Are there any living up there?" She said "she believed there were;" so I persevered, notwithstanding the close atmosphere, and on the top floor I sold a Bible.

" What kind of people live in such houses, and why do they live there?"

" The rents are cheap—only two shillings a week for a room. The people are a mixed folk—shoemakers, idlers, and smokers, women washing and gossiping. Many said ' they were not religious, and did not want a Bible.' I went up two branches of stairs, which must once have belonged to a grand old house. At the head of each were six rooms—very dark and dusty rooms, the windows stuffed up with rags. A great many of the people were Irish and Romanists, who said ' they were not going to be converted.' Still I found subscribers. I went through every room of a large public-house, let out in lodgings to a strange set of people. Here a fine lady opened the door; above, a shoemaker, who had once been a Sunday scholar, was glad to purchase a fourpenny Testament. I got twelve names in those courts; and here and there I met with decent women of the church-going and Bible-class order, living (I myself wondered why) in some of the foulest corners."

" *Perhaps these are the very people who might be*

called out to mend the rest. Your descriptions to-day are really worse than those of your walks in St. Giles's."

" I have, indeed, never seen such dirt as I saw yesterday. I have been into places where not even the City Missionaries visit, and where the people say, 'Nobody cares for *us.*' The residents are costermongers, pawn-brokers, keepers of little rag and bone shops, and I suppose there are many thieves—a mass of over six hundred families, living in a state of filth and destitution such as I could not have dreamed. I was sick and ill all through the night, and what must they be who always breathe such air ?"

As Shaw was passing a book-stall one afternoon in Gray's Inn Lane in the course of his rounds, he observed a blind man, led by a dog (to which he spoke as "Blucher"), turning over some little books, which the boy in attendance appeared to have reserved for him as a well-known customer. They were small religious books for children, and the blind man from time to time requested the boy to read him a paragraph here and there, selecting for purchase those from which a sentence seemed to please him.

After watching him for a little time, Shaw addressed some question to the blind man on the nature of the books he was buying, and a smile brightened over his face, though not in his eyes, as he recognized the dialect of a fellow-countryman. "Do you know Staleybridge and Dukinfield?" said he, in reply.

"How came you to think I did?" said Shaw.

"Oh! I knowed you by your tongue. I come myself from thereabouts. Let's come and talk over a cup of tea, and then *you* can read me some more of these books. Stay," said he; "how do you get your living?"

"I, too, sell books," said Shaw; "but they are all of one kind. I am a Bible-seller. I sell this book for tenpence (putting one into the man's hand). It is a beautiful-looking book, as you can feel, perhaps; but not one that you can read. You have not a Bible, I suppose?"

"Oh, yes, I have the Gospels in raised letters, and I sometimes carry one with me, and sit down to read it to the children in a quiet place, and they gather round and listen, and I want these little books to sell to them. I sell a great many, and so do some good, and turn a penny for myself, which sadly I want since poor Fanny died. Fanny was my wife, you know, and I lost her, last Christmas."

So Shaw went home with him to tea, not for the sake of the tea, but the companionship. He found he lived in a very clean back room in Portpool-lane. The tea was only herb tea, but it was given with a welcome. The man said he was well known in London as " Blind Jemmy," and that he had many friends. He had lost his sight twelve years ago, having been an engine-fitter on the London and North-Western Railway, and, in chipping metal facing another man, one of his eyes had been struck out, and the other not long after had decayed away. He had had the best medical aid afforded him by the Company, but the sight was irrecoverably gone.

"I had lost," said poor Jemmy, " my working sight, but not long afterwards God gave me my spiritual sight. I lived then with some uncles and aunts down in your parts, and they were pious people, and taught me the true comfort. I remember well a solitary place—a little running brook in Rochdale—where I first knelt down and could say, 'Thy will be done, O Lord, not mine;' and He has cared for me ever since. Soon afterwards He gave me Fanny, and He has never suffered me to want my humble crust. People often say to me, specially since I lost Fanny, 'Jemmy, why don't you go into the workhouse?' 'I do go there,' I answer, 'once a week, but it is to carry sixpence to a man who used, when he was able, to give me my two shillings, so I never forget him;' but may God keep me from abiding beneath that hard and heavy knocker."

"Your place is very clean, Jemmy," said Shaw.

" You tell me that you're out all day going your rounds with Blucher : how do you have it so clean ?"

" I am always up at five," said Jemmy ; " I can't sleep any longer. I have to wash myself and say my prayers. I clean it, as Fanny did, on a Friday, that I may not have so much to contend with on a Saturday, and that I may be ready for Sunday. I tie a cord across the floor, that I may know how far I have scrubbed, and not do it over again ; but ah, since Fanny died, I've often been in my difficults. If the button-holes of my coat are worn out I have to mend them myself."

Much more of interesting detail passed, and it seemed to Shaw that this man, from his wish and effort to do good among the children by the wayside, with his Bible-reading and his little books, might, though with one sense less than his fellows, in some way be made a missionary in his own degree, with a little help and guidance. This was a very pleasant leaf from life in Gray's Inn Lane.

Shaw's researches in this locality have been followed up by the visits of ladies, and a Bible-woman named Lydia has now been employed there also for twelve months. Her reports of the district were for a long time most disheartening ; yet she gradually obtained 280 Bible subscribers, and, after long perseverance and patience, is succeeding as well as her compeers in obtaining subscriptions for decent clothing. The following is a leaf from her Journal. She says:

"*July 27th.*—In going out this morning I prayed that I might be made a comfort to some one. In the courts at the back of Chancery-lane I find a moral waste; in many rooms dirt is almost the only clothing of the poor children. Here and there a tidy person seems like a green tree in the wilderness. I trust ere long that many of the people will be induced to read God's Word, as several have begun to pay for Bibles.

"In Baldwin's-gardens, another part of this district, more wretched than the former, sin reigns in every form. The people are generally very poor and depraved. Drunkenness is almost always the cause of the apparant misery. -

"*August 8th.*—I visited to-day a poor young woman who seems far advanced in consumption, very weak, and in great distress,—her husband, who is a law-writer, not having been able to obtain employment for some time. Spoke to her about her soul, and found her willing to converse upon that subject. She has had a Testament given her, in which she feels great comfort. I pray that the Lord will open the eyes of her understanding, and that ere death overtakes her she will be able to say, 'I know in whom I have believed ;' and then she will be able to give up her dear little boy and her husband to One who will never leave nor forsake them. I next went to a house where, for the fourth time, I found the man in bed, drunk. His unhappy wife, who appears a decent woman, said he had not been sober for a whole month, and that she was obliged to cut his food and put it into his mouth, or he would be starved to death, he was so unconscious of wanting anything but drink. Words are useless—he does not know that he is spoken to. O that the Lord would have mercy on this miserable drunkard!

"I then got into a house where I was obliged to wait up stairs for a long time, owing to drunken women qarrelling and fighting in the passage: hard names and harsh words were used, not fit to be mentioned. I often feel sick at heart. Lord, have mercy upon them, for they have none upon themselves!

"I have visited to-day the wife and daughters of another poor drunkard, who came home and threw almost all their things out of the window, and some of them fell upon a little child, nearly killing it. I strongly suspect that the wife is not much better than the husband. I have tried to show her the evil of such a course of life, and the bad example they are setting before their wretched children. Remonstrance seems of little use at the present time. Drink appears to be all they live for; but we must remember that the Lord's hand is not shortened, neither is His ear heavy that it cannot hear. Obliged to wait again upon the stairs: a man drunk, beating the room door with all his might, and using the most dreadful language; it was quite terrific to hear it. I am often asked by these people to treat them, or lend them a few pence."

Lydia soon began the Clothing and Bed Clubs. She found few at first willing to subscribe; but we went on in faith that this would be the most practical crusade against the gin-bottle.

Gray's Inn Lane always presents itself to our minds when we think of a district at first discouraging, and afterwards fruitful. We had almost doubted the energy of the agent, who did not happen to have found the help of a Lady Superintendent. Lydia now serves two of the City Missionaries' rooms with clothing, and the results of her visits to the family, where the man had not been sober for a month, are most cheering: she has induced him to become a teetotaler, "chiefly," she says, "by arguments from the Bible in Bible words." He says "nobody ever talked to him before." He is now grown "quite stout and happy." She has not yet succeeded in inducing him to attend a place of worship, but he has had a Bible, and has kept sober ever since. He did so even at Christmas time, so that the reformation now is of some standing. Here, also, the district presents altered features from the now better clothing of the people. "Even the costermonger women look so neat in their print gowns."

The City Missionaries of the district were not at first sure but that the new work might interfere with theirs. Those who have come to understand it have hailed it as the very thing that had so long been wanted among the people; and when we say this it conveys not the slightest reflection on any preceding agency. There had been District Visitors in Gray's Inn Lane. There had been Ragged Schools and Mothers' Classes, with *their* Clothing Clubs attached. There had been Visitors from the Christian Instruction Societies of various degree; but the whole number called in by these was nothing (and every earnest worker knew it) to the numbers *passed over* of those who were in the most need of being cared for.

It is visitation in their homes, and by those whom they will permit to enter, which is needed by the London poor. The clergyman himself is thought by a large class too good and grand; the visits of the Scripture-reader and City Missionary are objected to by many of the husbands, in their own absence. Of the Lady Visitor they will beg, and think she has no right to come to them except she brings relief; and they say, besides, that she is seldom punctual. But for the quiet, civil woman of their own class, who knows their difficulties and is surprised at nothing, for her they have evidently a very different welcome. Now, it is teaching the mothers in those homes—*the mothers who will not come out to learn*—the common arts of domestic life, of which their deficient education and their early thriftless marriages have left them totally ignorant, that is *the crying want of the times ;* and this is woman's work. It should be the work, under right direction, of *women of their own degree*, who must be *moderately paid and carefully superintended agents ;* and it is this beginning at the *roots* of society that would do away with the *need* of half our Reformatories, Refuges, and Ragged Schools, and double the efficacy of all the rest.

That such a range of efforts should be intimately associated with, and should, indeed, spring out of, the *offer of the Book of God*, is especially necessary. This must be *the visible mark of its distinction* from Romanist and Tractarian exertions. The church "which hides the Book" has no more subtle and extensive power over its members than is gained by its system of female charitable visitation. That church can find the women—that church lacks not the means to employ them ; and shall the Protestant strength of Christendom believe the same work impossible?

If there is one desire nearer to the heart of those who are at present extending this Protestant agency than another, it is that the work shall be wide in its basis, and that *union, prayer*, and *faith*, shall be its foundation stones ; "Union in which sects shall scarcely be named in the choice of the workers; Prayer that rests not night or day; Faith that takes no denial," and we have hitherto found none, whether as regards instruments or the funds, to supply their need.

CHAPTER XVI.

LEAVING Lydia at work in Gray's Inn Lane, and
Dinah in Portpool-lane and in Smithfield, let us pass
to Somers' Town, where we shall find an Esther, who
has been occupied in similar visitation for about the
space of a year, during which time she has had more
than 350 Bible subscribers, and has been made a blessing to many. To imagine the scene of her labors our
readers may follow Shaw into the Saturday evening
market, called the Brill.

This is held in a long narrow street of small shops ;
the stalls are placed beyond the pavement, and out in
the gutter, leaving space for but one cart to pass down
between them at a time. When this is a water-cart—
which is often necessary on account of the dust and
heat—plums, oysters, potatoes, &c., may be refreshed ;
but it is not so with books. However, a friend of

(224)

the Bible Society, acquainted with the neighborhood, pointed out the best place for a stall—a vacant spot in the front of a beershop.

"The master," says Shaw, "gave me permission to set up my stall in the front of this house, and said, 'You had better take your stand there Sunday mornings as well as Saturday evenings.' I said I was much obliged, but could not work on a Sunday. 'Well,' replied he, 'you might sell more on a Sunday morning here than any other day. There is a great need of Bibles here. We are a wicked lot; and I do not know what will mend us.'

"The first night I sold twenty copies—seven Bibles and thirteen Testaments.

"On the second Saturday I met with many remarks. One young man said, 'He did not want a Bible; it was all priestcraft; he could write a better book than that himself.'

"Another said, 'Can you tell me who wrote the Bible?' 'Yes, sir; holy men wrote it, as they were moved by the Holy Ghost.' 'I will have nothing to do with it. The Holy Ghost will not feed me. I am going on the other side to buy beef.' May the Lord open his blind eyes!

"An Irishman said, 'You are selling a dangerous book, master. Why, the people can't understand it all. They put a wrong meaning on it; and it is King

10*

Harry the Eighth's edition. He was a bad man, and he could not write a good book.'

"Then came a little encouragement. One said, 'Master, this is a step in the right direction.' Another man remarked, 'I am glad to see you here. My boy bought a Testament in the market last Saturday, and he tells me you are selling Bibles. I have come to look at them, and I hope you will sell many.'

"About nine o'clock a young boy who stood next to me, selling pictures in gilt frames at fourpence each, was taken by the policeman to the station. It was said he had been picking pockets.

"At ten o'clock the crowd was great, and as several persons were looking at my books, some one came and upset my stall. By the time I had gathered up my books from the pavement the offender was gone. Some said it was a drunken woman. Sold to-night eight Bibles and thirteen Testaments."

Somers' Town is generally known to be a poor and densely-populated neighborhood, whose origin is of comparatively recent date. Aged people are living who remember the time when it consisted of open fields, with here and there a house, and these fields were famous for the Sunday meetings of the Chartists. Now it is wholly built over, and the number of inhabitants exceeds that of Kentish and Camden Towns combined. In 1851 it contained more than 3500 persons; and while the population has been increasing so rapidly there has been, until lately, little increased provision for their educational or spiritual wants, so that we have to overtake the neglects of a past generation.

Somers' Town lies in the parish of St. Pancras, once the name of a solitary village in the fields " situated north of London, one mile from Holborn Bars." It was a parish before the Norman Conquest, and is called St. Pancras in Domesday Book. Stukeley affirms that the site of old Pancras church was occupied by Cæsar's Roman encampment, and traces the Brill in Somers' Town to a contraction of Burgh Hill, a Saxon name for a fortified place on an elevated site. The surface of old London lay fifteen feet below its present level ; and where a Roman general pitched his camp the floor of his tent became a tesselated pavement : buried coins, lamps, and vases, testified of his presence, and sometimes baths and watercourses, with the foundations of temples and of altars.

The low ground which skirts the western side of Islington, separating it from St. Pancras, is the traditionary scene of that destructive onset described by Tacitus, in which 80,000 of the Britons fell in slaughtered heaps before the enraged legions of Suetonius. The British queen, Boadicea, at their head, had, after a fierce onslaught on London, burnt the town and scattered the inhabitants ; but " Suetonius made a victorious stand in a fortified pass, with a forest in his rear."   By the help of the ancient historian and the modern poët, we may imagine the mingled and disorderly throng of Britons surrounding their queen, who, accompanied by her outraged daughters, harangues them from her chariot, inciting them to revenge upon her conquerors.

> " When the British warrior queen,
>   Bleeding from the Roman rods,
> Sought with an indignant mein,
>   Counsel from her country's gods,
> Sage beneath the spreading oaks
>   Sate the Druid, hoary chief,
> Every burning word he spoke
>   Full of rage and full of grief.
>
> " ' Princess, if our aged eyes
>   Weep not for thy matchless wrongs,
> 'Tis because resentment ties
>   All the terror of our tongues.
> Rome shall perish !   Write that word
>   In the blood that she has spilt—
> Perish, hopeless and abhorr'd,
>   Deep in ruin as in guilt.
>
> " ' Then the progeny that springs
>   From the forests of our land,
> Arm'd with thunder, clad with wings,
>   Shall a wider world command.
> Regions Cæsar never knew,
>   Thy posterity shall sway ;
> Where his eagles never flew,
>   None invincible as they.' "

The "spreading oaks" are no more, but the Druid's words are fulfilled. The Bible, which Boadicea knew not, has raised her country to be mistress of the nations; but it is sad to think that a spot thus haunted by historic memories should be one of the most heathen in the metropolis.

In those former days, the native Briton, from his hut among the copse-wood on the ridge of the Burgher Hill, might look over a wide plain to the still more elevated ground of High-bury and High-gate, parted by the Hollow-way. The author of "The Vestiges of Roman London" tells us that Suetonius retired to Barnsbury before the Britons; and adds that, until within the last few years, the remains of an encampment (for which the Romans always chose an elevated site) were to be found in what was called the "Red Moat Field," a little to the west of Barnsbury Park. The moat was twenty feet wide and twelve deep, and the embankment offered an extensive and beautiful prospect, northward and westward, to the eye weary of bricks and mortar; but insatiate London still extends its arms to devour its children, and has swallowed up all the suburban hamlets nestling near it. White Conduit Fields are no more; "Six-acre Field," with the camp of the Roman general, is no more; and Fort Cottage, a modern villa, usurps the Prætorium of Suetonius.

And what of the Brill ?   A congregation of knack-ers' yards, tile-kilns, dust-heaps, and a vast new cattle market, with rows of dingy houses, compose its present neighborhood ; and Battle Bridge, whose name is sup-posed to point to the memorable encounter above men-tioned, is the terminus of the King's Cross and Great Northern Railway.   The Brill is one of the poor man's great Saturday evening and Sunday markets.   There are hundreds of stalls, and every stall has, at dusk, one or two lights.   One man shows off his yellow haddocks, with a candle stuck in a bundle of fire-wood ; his neighbor, the boy who shouts, " Eight a penny, splendid pears !" makes a lamp of a turnip ; while the butcher's gas-lights stream in the wind like flags of flame.   Alike on Saturday night and Sunday morning may be seen " a riot, a struggle, and a scram-ble for a living."   Unless it is beheld, people can have no idea of the masses of unshorn and unwashed beings who weekly congregate here.

" The extent of Sunday trading is frightful," says " Esther," the Bible-woman ; " it certainly does get worse and worse.   People come with their barrows from the East End of London, and make sales of fruit, etc., all the day long.   The police look on, seemingly not knowing what to do.   Many a man, clever at his business, and earning good wages, has nothing left on Monday morning, for the Sabbath has been passed in drinking, cursing and swearing, fighting and quarreling. I called on the wife of such a one, and, happening to find her sober and at work, I told her the awful end there would be to such a life as theirs. She said her husband had led her to it by his ill-treatment. The sight of women lying senseless in the street from drink is sickening to behold. They are frequently carried off on stretchers to the police stations."

A person walking through the Brill on a Sunday afternoon would find the tumultuous business of the day partly over. The middle of the narrow streets is thickly strewn with cabbage leaves and other offal, showing how large a vegetable market has been held there. Fishmongers and butchers' shops are open all day, and the "holy rest" of the Sabbath is claimed bodily, at least, by the weary salesman snoring on a bench beside his periwinkles, and the butcher dreaming over his pipe amid the remnants of his veal and mutton. The service of Satan is hard service. The men are chiefly in their working dress, and many appear to have been drinking.

Esther's work refers, of course, to week days.

"When I offered the people the Bible," she says, "and they answer, 'Don't want any,' 'Got plenty,' 'No time to read it,' I often reply, 'Listen but to one verse ; that will not take long, and a word from this book is as needful to your soul as your daily food to your body.' Often where refusal meets me at first I get permission to call again. They are not altogether unwilling to have it said to them, in a quiet way, 'Stop, poor sinner, stop and think ;' but how can they think when they give themselves no Sabbaths? They often tell me I am the first person that ever spoke *to them*, and that they wish they could have listened years ago.

"With all their Sunday trading, they do not appear to enjoy much prosperity, for I may call week after week, and on decent people too, without getting a penny, because they are out of work. Most often, of course, drunkenness is the source of the prevailing misery, and sometimes sudden death gives a loud warning to all around who are living in their sins. An old woman, who had long been leading a most degraded life of deception, was called away at last, at the age of seventy-two, without time to cry for mercy. She was struck dead at the bar of a public-house, while in the act of asking for a glass of rum.

"People in the 'Brill' are very glad to hear of the clothing and bedding club, as they say it will do away with the tally bills ; they could not possibly buy the articles at once, or save the money to do it, and when they obtain the things they so much want, 'it comes to them like a gift.'

"Few of the people who can read, and are Protestants, are found without the word of God in some small form; but wherever the large-print Bible is shown, they desire to possess it, and readily promise to pay the penny 'when their husbands get into work.'

"Delivered a 2s. 6d. Bible to a poor aged woman, who stands in the market, and was extremely anxious for the Book. She has such a wicked husband, that his oaths frighten even the other profane persons with whom he may labor, especially his oaths at the Bible; and though she has not lived with him for some time, yet he is always annoying her in the market. As I went to her for the last payment, fivepence, he was close by. So desirous was she to get it, that she left her goods and came after me to a distance; borrowed a halfpenny, and made up the rest in farthings; then hid it under her gown, with 'Thank you, thank you, he shall not see it; I am so glad I have got it. May God bless it to my soul!' And so said I in my heart."

Another good female agent is started for Cromer street, in the St. Pancras district, which is also a radius of poor streets leading from the King's Cross Railway. She has had a long and fitting education for the work, as teacher in a Ragged-school: she is remarkably successful in obtaining Bible subscribers, even after the earnest voluntary work of ladies in the same district continued for years.

A fresh welcome awaits the Female Missionary in every locality. One woman told her that since she began to subscribe for a Bible, everything seemed to prosper, and that she hoped next week to pay up ; for, though she cannot read herself, she could get some child to read it to her. She was unexpectedly cheered in a second visit to a kitchen, which she had found in a most filthy state, but where the woman had been persuaded to subscribe for a Bible. The girl met her at the door, and said her father wished to speak to the Bible-woman. The kitchen was no longer dirty, and as the man pointed to the clean floor and bright fire, he said, " God bless the day you came into my place !" These people had no Bible at all, and a Testament has been lent till they secure their own. The girls were introduced to the Sunday-night Ragged-school, and in a third visit a poor woman was found teaching them to read.

"Harriet" stepped into a room in a close court, where three or four girls were taking a cup of tea for their dinner with an old woman, its mistress. The Bible-woman read to them the story of the crucifixion, in which all were so interested that they determined to buy the New Testament for themselves. " It would cost fourpence,—and would she bring it them next week? They could not take it home for fear of the priest, but they would come to listen to it again in

Biddy's room." On the occasion of the next call they bought, with their united funds, not a Testament, but a 10d. Bible. The sister of one of these girls also bought a Bible for herself, saving the pence out of the money allowed her to get her dinner.

"Harriet" believes the people are become so dirty for want of some one being kind to them, and helping them on to cleanliness. The District Visitors speak to them at their doors, but their dirt renders stepping within a great self-denial. The very tracts given have been found too dirty to return to the visitor's bag; and any disgust expressed only renders them unwilling to take it again. *Finding fault with them does not mend them—nothing short of offering them the opportunity of doing better.* The neighbors said the Bible-woman had done great wonders; for a certain man had, for the first time in his life, been seen sitting at his door in a clean shirt, reading the Bible. His wife is getting much tidier in her home. People in this district out at work all the week, are glad to come with their money in their hand to buy the ready-made articles of clothing on the Saturday night, which they have seen, and only been able to pay twopence for, at work meetings on the previous Monday evening. This money would probably otherwise have gone for drink. In this district, lately, a man was thrown off a water-cart, in the act of swearing at and beating his horse, and, being mortally hurt, died as he was being borne to the hospital. All the court was out to hear the report of those who had carried him away, and one of those men gave a terrible testimony. "I have often heard him," said he, "say, 'Strike me dead,' when he was angry ; and now God has just done it!" This appeared, "Harriet" says, to make a great impression for the time, and the people round were willing to let her read and pray with them, which seemed needed, and she was glad to be in the way.

This Bible agent being a woman of much prayer and simple faith, as well as sympathy, her journal abounds in encouragement, and her happiness in her work is written on her countenance. She has in four months drawn around her a most thankful class of women, some of them previously the terror of their neighborhood. They are fast learning "to pay for tidy gowns, and go without the drink." Many children are brought to school, others to a place of worship. Abuse on the first visit has melted away after a second and a third ; and now, in street after street, there is not a house where she is not welcome. Here, as in Church Lane, and at London Wall and in Limehouse Fields, there are great and visible changes in the appearance of the persons visited. "Harriet" has, after many efforts, penetrated into a court called by the neighbors "Little Hell," and deserving the name for

its perpetration of every kind of wickedness. She
found half-naked, filthy children peopling most wretched rooms, where they and their mothers bore evident
marks of savage treatment. She was first obliged to
listen to many a tale of cruelty, and then she spoke
of the MESSAGE FROM GOD ; and how, if they listened
to that, all would begin to mend with them. Some
"had Bibles, but never read them ;" and it seemed
strange, they said, that any one should care for such
as they were. "They heard gladly of a meeting to
get clothing, and promised to come to it, and some
have kept their promise. Truly here God's word
seems as if it will not return unto Him void, but will
accomplish the work whereto He sent it."

CHAPTER XVII.

OUR MORAL WASTES AND THEIR MATRONS.

WE left Marian at the close of her Midsummer Fête, and at the end of her first laborious year, when she certainly accomplished greater things in a certain space of time than by any of her sister workers has since been found possible. She had supplied 1000 Bibles and Testaments in St. Giles's by the people's own purchase, chiefly at the prices of tenpence and fourpence ; and very many homes in Church Lane testified, by the changed character and habits of their inmates, to the efficacy of her domestic mission. God had greatly honored her work for the sake of His Word ; and now, doubtless in love to her own soul, He caused that year of exemplary success to be followed by another of severe personal discipline. Her powers, mental and bodily, had been somewhat over-taxed. She became alarmingly ill, and was obliged to leave her district for many weeks ; and when she recovered, her sick and failing husband claimed the greater part of her time, so that she could visit very little among the people for many months before his death which took place on the 9th of May, 1859.

Her attention had, under these circumstances, been divided between her own home duties and a dormitory for the water-cress girls, the idea of which she had started, believing that, if a quiet home were provided for them in the centre of their district in St. Giles's, they would immediately embrace the opportunity of escaping from their own over-crowded rooms, and gladly render the undertaking self-paying. The kind readers of the "Book and its Missions" listened to this sanguine hope, and very shortly placed within our reach the means for rescuing and thoroughly repairing one of the worst houses in Dudley-street, furnishing and fitting it for the nightly occupation of twenty-four of these girls.

This was a pleasant experiment, and one from which we hoped much. It was, however, as we found by experience, easier to prepare the house than to fill it. The outlay hitherto has been large, and the returns very small, because it has been difficult to get the people to understand that the enterprise was intended to be self-paying. There were numbers of destitute girls, who looked for food, shelter, and clothing, and needed them; but this was not the design. We wished to find twenty-four girls who would prefer a clean and comfortable lodging-house for themselves to the ordinary mixed and crowded ones, and be willing to pay for it what they would pay elsewhere.

The work is still experimental, and it seems more likely to be acceptable to poor sempstresses than to the street-sellers of water-cresses, who all say they are too poor to pay threepence a night for their lodging, if they give up Sunday trading, which brings them more money than they receive all the rest of the week. Since needlewomen have been admitted, the house promises to fill, and there are now fifteen inmates, whose payments amount to £1 2s. 6d. a week. The annual rent is £40.

RECEIPTS.	£	s.	d.	EXPENDITURES.	£	s.	d
Donations to Dormitory	348	3	2	Repairs and gas fittings	109	2	1
People's payments	8	2	0	Rent paid	30	0	6
				Taxes and rates	12	8	9
				Furniture and bedding	108	10	2
				Salary, service, and Sunday meals	30	15	0
				Coals, tea-meetings, washing, and miscellaneous house expenses	23	17	8
				Balance	41	11	6
	£356	5	2		£356	5	2

It was not found practicable, when it came to be tried, for Marian to undertake the care of this dormitory, and also to continue her mission work. They are quite separate walks of usefulness, and she herself became thoroughly convinced of this. We shall, therefore, ask our readers to revisit her in a quiet room of her own, devoted once more to her separate Bible and domestic mission, gladly relinquishing the anxious care and guidance of the dormitory into other hands, though she yet takes a warm interest in its welfare; and her mission-room, our "parlor among the dens," is still a room in that house.

This little parlor is a pleasant and orderly meeting-ground for the inhabitants of the "dens" and the "squares," in small numbers. Three or four of the upper, and from thirty to forty of the lower, classes may there hold frequent interviews, for their mutual benefit, and during the last winter this kind of conference commenced very satisfactorily.

"Marian's" "mothers"—several of them reformed from ungovernable and drunken furies, through her long and patient Bible visits to them in their rooms— were here continually to be found on certain evenings in the week. Some brought their work, and some their babies, and having paid their instalments for their clothing or bedding, sat round the table, by the cheerful gas-light, to hear the Bible story, new to them as to many of the heathen abroad ; or the dormitory itself was a perpetual "object lesson," as much

11

needed as any taught in an infant-school, bringing before their eyes (and with them "seeing is believing") certain necessary provisions for cleanliness, health, and propriety, of which they had never heard from generation to generation. "Their mothers," they said, "did not know, so how could they teach better ways than those in which they had been born?" But they are very generally anxious that their daughters should have a different training. We were, therefore, in full communication with persons who, a year before, cared nothing for the Bible, and little for their homes. Here they sat, "clothed and in their right mind;" and we fervently hope ere long to add, "at the feet of Jesus." They still would have found it difficult to obtain a loan blanket, for want of proper security, or a box of linen in the hour of need, because they lie in the stratum of society, below that to which it has been considered safe to afford such loans; yet they want the help often more than those who get it. We therefore took "Marian's" word and knowledge of them, and tried the experiment of lending twenty-four blankets and fourteen boxes of linen, "upon honor"—the honor of St. Giles's. They have been returned during this summer, at the appointed season, very creditably.

They are a class of people, too, who hitherto have not been trusted with needlework, because no lady could venture to give them her ticket of reference ; so here again we experimented on a small scale. We knew half a dozen that we adventured to trust, and could put in their way a new help to a livelihood. One or two kind ladies were found willing to prepare garments for us, and to come to our parlor to give out and take in the work. With the shilling the women earned by their sewing they have often bought the article they had made.

To our "parlor among the dens" is attached A KITCHEN, where (though we still lent saucepans) we also last winter made soup, which was sold at its exact cost—one penny a quart—and was in great request. We hope, another year, to add other savory and cheap dishes ; and in the course of time, under the care of a lady who may devote herself to the particular superintendence of this department, it may expand into larger proportions during the day-time. In the evening the use of the kitchen must be limited to the lodgers. We have every hope that, as ladies group themselves in aid of special purposes around a Bible Mission-house of this kind to the inhabitants of " dens," they, or those over whom they have influence, will not forget their neighbors of the squares."

There are many of the latter who have hitherto been ignorant of the details of the wants that lie around them. How should *they* know that which they never see, and of which they never hear ? Numbers of them, we would hope, by their comfortable firesides, read and believe the Book which is now afresh penetrating downwards among the degraded and the wretched classes. Surely they will speed the way of God's Word at home and abroad!—THEY WILL HELP THE BIBLE SOCIETY WHICH SENDS IT FORTH!—ay, many who never thought of doing so before.

"Marian" has resumed her Bible work—not exactly as she formerly did, spending the whole of every day in her visits to the people (her own abated health since her illness, tried also by her long and faithful attendance on her husband, has prevented this)—and another female visiting colporter is nominated for a large portion of the wide district of St. Giles's. The influence Marian gained in the first year, however, remains, and the pence in her own now more limited district are in numerous cases brought to her. "What a heavy load you have there on your head, Mrs. B——!" said she to one of those whom she calls *her* women, and who was carrying a basket full of shrubs, not flowers, which seemed enough to bury her beneath their weight. "You surely cannot carry that home?" "Oh, yes, I can, and thank God for it," was the answer ; "and thank you and our ladies, who have made a sober woman of me. I shall get something handsome by these pots to-morrow, for I bought them at a good market ; and then I am coming to you with the money for some sheets and a gown. Thank God, too, you're come back amongst us. We are so glad to see you. Thank God, I've left off drinking." This case is by no means a solitary one ; and what a contrast to another as recent and as true !

A poor girl, having been out to the hop-grounds with her mother, had earned thirteen shillings of her own, and had wisely expended most of it in a pair of strong new boots. Her mother, having drunk up her own earnings, took the boots to pawn, and drank their price ; and not only that, but sold the pawn-ticket for sixpence more to drink. What wonder should a girl forsake such a home and such a mother? Girls so circumstanced we wish to shelter, and possibly to influence their mothers through their means ; and whatever small practical advances we may make in "social science," which is the study of the day, we hope always to connect them with the Bible.

By the leadings of God's providence through her second year's experience, " Marian" has been rendered willing and thankful to accept the help of ladies in her work. She had always been most docile and affectionate in all her intercourse with her first superintendent ; but as one Mission grew out of another, and the widely expanding General Work absorbed all thought and time, it became necessary to devolve special local interests on other ladies, whom God raised up for different departments. We have learned many things from our first experiment in St. Giles's. Because "Marian" was in herself what she was, and still is, she was listened to, more than was strictly prudent, when she begged for her poor, wretched neighbors, during the first year, to have clothing and bedding *in advance*, paying a little, and *promising to pay* the rest. Then followed her illness and absence, and the ordinary autumnal migration of the. people, numbers of whom never returned ; another winter, with, of course, its own daily wants ; and no money for *back debts*. Happily in no other district had this unsafe plan been followed. Nowhere else have garments or beds been advanced *upon trust*, and "Marian" is cured of answering for those whose name is legion. The whole details of the Mission are now carried on on an improved scale, and with the help of many experiences earned in other places.

In the course of a year and a half, with all the drawbacks alluded to, the people had paid nearly £76 for their clothing and bedding ; but more than 400 beds had been supplied, and, on the whole, a loss was incurred upon them of over £100. When fourteen O'Donoghues, a dozen Ryans, &c., with faces and voices much alike, were the parties in question, a few mistakes were likely to arise ; but these are now stren uously watched against, and the *lady* element of punctuality and perfect order in the accounts being added to "Marian's" good work, we have every promise of future success.   The "mothers" are just now "packing up for the hops once more, and, casting longing eyes on the closet full of garments which their own fingers have made and been paid for, have said, ' We shall carry those all off, Mrs. B., when we come from the hops.   Be sure you have plenty of them ready for us.' "

"Marian" has recently spent a month in a fresh visitation of every room in the old Church Lane, in which there is a very marked reformation.   Her own work has had not a little to do with this, but the place has also come under the eye and the help of the most devoted of pastors in Mr. Thorold.   The various arrangements which it has been in his power to make have all had the same aim, and Catholics and Protestants alike are blessing his name.

The south side of " the lane " having recently come into the hands of the ground landlord, through the falling in of the leases, extensive repairs have been instituted.   The District Board of works have also exerted themselves most laudably in making every sanitary arrangement in their power.

Mrs. Thorold, though in very delicate health, has during the last winter taken deep interest in superintending the affairs of "Ruth," a second Bible-woman, who is now traversing much of the same ground on which "Marian" sold her first Bibles. That more Bible work remained to be done is proved by the fact that "Ruth" has had 110 subscribers, and has still 88 on her list, many of them for large copies. She has also a Clothing Club, at which Mrs. Thorold has secured the presence and assistance of a valuable friend.

As our plans have developed, we have become more and more alive to the importance of the influence of a superintending lady, or some lady whom she may delegate, to the preservation of right order in such rooms; for, as the aim is to teach each individual to work, it is impossible for the Bible-woman, at one and the same time, to render this important service, and also to preside over the meeting, and turn it to spiritual profit.

There is surely in every neighborhood, if called forth, some lady who would gladly and regularly give an afternoon or evening to such blessed occupation. Now and then a gentleman is found attending these meetings, who has declared it his happiest evening in the week. We cannot refrain from inserting a letter from the friend who has been introduced to this service in " Ruth's" Mission, which will show the kind of help that LADIES may give in Female Bible Missions:—

"My dear Mrs. Thorold,—On the 14th of April your Mission began to develope itself into its further branches of usefulness. A few of the poor mothers were invited to take tea together, and to commence a series of meetings, to be held from week to week, at which these ignorant ones may learn how to mend and make clothing for themselves and their families, and have the advantage of buying the materials at reduced prices, and by small instalments.

" The first evening was very wet ; yet the prospect of tea and the novelty of the occasion brought seven out of the twelve guests invited, and any one who could have looked into that small back room about six o'clock would have been pleased to see the women gather round the plentifully-spread table.

" Some idea may be formed of the kind of people to be assembled at these meetings, when it is mentioned that one woman came late because she had to borrow the gown of her sister, and was compelled to wait not only till her sister came in, but until the one gown had been partially dried from the afternoon's rain. Another could not come at all that first evening, because she had been wet through, and had nothing to change. The attendance has, since that day, been gradually increasing, and we now number some twenty-six members.

" But while it is of incalculable service to give them

the means of procuring decent clothing, and to lead them to more industrious and thrifty habits ; to show them that we are interested in their welfare, and sympathize in their trials—this is not our chief aim. *That* is to teach them the ever sweet and ever new, though to us familiar lesson, that God loves *them*, that Christ died for *them*, and that He rose again to plead for *them*, and from His throne of glory ever watches over their sorrows and their interests.*

" The peculiar circumstances of the women brought to ' Ruth's ' meeting made it seem wisest that instruction should at first be conveyed by conversation rather than by reading. I have, therefore, narrated in simple and often scriptural language one of the beautiful histories of God's Word, leading our poor friends to draw from it such holy lessons as may be applied to their daily practice.

" I have been struck with the superior power of God's stories over any others, and I believe most people would be surprised to note the thrilling interest with which they are listened to. If any one

---

* For a specimen of the matured development of the work at which we are aiming in our Female domestic Missions, we beg to refer our readers to a very pleasant volume recently published, called " Ragged Homes, and how to Mend them." J. NISBET, Berners Street. Price 3s. 6d. It is the record of the practical work of a lady who has a deep and genuine sympathy with poor mothers, and whose book will do much to communicate that sympathy to other minds.

wishes to learn the present ignorance of our lowest
poor concerning the Scriptures, he should sit down in
such small mission-room, and listen to the remarks of
some of the most decent and respectable among our
mothers. 'Oh, ma'am, please don't stop just there!
I so want to hear. Was the poor child (Benjamin)
punished for stealing that cup he never touched?
How hard!' Or another day, 'Do, pray, go on. I
hope those frightful great beasts (the crocodiles) did
not eat the baby' (Moses). Sometimes one has said,
'I do think our lady knows everything. Edication is
a grand thing, but it seems she's got it most all from
the Bible. How she must read it, to have it so ready
like! I'm going to get one soon. I've paid fourpence,
to-day.'

"Each meeting closes with prayer; and when it is
remembered that some, probably, had never knelt before to ask from a God of love the blessings that they
need, do I think this bending with them in worship is no
small matter, and we may feel assured that in the coming day it will be found that a prayer-hearing God has
blessed and owned even these feeble efforts to win the
prayerless to the love of His Christ.

"I purposely avoid describing scenes of want,
misery, and sin, which I have visited at Ruth's request, and as arising out of these meetings. More
than once or twice I have stood in the midst of such

hopelessly wretched rooms, that when I lie down at night I have found it utterly impossible to forget the scenes ; yet I have found, in more than one instance, that somebody coming with loving, gentle words, simply to speak to them, without giving any relief, has roused them from the inertia of despair.

" They are often dirty, untidy, and careless, because in their crowded space they feel, do what they may, they cannot be othewise. Then they say, ' We're used to such ways : what's the good of changing them ? No one comes to see us, and *we* don't care. If we'd known now you was a coming, we'd ha' made things a bit straight.' "

But there is a district worse than Ruth's, which may truly be called the St. Giles's of St. Giles's, to which the refuse of the community were drafted when the new streets were built : it is in the neighborhood of Drury Lane—and here " Miriam," who is an offshoot from the happy and reformed community gathered together by Mr. Allen, the good Scripture-reader at Westminster, has paid visits scarcely describable. The colporter Shaw introduced her to her work. These are the dominions of " the children of the night," and at eleven in the morning many were asleep. The dirt and the stenches were hardly to be borne. Lodging-rooms were entered, bare of all furniture, in which were found twenty or thirty men, some sitting, some standing, many lying on the floor; some singing, some smoking—all idle—and some saying they had had nothing to eat for three days; all in rags, mostly Irishmen, who refused " Luther's book," or " King Henry the Eighth's book," and said they would " turn their backs on their holy religion for nobody."   Others, poor English people, declared they would get out of the street as soon as they could, and they thought perhaps the Bible might begin to mend them.   As to the vocation of the community, they were street folk, flower and brush-makers, sellers of hare and cat skins, and heaps of the latter we walked over in getting into their rooms.

" When the offer of the Bible did not find entrance, the mention of clothing did.   Very sad was the page of human life we turned this day," says Shaw ; " we walked in the midst of consumption and fever—of those here to-day and gone to-morrow.   We could scarcely get through one long street, inhabited by sorters of onions and oranges, for the orange peels and the cabbage leaves.   In few rooms did we see a bed, but this good woman will get into many a place where a man cannot ; and the fruit of our labors is already, in this direction, twenty-one Bible subscibers."

Miriam, after a month or two of work, found entrance and acceptance among the most wretched and reckless : she has thirty-eight subscribers for Bibles.

and a mission-room in Bloomsbury already well attended. The expenses of her domestic mission are cared for by the hand of private benevolence, which will be far less likely to be pierced by the thorns of ingratitude, in employing this intermediate class of agency, than in bestowing money, to ten-fold the amount, in gift to those who sought relief at its own door. The poor only really bless those who help them to help themselves.

CHAPTER XVIII.

WESTMINSTER AND ITS BIBLE-WOMEN.

" RACHEL," in NEWPORT MARKET, is traversing the
ground extending from Leicester square to St. Giles's,
and embracing Crown street, Soho, with its sundry
courts, where Marian first began. About five hundred
of the families resident on this district are visitable,
and of this number at least one hundred are Romanist, and a great many infidel. About fifty of them admit that they are without Bibles, and have no desire
to possess them. Persons who say they have them
very frequently cannot produce them, and the homes
where the precious book is professedly read, or where
the people attend any place of worship, are lamentably
few. At a meeting for exposition of the Scriptures
and prayer on Sabbath evenings which is held here,
and often conducted by Captain Trotter, about forty
attend ; and the numbers will doubtless increase, as
the attention of the people is called to it by visitation
from room to room.

[255]

The employment of the majority of women in the district is army clothing work, artificial flower-making, and shoe binding; and their absorption in these trades induces a state of careless indifference as to cleanliness, both of their persons and homes. When they are without work, idleness and gossip, combined with drinking, engross their time, and produce a state of things most difficult for the Bible-woman or Missionary to change for the better. On advising that a room should be cleaned, RACHEL has more than once been told that the walls and ceiling have not been touched for years—one for nine years. Another woman has said, "I do not know how to clean a room; it would be as easy for you to make my artificial flowers. I have never been taught to do it." Another, on whose table dirty linen was lying, said, "I do not know how to get it clean, so I have bought a new pair of stockings for my son;" and on RACHEL telling her how they might be washed, she said, "I should never be able to do that, I know." This, of course, has been followed up by showing her the process at another time.

Many of the families are extremely destitute of clothing. One man had no clothes left to attend a place of worship, and had worn his shirt a month since it had been washed. He was afraid to take it off, lest it should fall to pieces. A mothers' meeting has just been established to teach them to mend their clothes. In twenty rooms in P—— Row, thickly inhabited, no pretensions were made to anything in the shape of a bed, not even shavings or straw. Seven persons have begun to subscribe for cheap beds; others pleaded extreme poverty, which is the natural fruit of the drunkenness which so awfully prevails, both among men and women. The district rivals St. Giles's in its need of the simplest cooking utensils. "Rachel" has lent her own cotton gown to one woman three or four times (she always brings it back clean), to enable her to attend a Sunday evening service and Bible-class.

The City Missionaries occupied Westminster almost earlier than any other section of the metropolis, because it was known to be so "notorious for crime, poverty, and degradation." Bad as Old Pye street, Orchard street, &c., may be *now*, they were far worse twenty years ago.

Truly earnest and devoted clergymen in many such districts are being made willing that *all kinds* of agency *for good* should be concentrated upon them. No one mind, with the most perfect apparatus at its command, could compass all the spiritual and temporal needs of the lowest haunts of either St. Giles's or Westminster. The agency that most speedily serves and helps all present organization is the Bible-woman's steady daily ministration in and out among the " dens," so necessary even in aid of the two or three hours of weekly visiting which a lady can be expected to give, and which are all she probably *ought* to give, from the claims of her own home and circle. A month's experiment will tell on attendance at schools and on public worship, and will generally secure the glad reception of the after visits of the Pastor, the Scripture Reader, or the City Missionary.

Colporter WAYE, who has succeeded SHAW in London service, has made a thorough canvass of the lower parts of Westminster for Bible work.

The old Pye street district of Westminster affords a happy specimen of a vigorous and re-formed Ladies' Association for the BIBLE SOCIETY, working in conjunction with the Poor Woman's paid agency, and feeling that it is a most useful adjunct. " Were her labors withdrawn," they say, " the association would suffer." She has sold in nine months 171 copies of the Scriptures, and has 41 subscribers on her books. The voluntary collectors have sold in the same space of time £67 worth of books, and obtained £28 in free contributions, so that the immediate district is sown afresh with the seed of the Word. The ladies continue very active, and hope to arouse the attention of all around them to the duty and privilege of aiding in the circulation of God's Holy Book through the world.

Charlotte says, " The number of my subscribers on

the book has increased to about 150. I find a great many go to some place of worship, and I do hope, as religion increases among them, that cleanliness will increase also. They are very anxious to get beds and blankets for themselves and their children before the cold weather comes, and they are almost ready to force the subscriptions upon me; but I tell them they must wait a little till the ladies come home to arrange it. I do earnestly pray that those to whom God has given much of this world's wealth may help this effort in Westminster; and I pray God to bless me in my humble part of the work, that I may do it according to His will, not for the remuneration I receive, but knowing that He sees me in my walks."

It is declared, and too truly, that a less vivid sympathy is now shown in the London districts than in other parts of the country, towards the great and all-important object of supplying the Bible to the world. People are fully aware that it *is* important, and deserving of everybody's help; but very few will spare time to consider how they individually can help it. Yet opportunities will be evident to those who seek them. While, in what are called the "back slums," the well-chosen *poor woman* penetrates, under the blessing and protection of God, with His Word in her hand, up the dark, filthy staircase, braving rebuke and jest, and sometimes threats, from those whom her quiet mission will perhaps conquer after all—LADIES, with the love of the Word shed abroad in their hearts, will, in many an individual case among the poor, give effectual aid to the female colporter (we do not here speak of her one personal lady superintendent alone), and perhaps elicit, by well-bestowed inventive effort, the sympathies of persons in *their own class*, which now lie dormant. What object can be so high as to spread abroad the wonderful Word of the Lord, first and perpetually in our own ever-changing neighborhoods, and then to the wide world? Can we contemplate with delight communities of Bible-readers in Italy, and among the simple Karens, and not arise and make use of the same "Sword of the Spirit" among our own poor population? It is this alone that will cope with the advancing hosts of Rome.

We could, if space allowed us, extend our researches with an "Elizabeth" into Chelsea, and, crossing the river, find much to interest us with Phœbe in the New Cut, and Dorothy in Walworth ; but we have only time to revisit "Martha" in Paddington, and to observe the Cottage among the Dust-heaps, referring the readers, who shall not have been wearied by our simple life-sketches, for further and future detail to the little "Book and its Missions," a threepenny monthly periodical, which may be had of all booksellers, and whose title bespeaks its subject.

CHAPTER XIX.

AFTER a year's experience of the influence of a "Female Bible and Domestic Mission" among the Dust-heaps, those who have guided and assisted " Martha" are in a position to speak very hopefully and favorably of its general results.

It was thought desirable to take a cottage opposite one of the dust-yards, an upper room of which might be tenanted by "Martha," while on the lower floor another could be used for the bedding material, and for the women's weekly working meetings, and a third as a self-paying soup kitchen, and as a place of shelter and refreshment for the dust-people during their mid-day hour of rest.

During that hour hitherto they have been accustomed to take their meal, as the weather might be wet or dry, in the open air or under shelter of a cart; to make a fire of the cinders, which might serve half a dozen of them ; and prepare their coffee and red her-ring, varied by bread, cheese, beer, or gin, according to their taste; and very bad language is often used among them during this time of recess from their work.

In the cottage "no slang is permitted," and the improvement offered in their diet consists in a basin of good soup from "Martha's" copper, so good that it is declared, "This here is worth more than two pots of beer." The payment is three half-pence a quart, including bread, and the meal is taken on a table covered with interesting papers and tracts. The nourishing soup will really, it is hoped, wean them from the use of stimulants. Eighteen persons are now frequently numbered at dinner. A dustman dropped in one day, and as the City Missionary, who is frequently present, rose to go, the apparently rough, uncouth fellow cried out, "Don't go; I like to hear you read. If you'll sell a little spelling-book I'll buy it, and I'll buy a large Bible."

Since the 26th of January, 1857, "Martha" has delivered one hundred and eighty-seven Bibles and thirty Testaments, and her work of colportage among the people seems to have aroused in many of them a desire to learn to read, to meet which a lady, whose peculiar vocation seems to be the teaching of adults, has kindly offered them the opportunity, and several have embraced it gladly.

As "Martha" now finds the district nearest to her home fairly supplied with the Scriptures, it is proposed

that a certain portion of her time should be employed
for the purpose of colportage in an adjacent locality in Lisson Grove, "the St. Giles's of the West,"
another section of the Dust-heap region. An excellent city missionary devotes his whole time and ener-
gies to diffuse the true light through those dusky
abodes; but he has often declared his want of women's
help, and rejoices now to welcome it.

Here is another district of " dens," the dominions
of laundresses, scavengers, lamp-lighters, match-ma-
kers, " patterers," " utterers," " translators," and costermongers in ordinary. Let the Christians of London
go and look at them, in their Sunday-morning markets
for birds and rabbits, of a far lower grade than that
in Great St. Andrew's street, Seven Dials. It might,
last year, after " Boxing-day," have been seen in all
its frightful perfection, when the missionary could
scarcely find his way among the streets for a fortnight,
for the scenes of drunkenness and depravity.

The air echoes alike to the brawl of the swearer and
the cries of " boot-laces," " pipes," " 'tatoes," and
" greens ;" butchers roaring, " Buy, buy, buy, 4 lbs.
for 2d.," but of meat in what condition ! while poultry
is vended in all states of poisonous decay. Drunken
men crowd the pathway, tossing up their halfpence
till they have gambled away their jackets, and even
their donkeys, on which their livelihood depends.

The heart sickens at the sight of degraded lads and girls, lost to every sense of decency ; and one can only ask, Where were these brought up, and whence do they swarm forth, to mock the God of heaven, and defile the air they breathe ?

Whence ?   Let those who know them lead you to their homes, or, truly, their " dens,"—back kitchens, eight feet square, with broken floor and window, where the mother, drunk, sits on an old tin kettle in the midst ; she has on one garment and a tattered shawl, but her baby has nothing ; and a three-year-old child, crippled by a fall from a chair, and with one eye cut out, has nothing ;—or to rooms where each corner has its family, and where one lies dying of starvation and another of small-pox.   Such is the close of life to thousands in London.   City mission-aries and Scripture-readers know it ; medical men know it ; the clergy know it ; but the gulf of misery is immeasurable, and it is given up in despair.   These homes make these people generation after generation.

Would it have been thus if the Christian WOMEN of London had long ere this found their true mission, and fulfilled it ?   Mothers make homes, and mothers make " dens."   Women like " Martha P." might be sought out in every street, and, like salt in the cor-rupting mass, be used to purify it.   In a few weeks the work this agent has to do is visible.   She brings the people a Book, and says " it comes from God," and that it is " full of the words of Jesus." She quotes some of those words *to them*, and they prove like the " two-edged sword,"—they recall dim memories of a pious mother or of a Sunday-school. She tells them they may get the Book—that they may get clothing—that they may get beds—that they may make a home out of a "den." She is one of themselves, and, God blessing her, she is the most powerful instrument for recovering the recoverable. Once more, O Christians of London, let us find out such women, and employ them.

Martha paid a long series of visits to the house of a rat-catcher, whose wife was subscribing for a Bible. It is a terrible place ; half the room is occupied by a rat-pit : the creatures are caught in the sewers, and sold to be hunted by dogs. Sometimes their teeth are mercilessly broken out with pincers by the vendors, which is called " taking out the sting."

" ' We have not any to-day, sir,' said the woman to a customer, while Martha was waiting. ' Yesterday,' she added, turning to Martha, ' we sold two, and bought a quartern loaf. We should be glad to leave the trade if we could get anything else to do.'

" This poor woman seemed a broken-spirited creature, who had, however, been brought up in a Sabbath-school. She appeared comforted by a kind word ; and she could read, when her husband could not."

12

"Most of the subscribers," says the superintendent of this district, more recently, " are now beginning to make a clean and tidy appearance. Even the rat-catcher's wife attends the meetings regularly, and her circumstances are greatly improved. Here was as hopeless a case as could well be imagined, and often has Martha sighed with me over the apparent impossibility of raising this family from their misery and degradation. Yet the result of her labor of love is manifest. I might mention many others, but it is not wise to individualize more than is needful in order to represent the mode of working. Martha has always been herself a managing, provident woman, and she now very frequently succeeds in persuading her neighbors to refrain from pawning their things as long as possible. It is otherwise a habit they indulge in on the slightest pressure of want. I beg to offer a few words of sincere acknowledgment to all the kind friends who have combined this year to raise this Mission. Ladies residing far from London have helped me with the beautiful work of their hands, for sale on its account. There are many elegant forms of usefulness in this department, whereby the drawing-room may let fall crumbs of comfort into the den. In this way £20 has been added to our funds, while the tradespeople concerned in our expenditure have all most generously assisted by casting every advantage of purchase into the scale of the Mission. I trust yet to be sustained by the prayers of all contributors, that the Word of God may still further have free course, and be glorified, in this and all other dark and destitute districts around us."

We may add that Martha has a sister Jane, as well fitted for the work as herself, and that she also is employed in Lisson Grove. under the care of another lady.

CHAPTER XX.

THE friends of Bible distribution will probably be interested in observing the results of two years' experiment of a *Paid Female Agency* in the lowest districts of London. During the year 1857–8, comparatively few BIBLE-WOMEN were engaged, but their numbers now are considerably multiplied. The annexed tabular statement shows the totals, up to a given date, of money paid to them as salary by the Bible Society, and received by them for Bibles, as well as the amount of their sales of books.

The history of this Table is an interesting one. We must first look back for a moment to an original grant from the Bible Society of £5, made in June, 1857, and expended on ONE Bible-woman in St. Giles's (Marian), at the rate of ten shillings a week, in payment of the

ACCOUNT DELIVERED TO THE BIBLE SOCIETY, JUNE 13TH, 1859.

Postal District.	Name of Bible-Women.	District.	Bible Association or Depot through which Money is paid in.	Weeks at work.	Salary to Bible-Women. £	s.	d.	Sums paid in by Women for Bibles. £	s.	d.	Copies sold. Bibles.	Testaments.	Total.	Present No. of Subscribers.
E.O	I. Sarah	London Wall	City of London Ladies'	61	26	1	0	38	11	6	202	170	372	57
	Dinah	Smithfield	Brunswick Sq. Ladies'	28	9	18	0	7	1	5	121	42	163	87
	Miss Payne	Blackfriars	Earl Street depot	76	18	10	0	28	19	6	264	281	545	40
W.O.	II. Esther	Somers' Town	Harrington Sq. Ladies'	55	21	18	0	25	8	7	213	80	293	66
	Lydia	Gray's Inn Lane	Brunswick Sq. Ladies'	58	26	10	0	16	17	10	190	40	230	50
	Marian	St. Giles's	Do. do.	99	37	10	0	29	11	5	520	710	1230	80
	Ruth	Do.	Do. do.	16	9	4	0	3	18	0	19	3	22	88
	Miriam	Drury Lane	Do. do.	16	8	8	0	1	2	11	15	20	35	36
	Harriet	Cromer Street	Do. do.	12	4	9	0	1	3	2	6	8	14	50
N.	III. Lucy	Clerkenwell	Clerkenwell Ladies'	24	9	12	0	17	7	7	40	55	95	49
S.W.	IV. Charlotte	Westminster	Wesminster Ladies'	46	19	5	0	19	7	11	142	80	222	53
	Rachel	Newport Market	Brunswick Sq. Ladies'	19	5	18	0	4	10	10	23	20	43	60
	Elizabeth	Chelsea	Pimlico Ladies'	4	1	4	0	....			..	..	..	..
N.W.	V. Martha	Paddington	Paddington Ladies'	64	29	6	0	87	12	5	241	47	288	60
	Jane	Lisson Grove	St. John's Wood Ladies'	10	4	18	0	1	9	8	25	25	50	50
	Agatha	Edgware Road	Depot	4	1	4	0	....			..	..	..	80
	Joanna	Marylebone	Depot	5	1	4	0	....			2	7	9	26
E.	VI. Priscilla	Stepney	Stepney Ladies'	13	7	6	8	7	18	8	31	90	121	79
	Susan	Whitechapel	Depot	13	6	0	0	2	10	6	9	12	21	86
	Bridget	St. George's East	Depot	6	3	8	8	2	15	8	12	18	30	52
N.E.	VII. Hannah	Spitalfields	Depot	51	20	12	6	32	3	2	151	87	238	88
	Alice	Bethnal Green	Depot	22	5	15	3	4	9	6	26	47	72	49
	Sophy	Do.	Depot	12	4	16	0	8	19	4	25	49	74	35
	Mary	Victoria Park	Depot	23	7	8	6	7	19	1	38	43	81	43
	Rebecca	Haggerstone	Haggerstone Ladies'	12	4	0	0	6	4	6	30	23	53	109
	Dorothy	Shoreditch	Do. do.	4	1	0	0	....			..	..	..	..
S.	VIII. Phoebe	New Cut	North Lambeth Ladies'	20	5	4	0	7	6	5	27	36	27	40
	Deborah	Walworth	Walworth Ladies'	12	6	4	0	4	7	7	18	86	54	75
					311	14	7	337	16	4	2890	2029	4419	1438

Grants received from the British and Foreign Bible Society from June, 1857, to June, 1859, £306 17s. 8d
Expenditure, £301 14s. 7d. ; Balance, £5 2s. 8d.

occupation of the whole of her time in the sale of Bibles, in a low district unclaimed by voluntary collectors. She found in that district numbers of human beings, whose homes and persons, whose habits and condition, were such, that no one going to them with the Word of God in their hands, if the Spirit of God were shed abroad in their own hearts, could say, "I bring you the *Book*, and nought besides." It was impossible to visit in such a district with any spiritual purpose, and not see that the physical estate of its inhabitants required raising, in order to the acceptance of any offer of good to their souls. The continued visits of the above individual, under watchful guidance, were shortly, as our readers are aware, made instrumental in the reformation of many of these wretched homes ; and such improvement was, and is to this day, connected in the minds of the people with the Bible and the Bible Society.

The work did not stop in St. Giles's. What had been accomplished in one low district, it was thought might be tried in another ; and what one poor woman had been found to do, other poor women might be encouraged to attempt with equal success, always under the careful training of educated Christian ladies.

The Bible Society were, meanwhile, entreated to repeat their grants, and another £5, then £10, then £30, then £60, provided the salary for seven other Bible-women; and on the 20th of December, 1858, £128 of the Society's money had been dispensed in payments for *purely Bible work*, not only in St. Giles's, but in Paddington, Clerkenwell, Gray's Inn Lane, Somers' Town, Westminster, and Blackfriars.

It is a fact that cannot be denied, that, but for the Bible-women's agency, this number of between 5,000 and 6,000 copies of the Scriptures could never have reached a class who would not have come forth to buy them. The Committee, therefore, rejoice in the ascertained results, and on the 18th of July last they voted A CONTINUANCE OF THEIR GRANTS to this object, " though their now extended nature demands that in future they be made THROUGH THREE MEMBERS OF THEIR OWN BODY, who take special and practical interest in the subject, and who GUARANTEE that such funds are to be appropriated EXCLUSIVELY to the legitimate object of the British and Foreign Bible Society."

During the past six months twenty new Female Missionaries have been added to the staff, and each one is fixed in a suitable locality; they are almost all placed under good *local* superintendence, and are brought into communication with the previous or present Bible work of the district.

The Bible Society is considered to have a full and strong hold on their allegiance. They are preëminently BIBLE-WOMEN, in a way that they would not have been had their services been enlisted merely as Female City Missionaries. Then the distribution of the Bible, and possibly by *gift*, would have been the incidental purpose of the Mission—now it is its *chief aim*. The first three days of the week are claimed on behalf of the Bible Society, *i. e.*, five hours of each day. This is the peculiar and Protestant mark of the Mission, and distinguishes it from all other merely social work; but to the SOCIAL work we must now turn our separate attention

TO THE SUBSCRIBERS TO OUR FEMALE DOMESTIC MISSIONS.

The following Tables of Receipts and Expenditures have likewise an interesting story, known already to the readers of the "BOOK AND ITS MISSIONS."

To about the sum of one hundred guineas, received from the Bible Society in 1857–8 (and a grant more fruitful of good. perhaps, they never bestowed). addition was made, unsought and unexpectedly, chiefly by the means of recitals contained in the above magazine, which seemed provided, as it were, by the Hand that guides the world. In the year 1858, donations reached the editor to the amount of £644, which sum was de-

sired to be expended on the DOMESTIC purposes of
these Female Bible Missions to the homes of the poor
of London, *not* in *gift*, but in helping the helpless and
the thriftless to try and help themselves.

The account of the first year's expenditure is given
in the next page.

With each month's work came fresh experience and
introduction to new fields of labor. Counsel was taken
with practical co-workers ; a few rules were instituted,
and results of experiments compared. There are now
from two to five Bible-women in each of the postal
districts of London.

The receipts of the first *half* year of 1859 have, we
are happy to say, exceeded those of the *whole* year of
1858. They were previously £644. They are now
£766. The payments of the poor for their own supply of clothing and bedding were, in 1858, £109.
They are now £229, making a total of receipts,
from the 20th of November to the 20th of May, of
£995.

During the whole existence of the agency, the expenditure on the part of the Bible Society, as has been
seen, is £301 14 7
On the part of the Mission Fund   .   1,218 9 7

Of a small distinct fund, account remains yet to
be rendered, namely, of that one for MINOR EX-

FEMALE DOMESTIC MISSIONS FROM JUNE, 1857, TO NOVEMBER 20TH, 1858.

	Donations.			Payments by the Poor.			Year's Receipts.			Women's Mission Salary.			Advanced for Bedding.			Advanced for Clothing.			Aid and Loan.			Miscellaneous Expenses and Rent.			Balance.			Total Expenditure.		
	£	s.	d.	£	s.	d.	£	s.	d.	£	s.	d.	£	s.	d.	£	s.	d.	£	s.	d.	£	s.	d.	£	s.	d.	£	s.	d.
Marian, St. Giles's.	281	3	6	61	10	3	342	13	9	42	13	6	106	19	6	69	7	7	19	12	6	10	4	2	93	16	6	248	17	3
Martha, Paddington	166	16	1	21	6	4	188	2	5	7	16	10	33	13	6	54	0	8	8	10	8	6	11	5	57	9	9	130	12	8
Sarah, Clerkenwell	55	2	6	16	18	11	72	1	5	8	15	0	7	12	8	12	5	2	8	4	7	2	10	6	32	13	6	39	7	11
Lydia, Gray's Inn Lane	87	1	0	6	5	2	43	6	2	1	19	0	1	10	8	7	2	0	1	7	0	....			31	7	6	11	18	8
Esther, Somers' Town	35	10	0	2	10	0	38	0	0	1	6	6	3	16	5	7	18	6	....			....			24	18	7	13	1	5
Charlotte, Westminster	20	0	0	0	14	0	20	14	0	0	10	0	1	13	6	....			0	10	0	....			13	0	6	2	13	6
GENERAL FUND.	48	18	0	....			48	13	0	....			....			....			32	0	0	5	0	0	11	13	0	37	0	0
	644	6	1	109	4	8	753	10	9	63	0	10	155	6	8	149	13	11	70	4	4	44	6	8	269	19	4	483	11	5

PENSES, contingent upon carrying on a Mission work on the present scale and plans, to which personal friends of the Editor of "THE BOOK AND ITS MISSIONS" have kindly contributed the sum of £60 5s. Of this £41 10s. has been expended, and £18 15s. remains.

In this little book we have confined the attention of our readers to our own immediate circle of London; but there are large suburbs of London, such as Greenwich and

Blackheath, Islington, Lambeth, and Wandsworth, where these Missions are conducted on the same plans, and where the funds are provided *locally*. We likewise hear of similar agency at Brighton, at Newcastle, at Bath, at Cheltenham, and in the Wynds of Glasgow. In each case the two parties work together : they have no committee to harass them with formalities and resolutions ; but they are left to their own "inspired discretion," and to the guidance of experience as to the best methods of proceeding, which are learned by occasional meetings with other ladies and other Bible-women. "It is a sort of gospel of the scrubbing-brush," to use the expression of a fraternal pen, "which goes along with the presentation of the MESSAGE FROM GOD—an evangel of saucepans, and fresh clean beds, and tidy gowns, which tends onward to the washing of the soul in the laver of regeneration."

"The 'woman' goes where the 'lady' might not enter, and performs offices which are most fittingly rendered by persons of the working class. The floor is scrubbed by a good 'woman' better than by a pious 'lady.' Yet the lady can find the scrubbing-brush, and the soap, and materials for soup, and supplies of clothing, and the funds that are needful, and the sympathy and counsel which are indispensable, and be very blessed in her deed."

HALF YEAR'S BALANCE SHEET OF FEMALE DOMESTIC MISSIONS,

RECEIPTS.

Postal Districts	District	Name of Missionary	Balance from 1858	Transferred from General Fund	Donations since 20th Nov.	Payments by the poor	Half-year Receipts Total	Total Income
			£ s. d.	£ s. d.	£ s. d.	£ s. d.	£ s. d.	£ s. d.
E.C.	I. London Wall......	Sarah*...	....	....	64 14 0	17 15 4	82 9 4	82 9 4
	Smithfield........	Dinah....	....	7 0 0	6 16 2	0 7 1	7 3 8	14 8 8
W.C.	II. Somers' Town....	Esther ..	24 18 7	5 0 0	21 17 0	11 1 5	32 18 5	62 17 0
	Gray's Inn Lane..	Lydia....	31 7 6	....	7 17 6	20 12 11	28 10 5	59 17 11
	St. Giles's........	Marian. .	93 7 6	....	64 18 1	14 5 10	79 4 8	173 1 2
	King Street do....	Ruth ...	....	....	21 5 11	2 0 3	23 6 2	23 6 2
	Drury Lane do....	Miriam*.	....	3 9 0	....	....	....	3 9 0
	Cromer Street....	Harriet..	....	4 0 0	21 1 0	0 8 8	21 9 8	25 9 8
N.	III. Clerkenwell ...	Lucy ...	82 18 0	....	16 15 6	6 9 4	28 4 1	55 18 4
	Islington..	Anna. ...	....	....	14 12 6	11 7 9	26 0 3	26 0 3
S.W.	IV. Westminster......	Charlotte	18 0 6	....	22 16 0	40 10 7	63 6 7	81 7 1
	Newport Market..	Rachel ..	....	....	23 19 6	5 12 4	29 11 10	29 11 10
W.	V. Paddington	Martha.	57 9 9	....	111 16 8	37 14 5	149 10 8	207 0 5
	Lisson Grove.. ...	Jane ...	....	5 0 0	10 17 6	....	10 17 6	15 17 6
	Edgware Road....	Agatha*..	...	5 0 0	....	....	....	5 0 0
E.	VI. Stepney	Priscilla..	....	20 0 8	12 9 3	3 7 6	15 16 9	85 17 5
	Whitechapel......	Susan ...	....	9 0 0	5 10 0	1 14 5	7 4 5	16 4 5
	St. George East....	Bridget..	....	5 0 0	....	....	....	5 0 0
N.E.	VII. Spitalfields...	Hannah .	....	....	36 10 4	14 17 3	51 7 7	51 7 7
	Bethnal Green....	Alice ..	....	1 0 0	37 19 0	11 3 2	49 2 2	50 2 2
	do.	Sophy. ...	....	....	16 8 10	1 5 2	17 9 0	17 9 0
	Victoria Park......	Mary . ..	....	....	10 10 9	3 10 4	14 1 1	14 1 1
	Haggerstone.	Rebecca..	....	....	22 0 0	24 14 7	46 14 7	46 14 7
	Shoredich	Dorothy.	....	....	5 0 0	....	5 0 0	5 0 0
S	VIII. New Cut	Phoebe..	....	5 0 0	16 12 0	0 8 0	16 15 0	21 15 0
	Walworth........	Deborah.	....	10 0 0	3 7 6	0 11 0	8 18 6	18 18 0
	GENERAL FUND.......		11 18 0	....	190 13 1	....	190 13 1	202 6 1
			269 19 4	79 9 8	766 3 5	229 12 4	995 15 9	1845 4 9

"Examined and found correct "—W. COLES, J. H. FORDHAM, *Auditors.*

*Supported by private benevolence.

FROM NOVEMBER 20TH, 1858, TO MAY 20TH, 1859.

EXPENDITURE.

Name of Missionary	Woman's Mission Salary			Advance for Bedding			Advance for Clothing			Aid and Loan			Soup			Furniture, Rent of Mission Room			Stationery and Miscellaneous Expenses			Total Mission Expenditure			Balance		
	£	s.	d.	£	s.	d.	£	s.	d.	£	s.	d.	£	s.	d.	£	s.	d.	£	s.	d.	£	s.	d	£	s.	d.
Sarah....	7	14	6	8	12	2	27	12	7	9	4	9	1	16	6	9	1	6	9	19	8	69	1	8	18	7	8
Dinah....	1	12	0	0	7	0	2	16	8	0	15	0	....			0	7	6	....			5	17	9	8	5	6
Esther ..	4	10	0	8	2	7	17	19	4	4	7	1	....			0	17	0	....			35	16	0	27	1	0
Lyd a....	4	0	0	2	8	8	13	12	7	5	5	0	....			....			0	2	9	30	9	0	29	8	11
Marian. .	25	18	5	26	14	0	8	9	10	8	15	0	2	3	3	....			16	19	4	88	19	10	84	1	4
Ruth ...	0	14	0	....			3	15	9	1	17	0	....			....			3	1	5	9	8	2	13	18	0
Miriam..	0	13	0	0	12	0	2	2	0	0	2	0	....			....			....			3	9	0	....		
Harriet..	1	12	0	0	13	0	0	17	9	...			....			....			0	10	5	8	13	2	21	16	6
Lucy	4	9	1	5	9	4	6	0	0	2	13	6	....			....			0	19	6	19	11	5	36	6	11
Anna. ...	0	16	6	17	0	8	....			....			....			....			1	12	0	19	9	2	6	11	1
Charlotte	4	11	0	46	17	0	5	15	0	....			....			0	10	1	1	18	8	59	11	9	21	15	4
Rachel ..	3	5	0	1	8	0	6	8	5	0	19	6	....			0	17	0	....			12	13	8	16	15	2
Martha.	12	13	11	5	5	2	10	18	8	3	14	1	12	12	6	41	0	3	17	8	9	137	14	1	69	6	4
Jane	2	10	2	....			....			0	3	8	....			....			0	9	0	7	0	8	8	16	1
Agatha..	....			....			....			....			....			....			....			....			5	0	0
Priscilla..	3	13	3	0	11	9	23	3	0	0	5	2	....			3	13	0	1	6	8	82	12	1	8	4	7
Susan....	0	10	6	1	0	0	1	16	7	....			....			....			0	2	6	3	9	7	12	14	10
Bridget..	0	8	0	....			....			....			....			....			0	3	9	0	11	9	4	8	3
Hannah .	4	4	0	6	10	1	4	2	4	0	12	10	....			....			....			15	9	3	35	18	4
Alice ...	4	10	0	12	8	0	6	14	10	2	3	2	....			5	7	7	4	14	3	35	17	10	14	4	4
Sophy....	1	11	0	0	7	0	11	5	0	0	12	6	....			0	10	9	0	10	0	14	16	8	2	12	9
Mary . ..	2	2	0	....			9	15	0	0	10	0	....			1	8	7	0	5	6	14	1	1	....		
Rebecca..	5	17	0	6	8	0	20	10	0	2	2	1	....			2	1	6	1	2	0	37	15	7	8	19	0
Dorothy.	....			....			....			....			....			....			....			....			5	0	0
Phoebe..	2	19	0	0	9	0	2	13	3	0	5	0	....			0	16	5	8	5	0	10	7	3	11	7	9
Deborah	0	18	0	....			1	0	0	....			....			0	13	0	5	0	0	7	11	0	6	7	6
GENERAL FUND	....			....			....			....			....			....			59	10	5	59	10	5	141	15	8
	101	18	4	145	13	5	192	8	2	78	8	1	16	12	8	7	18	6	132	4	5	734	18	2	510	6	7

"Examined and found correct"—W. COLES, J. H. FORDHAM, *Auditors.*

It certainly seems that a NATIVE FEMALE AGENCY, drawn from the classes we want to serve and instruct, has hitherto been a MISSING LINK, and that such supplementary work might now perfect the heavenly chain, which shall lift the lost and the reckless from the depths of their despair. It should be forged by the universal church of Christ. In fact, the material is already in the hands of earnest Christians, and they have only to take it up and use it. So much of their past work has borne fruit, that this has only to " bring forth more fruit." " To him that hath shall be given," " and he shall have abundance" in the garner of God.

It is a common remark of those who are engaged in this agency, and whose hearts are warmed by perceiving the fitness of the instrumentality to the end designed to be accomplished, " Why was this Missing Link not thought of long ago ? "

CHAPTER XXI.

IN a recent estimate of the condition of classes of
the population in Glasgow it was discovered that while
two-sixths of the people were rising, two-sixths of
them were falling in their worldly circumstances : one-
sixth might be said to have risen; another sixth had
reached the lowest point, and were truly the " sunken
sixth."

Now, it is a very large class, this of our " sunken
sixth" in LONDON.   They have been reached commonly
but by the police.   The idea prevails concerning them
that they are a drunken and dangerous class as a
whole ; but there are many shades and varieties among
them.   Some live by their wits and daily shifts, and in
such habits of lying that they know not what truth is.
Brought up in dens of infamy, they know not what
virtue is.   Others earn daily what might be an abundant provision for their wants, but they mismanage it :
no one has taught them better, and they do as their
fathers and mothers did before them.

The Bible-woman agency arose amid this class. Rescued by the grace of God from sin, "Marian" could yet say to those she visited, "I am quite as poor as you are," and "I know your ways." When God has a work of salvation to do he always sends the right people to do it. Highly educated ladies would not have been the Missionaries for these Magdalens, whose doors were closed against all respectable approach. "Out," "out," "out," was said of them day after day to the Clergyman, the City Missionary, and the Lady Visitor—all too holy, and good, and clean for *them*—of no use to *them*, except as persons from whom they might beg. But let a woman draw near them just like themselves—not an ecclesiastical agent—coming from no church or party—without costume; not one of any sisterhood—simply a kind, good, motherly woman—and she may come and welcome; she may come with a "Message from God," and they will let her lift them out of their filth to hear it. She may point them to their forgotten duties, or to acts which they never saw to be duties; may show them how their children look when they are clean; may teach them the use of soap; instruct them in the preparation of food; get their windows opened and their floors purified; teach them the comfort of clean linen and clean beds; and bring them eventually "clothed, and in their right mind," to sit at the feet of all and any who may be in their degree

" the ministers of Christ." These people are tired of what they call " parsons " and " humbug ;" but they are not tired of kindness and sympathy. They perpetually say "nobody has cared for them," " they are surprised that any one will come down so low."

"Voices from the depths!" "Where is all that belongs to poor London?" we ask, as we enter its empty and comfortless abodes. Where? In the gin-shops and the pawn-shops! The earnings of every day go to the first, and all the tidy appliances of life's beginnings are lost in the gulf of the second. Are they quite lost? Is there any vestige of them? Yes! Ask for the pawnbroker's tickets. In a thousand cases you will be too late, but a hundred comforts you might restore. "I would give you twopence, mistress," said a woman in Newport Market to our " Rachel" there ; "but I have a good gown in pawn, and here's the ticket. Will you save the money for *that* for me? I can't."

" The general principle of the work above described is to present religion to the lowest class, the 'sunken sixth' of our society, at its first visit to them, as a gracious healing remedy for their actual miseries, and not as a thing merely of books, and tracts, and sermons. When the gospel goes to the door of an abandoned family in this guise it seldom fails to gain admittance. Illness is too common among the poor to be difficult to find ; and where there is suffering, help is soon welcomed. 'Shall I make you comfortable?' is a question which few poor women in their illness will meet with a negative. And, as 'Marian' says, one thing leads to another. Those who would be ashamed to be seen by a Clergyman, a City Missionary, or a Lady Visitor, have no objection to be a little cleared and set straight in their afflictions by one like themselves. And every such family visited in trouble becomes friendly when the trouble has passed away. A very few months thus spent establish an influence in the lowest and vilest neighborhoods which is irresistible. And it is an influence which opens a connection between the lost and the classes who can save them. In these cases the first penny saved from the gin-shop often becomes the commencement of a spiritual, interior and everlasting salvation. They begin to value what they have, and then they learn to value what they are."

The "sunken sixth" is a material that lies round about us almost everywhere, at least in towns and cities. Perhaps the sketches hereby given will be considered to have proved that they *can* be reached with a particular purpose, and by a fresh kind of agency. Perhaps the idea may be suggested by these facts that it requires but one great, wide-spreading, united effort of Christians *everywhere* to reach them, and to raise them. Some can give money, some time, some method, some teaching faculty, some heart sympathy, some fervent prayer. The work wants doing ; and shall it any longer remain undone ?

We wish clearly to repeat that, helpful as it may prove to all good ecclesiastical effort, the present movement is *not ecclesiastical*. In this it differs from all similar movements of a former day. It does some kindred work to that of the *Sisters of Charity* in the Roman church. They have ever proved the best supports of Rome, and have often truly followed out their name. Their services, however, have been very much limited to self-denying attendance on the sick, and to ministration among high and low in varied scenes of sorrow and suffering. Popery has been wise in its generation, and has always recognized the feminine element in religious work, even to the evil extreme of setting up to be worshipped " the Mother of God." The Roman Catholic Sisters of Charity have worked diligently *for their Church*, and they have their reward ; but they are not the " *servants of the Word*." They tell the people " they want something more or less than the Bible." They wield not the " sword of the Spirit." The " lamp" is not *their* " pitchers," and the world of the " sunken sixth" is still by them un-conquered.

While these pages are passing through the press

there has come before us a little pamphlet entitled, "The Kaisersworth Deaconesses," containing an account of an apparently successful experiment, on a limited scale, to restore the office of "Deaconess" in the Lutheran church. In a retired German village, Pastor Fliedner and his wife, having devoted themselves to this work, have, during the last twenty years, trained two hundred and forty "nursing" and "teaching" sisters of various ages, who take the benevolent care of a hospital, schools, and asylums for orphans, lunatics, &c., both at Kaisersworth and in similar houses at home and abroad.

These sisters are received from various ranks of society, and admitted on probation ; and if accepted, engage themselves to serve this institution for five years, and to observe a code of laws which appears to be very Christian and excellent. They wear a distinguishing dress, and are set apart to their work "as deaconesses," servants of the church, like Phœbe of old. (See Rom. xvi, 1.) This is done by an ordination service, " a holy solemnity, a solemn and joyful covenant." Much interesting reference is made in this pamphlet to the institution of the order in early and apostolic times.

But to meet the present need of the " sunken sixth," something more universal seems needed than would be compassed by the institution of any order. The number of women is comparatively few, whose duty it is to separate themselves from the ties of family and relationship, and to do nothing else but serve as "deaconesses," in comparison with the far greater number who, in the midst of private duties and of family life, can yet lend a hand, day by day, to raise "the sunken sixth ;" watching over and strengthening the NATIVE AGENTS who shall be given up to the service ; whose great first duty it is " to hold forth the word of life ;" and whose second, to lift up the hand of the " lowest of the low," to take hold on all the good the universal church of Christ has already provided for them ; and this is woman's work and mothers' work. It may spring up everywhere, and who shall hinder it ?

The woman is appointed for the physical civilization of communities. She is to " guide the house," whether small or great ; and this part of the education of the women of the working classes has been little cared for. The misery surrounding them is a voice from the depths saying, " Teach us to mend it." It is women of their own class who must answer this cry, just because of these only they will learn what is wanted to be known.

The City Missionary and the Scripture Reader cannot accomplish this Woman's Mission. They meet in their morning rounds chiefly with women, dirty, lazy, and drunken ; or, if industrious, at their work. Their husbands are generally " at work," and in some cases they complain of the spiritual visit paid to their wives, as "just hindering them and bothering them ;" but we do not find they have anything to say against our " Marians," and " Marthas," and " Sarahs," and " Rebeccas." These have all met with a genuine welcome from the Lower House of Lords, who know that their wives want teaching the common arts of life, and that even their own comfort depends upon the lesson being learned.

" Of mothers, whether rich or poor, it must be said, ' Woe to every woman who is not her son's counsellor to do him good.' In nine cases out of ten it is she who determines the course of his life's river. Alas! for one who does her duty by him, scores neglect it. The first idea a child has of goodness is from his education in a well-ordered house. Some houses are always in a chaos of confusion—only thunder and lightning to be heard amid their darkness ; in others, sunshine gilds the home, and brightens all the old furniture more than if it were inlaid with gold. A good mother ruling there teaches more than a cathedral establishment, and, holy woman if she is, receives an aureola like a saint in the hearts of her children. Her work is truly work for God, and so is that of the good nurse and teacher. It is possible to ascribe too much to ecclesiastical influences. Children are not thought religious ' unless they belong to the church ;' but there is a church in the house, and many a little child belongs to it. Some of the most real religion in this world, is that of little children, and some of the devoutest communion with heaven is uttered in their early prayers."

Now, it is this MOTHER'S INFLUENCE which wants carrying down among the "lost and degraded." Marian's first missionary walks in St. Giles's were directed with a sense that our Lord would thither have bent his steps were he still upon the earth ; and should we not follow, for the sake of Him whose blood, in the act of being shed upon the cross, drew with it that day to paradise the first soul it had redeemed, the dying thief, a member of the class of " the sunken sixth ?

CHAPTER XXII.

OUR AGENTS, AND THEIR SUPPORT.

A VERY general question asked us is, "Where do you find the women?—it must be so very difficult to do that;" and our reply may be, " We believe God finds them, and we perpetually ask him for a right judgment concerning those who present themselves." We by no means take all who come ; and we often have to watch against a kindly wish to oblige friends who only want a comfortable provision for their dear Mrs. So and So, and "think she may do." No ; this truly laborious and self-denying mission requires an agent still in the prime of life, and who evidences, after trying her for a month, that she has an especial call to this work.

We are often sorry to write to our country friends, and say that we cannot, at their request, "find them Bible-women." The kind of women who may be made useful we believe to exist *everywhere* among the communicants or members of our religious bodies. The Scripture Reader or City Missionary will often point them out, and where their services are required they must be sought by faith and prayer.

If we were asked to give a few details concerning the choice and guidance of the Bible-women, they would be these :—Next to piety, humility and docility are the most valuable traits of character. Courage and common sense cannot be left out of the question ; a quick, observant eye, and a ready hand for whatever is wanted, are important ; and a bright, cheerful view of things is a wonderful assistance in obviating the prejudices of the poor. But no *one* woman will possess all these virtues in perfection, and in some particulars more than others each will surely need cultivation.

We feel called upon to reject at once an evidently "pious gossip," or a weakly person who merely wants a place ; or a woman whose duty is to her own small family ; or a pretty, delicate young widow, unfit for rough work ; or any one who thinks evidently great things of herself, and is "sure she knows all about it before she hears ;" but a clean, tidy, humble, cheerful pleasant-spoken matron, with a good character—a character for real piety without " cant"—with a quiet, energetic missionary spirit about her, in her own small sphere, is what we want, and may be gladly accepted, at least for a month on probation.

She should certainly be able to read and to write,

13

and her lady may improve her in both particulars before she commences her work. She will not, of course, be an educated person ; but she must be trusty, conscientious, honest and truthful ; and, under a wise directress, she will improve and develope when she gets into her duties. In every one of our present thirty women there is something that one might wish otherwise ; it is the "lamp" in the "earthen pitcher :" but God works often with very imperfect instruments, or he would not work with any of us. The teachable person accomplishes most on the whole, especially if she has a large and loving heart that has itself known much affliction. We want these women for a practical purpose from a practical school.

This is truly a mighty work, and makes all engaged in it feel their own feebleness. They must ask daily and hourly wisdom from above, and go forth continually sustained by prayer. Those are the best superintendents who pray the most with and for their women, and who teach them most readily to unsheathe the "sword of the Spirit" which they bear,—to answer the people FROM THE BOOK. It is "the sword of the LORD and of Gideon ;" and we believe it is because of their earnest faith that they have a MESSAGE FROM GOD for the people that, simple folk as they are, they have been honored with success almost invariable.· In this success there have been three elements. THE BIBLE FIRST

—always the presentation of the BOOK, declaring what it is. When that has met with the faintest welcome, the door of entrance was open, the repeated visit has shown that THE BODY WAS THOUGHT OF AS WELL AS THE SOUL, for human souls live in bodies, and the bodies of these "lowest of the low" were very wretched ; and further, it has been a mission of WOMEN TO WOMEN, and of WOMEN OF THEIR OWN CLASS, which was very much wanted, as was evident by its ready acceptance : it was a Missing Link, and as such we have given its true and simple history.

The distribution of the Word of God, and the improvement of the homes of the poor, are both objects in which all Christians can unite. There is no need for sectional division here. Let every church of Christ, or congregation of faithful men and women, set itself to discern the fit helpers it possesses, and give them up to the work. The self-denial of not determining to keep them and use them *congregationally* is a high element in the matter, which a fresh baptism of the Holy Spirit might perhaps enable us to desire. If they are used congregationally, if the Bible-woman is only looked upon as another curate, and if her superintendent must be *necessarily* the clergyman or the minister's wife, then that is a very limited view of the scope of this new effort, and we think it must expect a limited blessing.

In this England of ours we live so much in classes and in strata of society, as observing Americans tell us, that we have hitherto been content not to enlarge our experiences, or to look beyond our own horizon. Before we can influence the sunken masses we want fusion in the great crucible of Divine Love.

A very interesting feature of this undertaking is, that it has been supported during the two years of its infancy by faith and prayer, and without an anxious thought. What God had done for "Orphans" he could do for the spread of HIS WORD, when he would have its witness carried among the lowest and vilest poor of London. The work is His, and he has used apparently weak instruments, that all the glory may be given to himself. He has found the women, and pointed out the willing and devoted lady superintendents, and sent the funds to commence each mission, often in the course of one week. The minute leadings of his providence have been unmistakable, and the answers to prayer innumerable. The machinery is so simple and so local wherever it arises, and it is of such importance that the work be secret and silent, that there is no necessity to clog it with extra apparatus, or to spoil it with platform compliments of man's device.

Nevertheless, the next remark that our friends make is this : " Well, then, if the work is genuine and good, we must surely extend it. Shall we not have a great society, a great Female City Mission, with the usual apparatus for collecting money, public meetings, committees, secretaries, and reports? Of course the thing will come to that in the end ; for when the novelty of the present movement is worn off, and the voluntary subscriptions cease, how is it to be supported?"*

To this we answer that our ONE resolve is, *never to get into debt ;* therefore, if the supplies cease, the work could always be transferred to those who will take it up, according to the rules of present routine. But it is a comparatively inexpensive undertaking, in part self-paying, according to its primary principles ; and by the general sense of the committee of the British and Foreign Bible Society, after much and careful discussion, it is pronounced in its commencement to be truly Bible work, and, as such, comes within their le-

* Amid the many salutary changes which might follow on the pentecostal outpouring of the Holy Spirit which we are beseeching from heaven, and which our Christian brethren in many parts of the world are already receiving, there might probably be numbered a holy *method* in our benevolent reserves of income for the work of the Lord, according to the scriptural indications given in the Old Testament. This would bring *enough and to spare* into the treasury of Him whose are *all* the silver and the gold. " He shall make His people willing in the day of His power." See "Gold and the Gospel ; or, Ulster Prize Essays on Giving Away in Proportion to a Man's Income."

gitimate province of *paid* labor, inspected by members of their own body.

For three days a week, therefore, the female colporter could go forth as from them, if her only duty were to sell Bibles ; but such is the Book, and such are the London heathen, that woman's civilization work must necessarily follow ; and to us it needs no argument to prove that for all " the Lord will provide."

It is necessary, even amid difficulties, we think, to keep the movement in full allegiance to that great and blessed association for the spread of God's Word. The social element might otherwise rise paramount, and the great first duty, the delivery of the message from God, singly and alone, on which he has showered his blessing, might at a future day be forgotten.

Our perpetual increase and change of population will make it a long time before London is fully supplied with half-crown Bibles, *in good type*, easily read by the ignorant, especially by small instalments.

Nevertheless, in proportion as the women are multiplied, and do their work vigorously, *a less portion* of their labor can be paid by the Bible Society, and therefore its payments must be on a sliding scale. It has also to care for the occupation of its voluntary helpers.

Those who are employing this agency have recently obtained the valuable assistance of a few " friends in council "—the Earl of Shaftesbury ; the Honorable Arthur and Mrs. Kinnaird ; the Rev. Anthony Thorold, rector of St. Giles's ; the Rev. Dr. Hamilton, of the Scotch Church ; and the Rev. William Arthur, of the Wesleyan body ; H. Hopley White, Esq. ; W. Coles, Esq. ; and J. Hampden Fordham, Esq., the latter gentlemen being members of the parent committee of the British and Foreign Bible Society.

These friends have all a genuine and heart interest in London " Female Bible and Domestic Missions." They will, from time to time, meet and consult with some of the ladies who are practically engaged in the work. The accounts of money received and expended will be submitted to their cognizance and inspection, and their various views consulted on any movement of importance. This Council of Reference will verify the business details in the public eye.

To ourselves the utterances of human life brought to us by the researches of our female colporters are of intenser interest every day. That timely teaching of a temporal character should be intimately connected with the Bible is not an element that these poor folk in their homes seem to shrink from. Most of them acknowledge the Bible to be a good book, and one that ought to be in every house ; but they know very little about it. They have heard a text taken from it for a sermon that they did not understand ; but Bible stories, well selected, and explained to them as if they were earnestly believed, go straight to their hearts. The story of the Book, as a whole, will all be new, and of the deepest interest to the mass of the lowest orders in this our nineteenth century.

The influence that shall redeem them from their bad habits must be a resident influence; and the more nearly it is allied to the condition and sympathies of its objects the more effectual is its aid. "Ladies" will not be found residing in St. Giles's and the Seven Dials; or, if they were, they would find the dwellings inaccessible; but the different orders of intelligence belong to each other in Christ's church. "The foot and the hand cannot say to the eye or the head, We have no need of you;" and it has been found always that union is strength. May the two henceforth work lovingly together in the vineyard of the Lord, and may He vouchsafe to give the increase!

APPENDIX.

[We here insert two or three papers deemed necessary and helpful
in the information of this Bible Agency, which friends in the
country are at liberty to reprint and modify to their own local
circumstances.]

LONDON FEMALE BIBLE AND DOMESTIC MISSIONS.

GENERAL RULES.

1. The work having now considerably extended itself, it is
thought desirable to give it the general designation of "LONDON
FEMALE BIBLE AND DOMESTIC MISSIONS."

2. The *objects* of these Missions are twofold, viz., to supply the
very poorest of the population with copies of the Holy Scriptures,
and also to improve their temporal condition by teaching them to
help themselves rather than look to others; the former to be attained by taking payment for the Bible in small weekly instalments, and the latter by assisting them to procure better food,
clothing, and beds in the same way.

3. None shall be employed in this Mission but women of
thoroughly respectable and Christian character, of active habits,
kindly manners, and but little encumbered with family cares.

4. The Districts shall be of regulated extent; and the Bible-
women shall reside in or quite near their respective Districts,
having a room in a central position for the general purposes of
the Mission, for which the rent will be paid by their Superintendent.

5. Each Bible-woman shall be placed under the careful superintendence of a Lady who may be found willing to undertake the

work, and who is a resident on the district, or within a reasonable distance from it.

6. The Bible-woman shall present a Weekly Report of her labors to the Superintending Lady, who will receive such Report, pay the salary, and give such directions as the local circumstances may require.

INSTRUCTIONS TO THE BIBLE-WOMAN.

1. Your first and principal work is to ascertain who are without the Holy Scriptures, and willing to purchase at a cheap rate.

2. Take with you in a bag, with which you will be provided, a variety of Bibles and Testaments, and should any of the parties you visit be able and willing to pay the whole price at once, take it; if not, offer to receive payment by small weekly instalments, for which you will regularly call.

3. Let the people understand that you are not supplying them at a profit, but, in many instances, at a loss to the Bible Society, and that the good people who employ you are only seeking to promote the benefit of the poor.

4. You will be expected to devote five hours every day, Saturdays excepted, to your work, for which you will receive 2s. per day. The Bible Work is to be done by itself, and the Domestic Mission Work at another time. You will follow the directions that will be given you as to the localities in which you are to labor for both objects.

5. As the Bible Work leads to other benevolent schemes, you will be directed by your Superintendent how to proceed in taking subscriptious for clothing and bedding, also inducing the poor no longer to live content with dirt, rags, and discomfort. You will then be able gradually to instruct them in needlework, cooking, and cleanliness.

6. It will be expected that you will live in or near your district, and a room there will also be available for the purposes of the Mission.

7. If you are able, it is desirable that you should keep a

Journal, in which you will give true statements of the things you meet with.

8. You will present to your Superintendent a Weekly Report of all your proceedings, at the time and place appointed, and according to a form with which you will be furnished.

9. The lady who has kindly promised to superintend your work is ———

SUGGESTIONS TO PROPOSED SUPERINTENDENTS OF A FEMALE BIBLE AND DOMESTIC MISSION.

It seems undesirable that a Lady should undertake this work if she is not able to promise a fair share of time and interest to its claims, which, though at first very simple, are sure to increase in many forms. We would suggest that a Lady Superintendent do not offer her services as merely honorary or intermitting: she must be depended upon for the vigilant performance of her own particular duties. No bills should be paid by the Bible-woman, or any material purchased except through written orders from her lady; and great care should be taken in selection if at any time a deputy is left in charge.

As the nature of the Mission is undenominational, and it need not be conducted within Parochial boundaries—though it often may, most conveniently, be so arranged—only those can undertake its general guidance in any neighborhood who are not necessarily limited by such considerations.

It appears always desirable that the Superintendent should become a member of the Ladies' Bible Association of the locality, and should herself pay in monthly to their funds the instalments received by the Bible-woman for copies of the Scriptures; of course, conferring with them on the districts in which, from time to time, this sub-agent should be occupied in Bible Work.

Regularity of payments to the Female Missionary, with kindly, and often helpful inspection of the varied accounts she renders, should be considered a duty to be fulfilled at least weekly, and at first even oftener. Her payment from Bible Funds must be exactly proportioned to her purely Bible Work, at the rate of 2s.

for five hours.   Her salary for all other service will proceed from Funds set apart for Domestic purposes.

It is very important for the Superintendent to understand the due administration of these respective funds.   The Bible-woman may be employed for two, three, four, or five days, ONLY IN SELL- ING BIBLES, according to the needs of the particular district, and for this ONLY the Bible Society can pay her.   She must not do any other work at the same time.   If the people offer to subscribe for clothing and beds, she will say, "I only do one thing at a time," and "the right thing first.   I bring you now the Message from God.   I shall be glad also to provide you with clothing, &c., at the lowest prices, and for this you can pay as you do for the Bibles, in small sums weekly; but you must COME TO ME to do this, at a certain hour, in my Mission-room."   There would be great evil in mixing the two departments of labor; the Bible Society would never know what they paid for, and mistakes would be made in the accounts; while a particular benefit to be gained, by assembling the Women at a given hour at one place, would be lost likewise.

Although it is found best that each Bible-woman should be made responsible to ONE Lady, rather than to a Committee, still, as suitable individuals may willingly come forward, saying, "What can we do to help you?" it should be the aim of the Lady Super- intendent to enlist their various activities in the regulation of special departments, such as weekly visiting of the clothing and bedding club—reading or speaking to the subscribers at mending or tea parties—purchase of clothing materials—fixing and giving out of needlework—arrangements concerning bags of linen—soup making—timely loans—visitation of special cases, &c., &c.   All these things gradually form a part of the Female Bible and Do- mestic Mission and when money may have to be expended, account must, of course, be rendered by each Lady to the Super- intendent.

Without interfering with any existing organizations, this Mis- sion is intended to carry down among the Neglected Outcasts of society the different measures for their benefit, which have long been familiar to the Decent Poor.   The lowest classes have said that "nobody cared for them," a complaint which it is the aim of this Mission to obviate.

Each Superintendent will see the importance of securing funds for the temporal purposes of her particular Mission. The Bible Society commences and pays for the Bible Work, and, with ten or twenty pounds besides, a good beginning may be made; while the various elements of the undertaking are intended to be *self-paying* as far as possible. If several Female Missionaries are engaged for an extended district, a quarterly conference of their Superintendents is recommended, to secure unity of design, with independence in details.

Frequent reading of the Scriptures and prayer with the Bible-woman will be found her most effectual preparation for the work she undertakes. Her great power is in apt quotation; and the Lord is proving that he blesses His own Word day by day. "The entrance of Thy word giveth light; it giveth understanding to the simple." ·

COOKERY FOR ST. GILES'S.

CHEAP SOUP, AND VERY NOURISHING.

Two ounces of dripping	1d.
Half a pound of solid meat, at 4d. per lb. (cut into dice one inch square)	2d.
Quarter of a pound of onions, sliced thin; quarter of a pound of turnip, cut into small dice; two ounces of leeks (green tops will do), and three ounces of celery, chopped small	1d.
Half a pound of rice or pearl barley	1d.
Three ounces of salt, and a quarter of an ounce of brown sugar	½d.
Fuel to make it	½d.
Six quarts of water.	
	6d.

How to make it.—Take an iron saucepan (a tin one will not do); put into it, over the fire, your meat cut small, with two ounces of dripping and a quarter of an ounce of brown sugar;

shred in your onions, and stir with a wooden or iron spoon till fried lightly brown; have ready washed and sliced your turnips, celery, and leeks, add them to the rest over the fire, and stir about for ten minutes. Now add one quart of cold water, and the half pound of barley or rice, and mix all well together. Then add five quarts of hot water, made ready in the kettle, season with your salt, stir occasionally till boiling, and then let simmer on the hob for three hours, at the end of which time the rice or barley will be tender.

This soup will keep two or three days if poured into a flat pan, but it is best made every other day. You must stir till nearly cold when you take it off the fire, which will prevent its fermenting. A little bread or biscuit eaten with it makes a supporting meal, much better than a cup of tea, and would go far to prevent the craving for gin.

CHEAP BEDS FOR THE POOR.

TICKING FOR BEDS may be bought (in quantities of not less than 100 yards) at 4d. a yard. Eight yards make a tick, and 30 lbs. of flock fill it. The flock is 9s. 3d. per cwt. and upwards. The bed is sold at six shillings, and paid for before receipt by sixpenny or shilling instalments.

NOTICE TO SUBSCRIBERS.

Friends wishing to subscribe to these Missions may send Post-office orders to Mrs. Ranyard, 13 Hunter street, Brunswick-square, London, who is their Honorary Secretary. The orders should be made out for the office in Great Coram street, Brunswick-square, and in the Christian name of "Ellen." The Hon. A. Kinnaird, M. P., will also receive subscriptions, as Treasurer, for the General Fund, addressed to the Bank of Messrs. Ransom and Co., No. 1 Pall Mall East.

The "Book and its Missions" may be had of W. Kent & Co., 21 Paternoster Row, and by order of all booksellers. Price 3d., monthly.

www.ingramcontent.com/pod-product-compliance
Lightning Source LLC
Chambersburg PA
CBHW020937120726

47905CB00008B/2557